FESTIVE SOMMER

NORA SOMMER CARIBBEAN SUSPENSE - BOOK SEVEN

NICHOLAS HARVEY

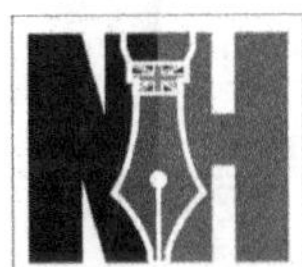

For my stepdaughter Lindsey and her husband Dave.
Nora has very few friends, but if she really existed – and boy we wish she did – Lindsey and Dave would be two of them.
With lots of love, your fake dad.

FOREWORD

BY USA TODAY AND WALL STREET JOURNAL
BESTSELLING AUTHOR LISA REGAN

When Nick asked me to make a cameo in Festive Sommer, I was elated. The Nora Sommer Caribbean Suspense series is one of my favorites. Nora is such a wonderful character. She's fierce without even meaning to be. It's built in, a part of her makeup, as natural as breathing. Her tragic past haunts her, and yet, she shows up every day for others even when she feels like she's failing. She's a warrior, and yet, simple social conventions often confound her. She's always learning how to navigate relationships even after so much has been taken from her. In addition to that, Nora is just plain hilarious at times. The no-nonsense way she views the world keeps a smile on my face through every book. I absolutely adore her, so making a cameo in this book—being able to interact with one of my favorite characters—was a no-brainer.

I wasn't disappointed when I got to read an advanced copy of the book. Living vicariously through this fictional interpretation of myself and being in Nora's world was awesome. There's a particularly sweet moment near the end that made me tear up a little. Or maybe it was just allergies. Read and see for yourself! Also, I'm thrilled that Mr Phillip came along for the adventure with me, though I must say, as always, he stole my thunder. I just know you're going to love this book so stop wasting your time on this foreword and read on! Nora is waiting!

PROLOGUE

The Bookworm and the Visitor

Five Days until Christmas

The Bookworm loved Christmas time. It was the only holiday where he found himself missing his native New Hampshire. The usually welcome Florida warmth starkly contrasted the wintery feel he longed for, so he cranked his air conditioning to chill the house, just so he could turn a fire on in the living room. The fake electric logs were a poor substitute for a real wood-burning fireplace, but he could lose himself in a book with the radiant heat on his legs and pretend.

A retired schoolteacher, the Bookworm missed his daily routine and those few students who truly enjoyed and participated in his English classes. He was happy to leave the others behind. Those who found no fascination with the language or the written word. Volunteering at the library helped fill the void, and he found the majority of folks coming by the library were as keen on reading as he was.

Mysteries and thrillers were the Bookworm's genres of choice, from the classic authors such as Agatha Christie and Ian Fleming, through the hugely popular works of Tom Clancy and Clive Cussler, and now the modern boom in crime and psychological thrillers by the likes of Freida McFadden, Karin Slaughter, and his all-time favourite, Lisa Regan. His consumption of literature was voracious. Most days, he read a complete novel. He'd reluctantly broken down and purchased a tablet on which to read ebooks, as his social security income was not sufficient to support hardcovers or even paperbacks of all he read.

One benefit to the ebooks was receiving them a second past midnight on release day. For his favourites, he would set an alarm for twelve and open the new book the moment the file appeared. Often, the Bookworm would power through the exciting new story by breakfast, after which he'd go back to bed and sleep for a while. Because he could. Apart from the library, and a handful of online book clubs he participated in, he had very few obligations and commitments.

But those special books by his favourite authors were the ones he still splurged on and purchased in print edition. He would reread the novel once the physical copy arrived and discover he'd missed bits and pieces in his sleep-deprived overnight binge. Those surprises gave him great pleasure, and he'd share his new observations in the reader groups, and with his sister, who shared his passion for books.

The Bookworm had been divorced for over a decade, and was happy to be so. He'd married a woman who'd shown interest in him when few did, and their relationship had been more companionship than passion. She was a fellow teacher, but her love was geography, and her reading interest was solely nonfiction. Over the years, she would travel with friends while he stayed home and enjoyed the peace and quiet to consume more books. Apparently, one of these travelling partners became more than just a friend. The

Bookworm didn't mind. In fact, her leaving saved him the awful business of discussing a separation and counselling and all the other drama he watched couples go through before the inevitable finally happened. He didn't miss her and doubted she ever missed him.

Settled into his favourite reading chair, the Bookworm was two chapters into a thriller by Kiersten Modglin, a young American author he'd recently discovered, when he heard a knock on the front door. He sat there for several moments, contemplating who it might be. He almost never had visitors, and when he did, they were always scheduled in advance. Not once had he ever socialised with his neighbours. In fact, he only knew a few of their names. Ordinarily, he would ignore the knocking and let whoever it was selling religion, cookies, or subscriptions go away, but occasionally at this time of year, carol singers had been known to come by. And the Bookworm loved Christmas music.

He walked to the door and took a quick look through the peephole. He could not have been more disappointed. Or surprised. Opening the door, he looked over his visitor.

"Hello," he said flatly. "What do you want?"

"Hardly the way to greet me," came the reply. "Are you going to invite me in?"

The Bookworm considered his options, which seemed rather simple. Either deny entry or step aside. Hating conflict and generally seeking the path of least resistance, he moved out of the way so the Visitor could come in.

"Tea?" he offered, hoping they wouldn't be staying that long.

"You know I don't drink tea."

Perhaps at one time he did know that the Visitor didn't drink tea; he couldn't recall. He'd given the sum total of zero thought to the subject or the person for too long.

The Visitor ran a finger along the spines of a row of books on the overflowing shelves in the living room. Alphabetically sorted in genre, of course.

"Are you still going on this trip of yours?"

The Bookworm nodded. "Leaving in the morning."

Which was obvious, seeing as they'd both walked around the packed suitcase in the hallway. The Bookworm couldn't recall the last time he'd spent the night away from the house, so a week-long adventure to a foreign land was a major life event for which he'd packed, unpacked, repacked, and repeated, multiple times.

"She's a hack, you know," the Visitor said, pausing by the collection of Lisa Regan's Josie Quinn thrillers. "So little understanding."

The conversation was taking the same turn their last one had spiralled into, and the Bookworm had no interest in going there again.

"What do you want? I was in the middle of something I need to get back to."

The Visitor laughed. "No, you weren't. Unless you consider reading these childish works *something*. But as that's all you ever do, I suppose you have to look at it that way."

The Bookworm didn't respond and stood with hands on hips, waiting.

"Leaving tomorrow?" came the question he'd already answered.

"Yes."

"To Miami?"

"That's where the yacht leaves from."

"How many days at sea?"

The Bookworm had no clue why he was being asked any of these questions, but he preferred this conversation over arguing about literary critique, which he considered The Visitor to be ill equipped to speak sensibly about.

"Two."

"And how long there?"

While the subject was less infuriating, he was still growing impatient. He'd left the protagonist in a particularly sticky situation in the Modglin book.

"Why are you asking all this?"

"How long there?" the Visitor repeated.

"Three days. Now why on earth are you here and asking me all these questions?"

The Visitor grinned. "Because you're not going on this trip."

The Bookworm laughed. "Oh yes I am, and I think you should leave now."

But the Visitor didn't leave, and the Bookworm stopped laughing when the gun was raised and aimed at his chest.

1

PUNCH CARD

Three Days until Christmas

I'd figured out the trick was to answer a question early in the classroom session and then Driscoll would leave me alone. Although in a class with only four students, my chances weren't great. After that, the challenge was staying awake. All the procedural *dritt* was so boring, and from what I could see, did nothing but help the criminals. I guess it's mostly necessary to protect the innocent, which was fine – I didn't want to lock up an innocent person – but the people we dealt with weren't innocent. Regardless, I was relieved to finally be enrolled in detective training, so if I had to listen to Driscoll drone on about correct procedures and form numbers for this, that, and the other thing, I'd suffer through it.

I rested my face in my hands with elbows on the desk, hoping Driscoll didn't notice when my eyelids refused to stay open occasionally. I'd been burning the matches at both ends for weeks. That didn't sound right. Burning something involving ends. Anyway, I was knackered. Mostly classroom during each day, and then helping with a task force in the evenings and on weekends, plus my foster kid Jazzy's school and athletics.

"Constable Sommer?"

"Sir?" I replied, realising I had no clue what he'd been talking about.

Which apparently he'd noticed.

"Simple question, Constable Sommer. Under what circumstances may a suspect be held without charges for more than 48 hours?"

"When extra time is required to preserve evidence in the case, collect evidence, or carry out investigations. Sir," I answered, relieved he had repeated the question.

"For up to how long?" Driscoll asked, still looking at me.

"Seventy-two hours, sir."

He nodded, but his eyes didn't shift from me. "And who can authorise that extension, Constable?"

He liked saying 'constable' a lot to remind us all we could fail his course and remain at what he seemed to consider a lowly, unworthy level.

"An RCIPS officer with a minimum rank of superintendent, sir."

"Has it always been that way?"

Who cares? is what I wanted to say, but I didn't. Seriously, what does it matter how the law used to be? All that's important is what the law is now, so we don't screw up and give a douchebag lawyer the opportunity to set free an even bigger douchebag criminal. But fortunately, I'd read the section he'd told us to review.

"The amendment to police law in 2014 shortened the extension period, sir."

Driscoll turned and walked back to the big dry-erase board on the wall without acknowledging my correct answer. He started rambling on again about more things in the sections he'd told us to read last night. I yawned and took a sip of the coffee-flavoured energy drink whose contents were the only thing keeping me awake and preventing my forehead hitting the desk.

From behind where I sat, I heard the classroom door open.

"Forgive the interruption, Arnie," came the familiar voice of Detective Whittaker with his tint of Caymanian accent.

"How can I help you, Roy?" Driscoll asked.

"May I steal Constable Sommer from you?" Whittaker responded, and I felt like cheering.

Although that was based on boredom and the assumption I was being called to do something more active and interesting. The idea that I was actually in trouble for something once again quickly dashed my eagerness.

"Sure," Driscoll replied. "I believe she did her studies covering what we're discussing this afternoon."

At least he noticed that.

"Besides, she was about to fall asleep, so if you have something more useful for her to do, then be my guest."

And unfortunately, he'd noticed that too.

"With me, Constable Sommer," Whittaker ordered, and I scooped up my rucksack and followed him out of the classroom.

"Napping in class?" he said once we were down the hallway.

"It's boring, sir. He rehashes the same stuff we had to read the night before. If he just asked, I could tell him I read it and we could move on."

"His job is to make sure you know all the information, Nora," Whittaker said, as we crossed the lobby at Central Station. "Going over it shows him you do."

"Asking me would be faster."

We walked past the Christmas tree with its glittery decorations and Whittaker held the door to the car park open for me. The December heat hit me as I stepped outside. At least the humidity dropped from full-on sauna to just clammy in winter.

"Everyone will say they did their homework," Whittaker pointed out as we continued to his car.

"I would tell him if I hadn't."

"Yes, I dare say you would, Nora. But you're not typical of the young men and women Arnie has to shape into detectives."

I thought that might be a compliment, but I wasn't sure, so I changed the subject. "Where are we going, sir?"

"We have a lead on the West Bay gang we've been after," he replied, unlocking his Range Rover with the remote.

I walked to the passenger side and climbed in.

"The Bush Bros?" I asked.

Whittaker shook his head. "That name makes me cringe. But yes."

I put my belt on. "I agree. They should be arrested for such a shitty name."

"Is that covered in Driscoll's curriculum?" Whittaker said without any humour in his voice as he backed out of the parking spot. "Arrests for poor marketing skills within street gangs."

"I'll let him know you suggested he add it, sir."

I'm pretty sure he snickered a little, but he tried to not let me see.

"Who are we joining, sir?"

"Sergeant Williams with the firearms unit," he replied. "They're waiting for us at West Bay station."

Detective Whittaker, my mentor, and one of the few people who'd believed in me when I'd been at my lowest a few years back, was being polite as usual. The firearms unit were waiting for him. I was given the chance to tag along because I'd put in a good deal of legwork on the gang he was talking about.

I wasn't sure what officially entitles a group of individuals as being a 'gang'. If the criteria were like-minded adults with similar goals and methods of doing things, then the local bingo club could be classed as a gang. I suppose having unlawful intent came into the equation, which would get most of the bingo-playing crowd off the hook.

Anyway, Grand Cayman had a few unsavoury types who liked to call themselves a gang, and as most of their activities were focused on their rival gang, I didn't care too much. If they wanted to steal from, shoot, and stab each other, that seemed fine to me. Saved us a lot of work and kept their numbers down. The problem was these idiots had begun having their brawls in more public places, and the gun violence was escalating.

The Cayman Islands had a reputation for being one of the safest destinations in the Caribbean, and no one except these *drittsekker* wanted to ruin that. More guns were showing up on an island with very strict firearm laws, so for all those reasons, the Royal Cayman Islands Police Service were under a lot of pressure to find the ringleaders of the Bush Bros and the other gangs.

The dumb name came from the streets where at least some of the gang members resided. Which made things somewhat easier. This wasn't New York with high rises containing thousands of flats all crammed into a few city blocks. Someone had named a series of short streets and cul-de-sacs after Bush family members. I had no idea when this was done or how the neighbourhood used to be, but now it was a few dozen run-down, block-built homes with all kinds of rubbish and dead machinery lying around.

Williams and his team had been ready to get on with it when we'd reached West Bay station, so now I put on the bulletproof tactical vest they handed me in the back of the unmarked white van and listened to their plan. Another vehicle with four officers would take the rear of the building while Williams and his group went through the front. Whittaker and I were instructed to stay in the van until we were given the all-clear. Which made me wonder why I had to wear the vest, as it was hot as hell in the van.

The officer behind the wheel drove the van slowly into the neighbourhood, picking out the house we'd been tipped off about. Coming in quietly gave the guys a chance to be entering through the front door before the suspects knew we were here. Tyres screeching and sirens blaring made for exciting viewing in the movies, but rarely helped in a real raid.

A few of the homes had half-hearted attempts at Christmas decorations, but overall the neighbourhood appeared to be void of holiday spirit. Stopping one home away, Williams slid the side door open and he and his men covered the 30 metres to the front porch in seconds.

"Police! Coming in!" Williams yelled, and one of his crew stood ready to swing the Enforcer – the official name of the custom-designed police battering ram.

But he didn't need to. Williams turned the knob, and the door swung open. His men disappeared inside, announcing themselves once more.

I sat in the open side door watching the house, unsure what to expect. There was every chance the occupants were stoned out of their skulls and still hadn't noticed or cared about the guys in tactical gear carrying assault rifles and yelling loudly. But at least one of them cared. From a side window, a dark-skinned young man in baggy shorts, high top trainers, and an American football team jersey leapt to the ground and ran.

"Wait, Nora!" I heard Whittaker shout, but I was already three strides from the van.

The three houses on this street were backed by three on a parallel street where I could see the other police car parked. So could Raiders man as he sprinted between the rows of houses, jumping over children's yard toys and a rusted car engine. Maybe this was the scenario Williams foresaw when he gave me the vest, but I still felt naked without my utility belt holding my truncheon and Taser. Wasn't much call for it in the classroom, so it was in the lockbox in the back of my Jeep back at Central.

Raiders ducked left behind the last house on the block. He had ten metres on me, but I liked my chances if he kept running. Sprinting around the corner, I slowed and looked all around. He'd vanished. The house was on the corner of the street and he hadn't had enough time to be out of view if he'd crossed in either direction. The back door to the home was open inwards, and a torn and shabby screen door let whatever breeze made it back here into the house. I squinted against the bright sunshine to focus inside on what appeared to be the kitchen. A pair of eyes stared back at me.

The young man was hard to make out, but he wasn't wearing a Raiders jersey or baggy shorts.

"Police. Did a man come inside?"

The youth lifted his chin and didn't move. I could now see he was leaning against a refrigerator.

"Nope."

I reached for my radio, which of course was also in the lockbox back at the Jeep. *Dritt.* These may have been some of the reasons Whittaker had told me to wait.

"Mind if I come inside?" I asked.

The young man shrugged his shoulders. "Suit yourself, lady."

I pulled the creaky screen door open and at the same time heard movement from outside the house. I stepped back and saw a window swing open. Leaping that way, I committed too soon, and couldn't avoid the body jumping towards me. Raiders led with his forearm and then…

"Nora?" Whittaker's voice echoed around me.

My head hurt and my eyes burned at the brilliant sunlight scorching my face. I had the salty, metallic taste of blood in my mouth. Running my tongue around to find the source, I quickly stopped when I realised my tongue *was* the source. I must have bitten it when Raiders clocked me.

"You okay?" Whittaker asked, leaning over me.

I propped myself up on my elbows. "Did you get him?"

Whittaker shook his head and Williams walked up and grinned at me.

"He gotcha good," the sergeant joked. "You alright?"

"Give me a gun next time," I muttered and tried to get up.

The two men helped me to my feet. My body felt like I'd put on 20 kilos and I wasn't altogether sure I wouldn't vomit. Just what I needed, another damn concussion. If I wasn't careful, I'd be getting a frequent flyer punch card at the hospital. *Merry Christmas, Nora.*

"Hey, where's the kid?" I asked, remembering the youth in the kitchen.

"What kid?" Whittaker asked.

"There's no one in the house," Williams added.

I shook my head and regretted the movement, but I was annoyed at myself.

"I can give you the description of two men we need to find."

"Pretty sure the guy in the Raiders jersey was Clifton Bush," Williams replied. "Best we know, he's the leader. You saw someone else?"

"*Ja*. Younger guy. He helped him get away."

"What did he look like?" Whittaker asked.

I thought for a moment. I'd just told them I could describe both men, but in truth I realised I couldn't. Raiders had his back to me until he smashed a forearm into my face, and the youth was in the dark kitchen on the other side of a screen door for most of the brief time I saw him.

"I'll look through the mugshots at the station," I replied, although I doubted it would do much good.

But in my gut, I knew I would recognise the kid if I saw him again. He had a cocky confidence and a look in his eyes when he lied to me that I wouldn't forget.

2

GUNS, WEED, AND A NEW OUTFIT

"What happened to your face?" was how Jazzy greeted me when I arrived home.

"A work thing," I replied, tired of talking about the bruising and whether I had a concussion or not.

Whittaker had insisted I go to the hospital and be checked over, where they prodded, poked, and grilled me about how I felt. Fortunately, he had a uniform drive me who stayed in the lobby, so I lied and told them my head didn't hurt, my vision was clear, and I wasn't in the least bit nauseous. I may also have given them the impression that I hadn't lost consciousness at all. Possible Grade 1 concussion was their conclusion, which was better than the Grade 3 which it probably was. That would mean all kinds of days off and follow-up appointments. I didn't have time for that. I thanked them and did my best to walk a straight line out the front door.

"Hope you got whoever did that to you," Jazzy added.

She was sitting on our little deck in front of our shack feeding Edvard the endangered blue iguana who had adopted us. Her voice was even, but her eyes seemed full of concern as she winced at the bruising on the bridge of my nose. I think it was concern. I couldn't focus that well, so perhaps that was wishful thinking on my part.

"He'll have a nasty bruise on his forearm," I replied, opening the door to go inside.

My entire house was only the size of most people's living rooms, but it was mine, courtesy of a kind old man named Archie Winters. He'd had to leave the island in a hurry and deeded the property to me to make sure a greedy developer didn't get his hands on it. There was no direct access from the road as the little dwelling had been the caretaker's cottage as part of a large resort, which had long since been torn down. Most of the time I parked my Jeep by the road, ducked through a hole in the fence, then hiked through the woods to where the shack sat overlooking the Caribbean Sea.

Even with its easement issues, I couldn't imagine what the property was worth now, as prices for lots and homes on the island had skyrocketed over the past few years. New condos and big homes seemed to be going up everywhere. West Bay had always been a sleepy little town where mostly locals lived to the north of the world-famous Seven Mile Beach. But now the rocky ironshore coastline was starting to look more like a continuation of the multi-million-dollar price tag places on the west coast.

I poured myself a glass of wine, ignoring the doctor's no-alcohol directive, and stared out the window. Beyond the deck, the late-afternoon sun shimmered on the wind-chopped surface of the ocean. It was my shack, and I'd never sell it, but I'd deed it back to Archie the moment he returned. If he ever did, which I doubted would happen. I received postcards every once in a while from various places around the world, never in the same handwriting, unsigned, but the message was always the same. 'Still kicking. Stay out of trouble. Mostly. Use them if you need them.' They made me smile every time a card showed up in my box at the post office. The *use them* part referred to the diamonds hidden in an urn on Spanish Bay Reef out front of the shack. They were also the reason Archie fled the island.

I took my wine outside and sat in the other chair. Edvard eyed me suspiciously but held his ground. It had taken a while for him to trust us enough to take lettuce from our hands. His lizard brain seemed to still think it was a cunning ploy to lure him into becoming a pair of shoes.

Letting out a sigh, I relaxed, sipping the wine and enjoying the breeze off the water. My head ached and the bridge of my nose throbbed, but the dizziness had subsided and my eyes appeared to be focusing properly again. I attributed that to the wine.

"I have a run meet tomorrow," Jazzy said, sitting back in her chair, having run out of treats for the lizard.

"Where?" I asked. She'd been doing really well in the 100-metre and 200-metre sprints.

"At my school. It's a Christmas fun event. Ten until two."

"You're not racing?"

"We are, but it's just for fun," she replied.

"Then it's not a race," I pointed out, as it seemed obvious to me. You're either trying to beat the other runners to win the race or you're goofing around having fun. You can't have both.

"I don't know," Jazzy said. "I've never done one of these before."

"Why are they having it tomorrow?" I asked, frowning, which I quickly stopped as it hurt. Today had been her last day of school before Christmas break. She didn't go back until the new year.

She shrugged her shoulders as teenagers are prone to doing, accompanied by a grunt which may have meant 'I don't know'.

The kid was fifteen now. Having grown up fending for herself on the streets for several years, she was far more mature than her peers in many ways, but behind in a few others. I was doing my best to bring her social skills up to par, but as I didn't have any myself, it wasn't going that well.

My mobile rang in my pocket, and I took it out to check the caller ID. It was Whittaker.

"Sir," I answered.

"How are you, Nora? What did the doctor say?"

"I'm fine, sir. He said it might be a low-grade concussion but nothing to worry about."

"Really? They don't usually use the terms *concussion* and *nothing to worry about* in the same sentence, Nora."

"He didn't seem concerned, sir," I assured him, feeling slightly guilty about bending the truth.

"Did he say you could work?" Whittaker asked.

"Sure," I replied. Which was a lie. He hadn't specifically told me I *could* work, but he hadn't said I *couldn't* either. He'd asked me if I had duty over the next couple of days and I'd told him the truth. I didn't. The classes were during the week and I didn't have any shifts assigned over the weekend. The doctor had said something about that being good and I was to come back in if any symptoms worsened. Then he was called away for some kid with a finger hanging off, so I left.

Whittaker was quiet on the line.

"What did you find in the house, sir?"

"Five handguns and close to ten pounds of weed. We'll see if we can trace the origins of the firearms. Maybe we can get an idea of the path they took to get here."

We both knew that was a long shot. The guns would have almost certainly started life in America, but may well have arrived via Jamaica or Mexico. The market for guns and drugs wasn't huge, with a population somewhere around 80,000, but large enough to have boats sneaking in under the cover of night. We were beginning to suspect the gangs were flying crew members overseas to buy the guns, who then returned by boat.

The immigration services were monitoring for people who left the island by plane but didn't return the same way. The problem was we had no idea if the individuals were back on the island or not unless they popped up in the system somewhere for a parking ticket or arrest. Most were students or innocent people spending the summer with family somewhere. Wide-net searches like that quickly overwhelmed the limited resources we had at our disposal.

"That's five guns off the streets, sir," I commented, as it was true. In many places, five weapons meant nothing, but on our little island that number put a dent in the problem.

"Indeed," Whittaker agreed, somewhat absentmindedly. His thoughts were elsewhere. "Are you sure you're cleared for duty, Nora?"

"Why, sir?" I replied, avoiding the question. "What do you need?"

"Have you ever read anything by Lisa Regan?" he asked.

"Read, as in books, sir?"

"Yes, Nora, as in books. She's a very famous author."

She can't be that famous, I thought to myself. I've never heard of her. But I suppose that wasn't fair, as I hadn't heard of anyone who wrote fiction books, starred in movies, or made music. I didn't own a TV, have music on my cheap mobile phone, or have time to read books. If I did, I'd read nonfiction about something useful. Like psychology, fixing Jeep parts, or picking locks.

"What did she do, sir?" I wondered. If the woman had turned from writing books to killing people, she might be interesting after all.

"It's what she's about to do. Seriously, you haven't seen anything in the paper about her?"

"No," I said, trying and failing to hide my impatience. My head still hurt, although I wasn't about to tell my boss.

"Her latest thriller book is set for release on Christmas Eve, here on Grand Cayman. *The Compass* has been running articles all week about it."

"I don't read the paper, sir," I reminded him.

I heard him sigh into the phone. "I do know that, Nora, but it still surprises me sometimes. There are things going on worth knowing about."

I hoped he wasn't pressing for some author launching a book as being a compelling reason for me to read the paper or watch the news. Russia invades Norway would be news I should know about, not some lady making up stories.

"What does Lily Fagan have to do with us, sir?" I asked, preferring to get to the point.

"Lisa Regan," he corrected. "The megayacht cruise with her fans arrives tomorrow morning, and she flies in after lunch. There'll be events on the yacht every day while it's here. The governor is a big fan and has committed the RCIPS to provide security."

"Security against what, sir? Paper cuts at a signing?"

Whittaker laughed. "It's just a presence to make sure Mrs Regan feels safe while she's here. I had two constables lined up to split the shifts, but one of them has the flu. Can't have him getting everyone on the yacht sick."

"And you want me to babysit this woman?" I said, somewhat surprised. It sounded more like a PR exercise than police work. Definitely not my forte.

"The notion had occurred to me when you said you're cleared for duty. But on second thoughts, it's probably not the best idea."

Dritt. It sounded like a horrible assignment. Sitting around for twelve hours a day while this old lady author signed books and pretended to like a bunch of people who'd paid to spend their Christmas with a stranger.

"I'll do it," I said.

The washing machine had died last week, so I'd replaced it along with the dryer, which had been making terrifying clunking noises at various times during its efforts to never completely dry anything. At a guess, I figured they were almost as old as Jazzy, so it was hardly surprising. Anyway, I still hadn't bought the kid anything for Christmas, which apparently fell under duties of a foster parent, so I needed the extra shifts. Especially if it meant holiday pay.

"That's okay, I'll find someone," Whittaker responded.

"I doubt it," I pointed out. "Unless you really want to piss them off."

"Excuse me?" he said, and I cringed.

"Sorry, sir. I just meant that the shifts over the holidays were set ages ago, and people with families like Jacob either scheduled the time off or traded shifts to be home with their kids. At this point, you'll be pulling someone away from their family for Christmas, sir."

The line was quiet while my boss chewed it over. I was right on both counts. He'd be ruining someone's Christmas, and I was a shitty option for the gig. Which he knew. Now he had to decide which choice was least bad in the big scheme of things.

"You'll be required to be polite, Nora."

"Yes, sir. I'll be the nicest Nora ever, sir."

"Hmm," he grunted. "I doubt that'll be enough, but fine. Meet me at the harbour at 2:00pm."

"Two, sir?" I said, looking over at Jazzy, who of course rolled her eyes.

"Yes. She lands at noon. Constable Foster and I are meeting her at the airport. You can join us at the yacht and we'll introduce you to Mrs Regan. You'll have the 6pm until 6am shifts."

It sounded like I was getting the 2pm until 6am shift to kick things off, but I'd already talked him into me taking the assignment, so I couldn't fuss now.

"Uniform, sir?"

"No, plain clothes. Wear whatever you have ready for detective duty."

"Yes, sir. Thank you," I said, and hung up.

I didn't have anything picked out for detective duty, as I wasn't a detective yet, which Driscoll constantly reminded me. My wardrobe consisted of uniforms, leggings, tank tops, and a rain jacket. Great. Now I had to buy clothes in order to make money to pay for the washer and dryer and Christmas gift. After covering the clothes.

"Ten until two," Jazzy reminded me with a frown.

"Ten until one forty-five," I replied. "I have to babysit some big-shot author."

"Lisa Regan?" Jazzy responded excitedly.

Maybe I should look at the paper every once in a while.

3

OVERCOMMITTED

Fortunately, the Cayman Islands Humane Society Thrift Shop opened at 9am on Saturday mornings. With plenty of wealthy homeowners around, the charity shop could be a gold mine for picking up high-end designer clothes for a steal. So I'd been told. I wouldn't know a designer outfit from one stitched together in a Chinese sweat shop. Somewhere on the RCIPS server was a dress code guide for all ranks and roles, but I'd forgotten to check it out. I figured basic trousers and a blouse ought to get the job done. No way was I about to start wearing a blazer in this heat. Or a tie. Unless they were in the style guide, in which case I'd have to, but not today. Whittaker wasn't about to send me home because I didn't have a jacket on.

"Here," Jazzy said, holding up a white blouse with flowers all over it in various shades of red.

"*Nei.*"

She grinned at me.

"Help me find something I can actually wear."

Jazzy put the flowery shirt back on the rack and continued rummaging. I thumbed through the trousers which had far less on offer than skirts and dresses. A navy blue pair was perfect except the length was a bunch too short for my 175 centimetres, or 5 foot 9 inches, as the island used imperial measurements for most things. I finally came across a dark grey pair of trousers which looked like they might work. I kicked my trainers off and pulled down the leggings I was wearing.

"Use the changing room!" Jazzy hissed at me, looking around to see if anyone was watching.

"I have underwear on," I muttered, pulling up the trousers. They were a size too big around the waist, but at least they were the right length. I could cinch a belt and make them work.

But I'd brought the plainest pair of trainers I owned and they were not going to work. White with purple and orange looked like a couple of flavourful ice lollies at the bottom of my legs. In uniform, I wore black boots, but that certainly wouldn't go unnoticed.

"How about this one?" Jazzy asked, holding up another blouse.

It was pale bluish grey.

"Would it fit you?" I asked.

She shrugged. "Close. Probably a bit big."

I reached out and Jazzy handed it to me. She was a lot shorter than me, but otherwise getting to be about the same size. She'd always been skinny, but since joining the running team, her figure had taken on more muscle.

Peeling off my T-shirt, I put the blouse on and buttoned it up. After tucking it into the trousers and pulling my hair out from under the collar, I looked at the kid.

"What do you think?"

"I think you could wear pyjamas and no one will notice anything except the weird colours your nose and face are turning."

"*Takk,*" I muttered and found a mirror.

The outfit would work if I found some shoes, but Jazzy was right, my face looked like… well, it looked like I'd been clobbered between the eyes.

"I need shoes. Plain trainers, not dress shoes. I can't run in dress shoes."

"I thought you said you were babysitting the author lady? Shouldn't be too much running involved."

"You never know," I replied, scouring the shoe shelves. Most of the trainers were multicoloured or at least had stripes. A black pair I came across were too small.

"It's quarter to ten," Jazzy informed me. "I shouldn't be late."

"Ja, okay."

Nothing would be open on Sunday, so I'd have to make do until I could try another shop on Monday. Which I remembered was Christmas Day. *Dritt*. It was either the ice lollies I already owned or a pair of only slightly less colourful second-hand trainers which were half a size too small.

Leaving on the trousers and blouse, I hurriedly paid for them, and we left. By the time we reached the Truman Bodden Sports Complex where the high school held events, it was 9:59am. Jazzy hopped out while I searched for a place to park the Jeep.

The first thing I noticed when I walked back to the field was the abundance of Christmas theme. I could get with the spirit after dark with the colourful lights and decorations, but seeing kids running around wearing Father Christmas hats and elf outfits in the middle of the tropical day was weird. Everyone was sweating from the intense sun and humidity. Apparently, someone must have loaned Jazzy a red bobble hat too when I spotted her with a group of friends.

After a few hours, I now understood what the school meant by a friendly event. Most of the kids competed with some form of holiday adornment attached to their bodies. Runners sprinted across the line holding hands instead of dipping their chests to beat each other, and I watched a boy fail the high jump when his green, red, and white scarf dragged the bar off. It took me a while to get past my natural annoyance at the pretence of competition, but Jazzy seemed to be having fun, so I eventually relaxed and found a shady spot to watch.

I wished I'd put my leggings and T-shirt back on as I was sweating in the blouse which I'd be wearing all night, but after lunch a breeze kicked up and knocked the edge off the heat. At 1:30pm my friend AJ Bailey showed up as arranged. She led a busy life running a dive boat operation and Saturdays were usually her only day off during the week. I'd felt bad asking if she could take Jazzy home, but she swore she had nothing else planned. That may have been true, but it was equally likely that she had frantically called around after getting off the phone with me and cancelled or rescheduled a million things.

"How's she been running?" AJ asked as she sat next to me in the stands.

"They're just screwing around," I replied.

"Oh, everyone's dressed up. How fun," AJ exclaimed. She was one of those people with an infectious enthusiasm and joy. Except in the early mornings. She needed the sun to rise and at least one large cup of coffee before her positivity kicked in, and then she was unstoppable. Although I prided myself on being generally impervious to her overzealous glee. It wasn't that I tried to be even tempered about everything, it was just the way I was wired. It was partly a Norwegian thing, but mostly a me thing.

"I can't believe you'll be meeting Lisa Regan," AJ continued. "That's brilliant."

"So people keep saying."

"You've never heard of her, have you?" AJ teased.

"Of course I have. Whittaker told me who she was last night when he said I have to watch her."

AJ laughed. "She writes the Detective Josie Quinn series. I love her books. Do you think you can get one autographed for me?"

"I doubt it."

"Why? You're guarding her for days," AJ responded. "That's what she'll be doing here, signing books. I'm sure she'd scribble in one more. I'll leave a copy at the shack."

I grunted a non-committal response. I was supposed to be babysitting the woman, not getting her to sign her name all over the place. Autographs were something I didn't get either. *Why was it so cool to have the signature of some celebrity? Where does that end?* I'd be more inclined to get the signature from a doctor who sewed a limb back on than a lady who made up a story.

"I was thinking I'd take Jazzy to the cinema later if that's alright with you?" AJ asked.

"Sure."

"You don't want to know what film we'll see?"

"*Nei.*"

"I think that's supposed to be one of those parental things you have to ask, Nora. You know, to make sure they're not seeing bloodthirsty stuff and naked willies."

I looked at her and frowned. Which still hurt. "They show films with naked willies at the cinema in Camana Bay?"

"Probably not," she admitted. "But it's still a parenty thing to ask."

"I trust your judgement," I replied.

"Great. That makes me sound super boring."

"*Ja.*"

"Hey, I'm not a boring pretend auntie. And by the way, I swore I wouldn't say anything, but I'm having a hard time looking at you. That must really hurt."

I touched a hand to the swollen bridge of my nose. "And I was thinking it wasn't very noticeable."

AJ busted up laughing, and this time I couldn't help but laugh too.

I stood up. "Keep the kid away from willies, please. I have to go."

"Fine," she replied as I began to leave. "We'll have a boring, willy-free evening."

I grinned again as I noticed several parents turning their heads to see who was talking. AJ was now blushing.

At the bottom of the stands, I tried to catch Jazzy's attention so I could wave goodbye. She was getting ready for her last race on the far side of the field. The 200 metres final. I recognised several of her friends standing nearby and then spotted a boy with his back to me. Jazzy was talking to him. I called him a boy, but I suppose he was really a young man. He was quite tall and athletic looking, although he wasn't competing. Or he'd already changed out of his kit.

Jazzy put a hand on his arm and smiled at the young man before turning away and going to the starting blocks. AJ and I had been joking about men's appendages, but maybe I needed to pay better attention to what was happening around my foster kid. I turned away and walked briskly to the Jeep. Some of these *parenty things*, as AJ had called them, were coming at me a little too fast for my liking.

I parked illegally and stuck my police sign in the window of the Jeep. Undoubtedly, some jerk would steal the sign as my car was topless, but maybe I'd have time to come back and move it later. On the south side of Hog Sty Bay, against the dock where the old Nautilus submarine used to moor, was a large luxury yacht. It had to be around 50 metres, or over 160 feet, long. I could see the name *Maureen* on the side. Christmas lights and decorations were strung along the railing of each deck and a large inflatable Father Christmas holding a book sat on the roof, tethered in place by several lines.

"Constable Sommer," I heard Whittaker's voice from behind me. "Have you met Constable Gabriel Foster before?"

I turned and recognised the officer's face, but I didn't think we'd met before. He extended a hand and stared intently into my eyes.

"Pleased to meet you," he said with a soft Caymanian accent.

"Hi," I responded, noticing Whittaker was also gawking at me strangely.

"Are you sure you should be on duty?" the detective asked.

I guess I should've tried to cover the bruising up with makeup, but I almost never wore any and when I did, it was usually a touch of eyeliner. I'd have screwed it up worse if I'd tried plastering foundation all over my face.

"Good to go, sir," I replied.

Whittaker nodded and turned back towards the road where a large black SUV had pulled up next to my old Jeep. The driver got out and opened the back door. After a few moments, a woman with long brunette hair appeared. She was younger than I'd expected, and surprisingly normal looking. Turning back to the open door, she reached in to get a bag or something.

"We'll do the introductions and then we'll have time to talk about the role with Mrs Regan, and between ourselves," Whittaker said.

"Yes, sir," Foster and I both acknowledged.

When I looked back, the author was walking towards us. Trotting beside her on the end of a lead was the ugliest dog I think I'd ever seen. If you took a 10-kilogram terrier and ran it into a wall at high speed, this would be what I imagined the result to be. His tongue lolled out of one side of his mouth.

"Hello again," the lady said in an American accent. "Is this the other officer you mentioned?" she asked and extended a hand in my direction.

I shook. "Constable Sommer, ma'am."

"Lisa Regan," she replied. "You're younger than I expected."

"You're younger than I expected," I responded.

She winced. "Are you okay? Looks like someone popped you a good one."

I looked down at the dog and was about to ask if he'd been smacked in the face too, but Whittaker spoke up and herded the author towards the yacht.

"Let's get out of the sun. I believe your suite is ready on the yacht, Mrs Regan."

"Please, call me Lisa. Come on, Mr Phillip, let's see where we're staying for a few days," she said to the ugly dog as they walked down the dock to where several crew members awaited.

"Nicest Nora, remember?" Whittaker whispered as we followed.

"About that, sir," I whispered in return. "I think I may have overcommitted."

4

FANCY HATS AND BOXING DAY

The captain, who spoke with a highbrow English accent, greeted Lisa as though she were royalty, and then turned to us for introductions. I learnt that Captain Elliott Marston had been in charge of the MV *Maureen* since she'd been launched four years ago. He explained that the passengers were currently on an excursion to Hell, the black limestone rock formation in West Bay, named for its jagged and daunting appearance, so Lisa was safe to look around the yacht without being ambushed by a fan.

A few steps from where we stood was the best suite on the vessel, which would be Lisa's for the next three days. It had its own entrance from the upper cabin deck at the stern. Her berth was spacious for a room on a boat, with a queen-size bed and a full en suite shower and bathroom, but still felt very congested with the three of us crowded inside with her. The captain shuffled outside once he'd shown Lisa the amenities.

"This is all a bit silly, really," she said, petting the dog, who'd immediately jumped onto the bed. "My publisher insisted on all this security, but it's quite unnecessary. I'm a novelist, not some controversial nonfiction writer penning exposés on political figures."

"Think of it as an extra blanket to make sure you're comfortable," Whittaker responded. "Purely for peace of mind."

"I'm plenty warm enough, thank you, Detective. Your island is certainly tropical. It was a few degrees above freezing when I left home this morning." Lisa wiped her forehead. "We're running heaters and you have the air conditioning on full blast."

I thought it was downright frosty in the cabin. The perspiration from spending hours outside at the athletics field was now chilly against my skin. The staff must have turned the temperature way down before their guest had arrived.

"Anyway," Lisa continued, "I appreciate everyone's concern, but it's all rather embarrassing, to be honest."

"Have you ever received any threats?" Whittaker asked.

Lisa waved a hand at him. "One or two, but nothing serious. A fan of the series got mad because Josie dumped one character and ended up marrying another one. I guess they didn't like that and sent me a few nasty letters."

"Letters or emails?" I asked.

"Letters in the mail," Lisa replied.

"Did the police run fingerprints? Trace the address or at least the postmark to get the area?" I pressed.

Lisa laughed. "I threw the first one away, but I thought about contacting the police when the second one arrived. Then they stopped, so I forgot all about it."

"How long ago was this?" Whittaker asked.

"A few years back," she replied. "Three or four, I suppose. I shouldn't have even mentioned it, really. I'm perfectly safe here, I assure you. These people have sacrificed their Christmas with family at home to spend time with other readers and get to be part of the book launch. The worst anyone here will do is trap me in conversation for hours."

Mr Phillip waddled across the bed and stood in front of me. Foster reached out to pet him, but the dog made a low rumbling growl. Foster quickly rescinded his offer of pets.

"Oh, don't be silly, Mr Phillip," Lisa said, patting the bed.

"Come here and leave the nice people alone. They're here to look after us."

The dog kept looking up at me for some reason. Maybe he was joining the long queue of people wondering who hit me. Regardless, I didn't consider that my job extended to looking after the mutt, so he'd better find his own protection.

"As I mentioned at the airport," Whittaker said, "Foster and Sommer will be with you throughout your stay. They will try to blend into the background, but please let them know if you notice anything unusual or suspicious they should be aware of."

Lisa looked at Foster and then me.

"When you say throughout my stay, what exactly do you mean? At night as well?"

"Yes, ma'am," Whittaker replied. "They'll work twelve-hour shifts, trading at 6pm and 6am."

"Twelve hours?" Lisa's eyes widened. "That's a long day for both of you. Surely I don't need guarding at night? I was told the island is very safe."

"We pride ourselves on our visitors' safety, ma'am," Whittaker responded. "But one should never be complacent. You'll hardly know they're here."

She glanced around the room and then at the door. "You won't be inside my room, will you?"

Whittaker smiled. "No, ma'am. Just outside."

"All night?"

"Yes, ma'am."

Lisa looked at me. "If you hear snoring, it's Mr Phillip, not me."

"I hope I do," I replied.

The woman looked puzzled. "You like hearing snoring?"

"I'll know you're still alive."

She stared at me. I waited a few moments until I grinned.

"Oh my gosh," she said, laughing. "You had me going there."

I felt Whittaker's eyes burning into the side of my head. I thought I was doing a good job of breaking the snow. It was the best I could do with a sore face and a concussion.

"Shall we take the captain up on his offer of a tour?" the detective suggested, and I was glad to funnel out of the confined cabin.

"Stay there," Lisa told the dog, who looked up at her with his buggy eyes and short snout. "Don't give that look, Mr Phillip. I'll only be a few minutes."

She pulled the door closed, and I heard a whine from inside the cabin.

"He'll be far more settled once my luggage is here and he has his bed and all his toys," Lisa said. Perhaps she thought I shared her concern over Mr Phillip's state of mind.

"Okay," I said, remembering I was under orders to be nice, and nice people acknowledged things like that.

The yacht was a warren of rooms and corridors over four decks. The lower cabin deck contained the crew's quarters and the engine room fore and aft, with guest berths in the middle, and the upper cabin deck was all guest rooms. The salon deck housed the bridge, captain's quarters, galley, crew mess, and a large salon for dining and a meeting area where most of the daily events would take place. Outside the double doors to the stern was a covered sun deck with ample seating for the group, where more events were scheduled to take place. Above was a sun deck with lifeboats on davits towards the stern, a hot tub, and the inflatable Father Christmas.

"Will the yacht remain at dock?" I asked when the captain finished walking us around and we stood in the salon.

"We have a snorkelling trip planned tomorrow morning, and a sunset dinner cruise tomorrow evening," the captain explained. "Otherwise, we'll remain in port until we depart on Boxing Day."

"I saw Boxing Day on my itinerary," Lisa said. "That's an English thing, isn't it?"

"It's the name we use for the day after Christmas," the captain replied.

"Ooh, I like an extra vacation day. I'm all for that," Lisa grinned and turned to me. "Where are you from, Constable Sommer? Do you have Boxing Day?"

"Norway," I replied. "Boxing Day is just a British thing. The rich used to give the peasants a gift in a box, but I don't think they do that anymore. They have football matches and eat leftovers instead. We have Stefansdagen."

The captain shuffled uncomfortably. I guessed his family tree contained a bunch of posh landowners who tossed their servants a token gift or two over the years.

"Stefan… whatsit?" Lisa questioned. "What is that?"

"St Stephen's Day in English."

"Like in the Christmas carol?" she asked excitedly.

"Huh?" It was my turn to be stumped.

"Good King Wenceslas," Whittaker offered. "On the feast of Stephen."

Lisa continued the tune in a half-hearted, self-conscious effort at singing. "When the snow lay round about, deep and crisp and even." She blushed. "I like that one."

"I'm sure it'll be in the playlist of Christmas music we have prepared, Mrs Regan," the captain assured her.

Somebody groaned, and everyone looked at me. I guess I'd been the one who'd groaned. I didn't mean to, but I was already sick of hearing Christmas music playing everywhere. In fact, I'd been fed up with it before December had even begun. This is why we had too many rules and laws in the world. When we don't, some corporate *drittsekk* decides pumping holiday music out a month too early will get us all to buy more junk we don't need.

"Does the gangway remain in place overnight?" Foster asked, and I was grateful to him for pulling the attention away from me. And I considered it a good question.

"It does," the captain replied. "Safety protocol in case of an emergency."

He was now looking down, and it took me a moment to realise the captain was staring at my trainers. Apparently, he'd torn himself away from my bruised face to discover my next flaw.

"Does the yacht have any other access points?" Foster asked.

"Not directly," the captain replied, lifting his gaze.

"But anyone could approach from the water or below the

water," I pointed out. "I assume you have someone on duty at all times, but not on security watch."

"My gosh," Lisa scoffed. "They say we writers have to think like a villain to come up with our plots, but I suppose you do too. This would be fun if we weren't talking about me being the target."

"There's absolutely no cause for alarm, ma'am," Whittaker quickly assured her. "It's our job to think ahead and consider all the angles, but perhaps we should continue this conversation in private and let you settle in?"

"That's quite okay. I may pick up a good storyline from all this," Lisa said, looking slightly uneasy. "I won't sleep a wink tonight, but I do that to myself sometimes after I write a really juicy murder scene."

"Is that the guests coming back?" Foster asked, and everyone turned to look out the salon windows towards the entrance to the dock.

Several vans had parked where they shouldn't, and huddles of people had formed.

"Oh dear," Lisa muttered, looking at her watch. "I wish my publisher would get here. She must have gone on the tour with the guests. She handles all this nonsense."

"What is *this nonsense*?" Captain Marston asked.

"Press," I offered.

"Yup," Lisa confirmed. "Necessary evil, I'm afraid. We can't have a book launch without the people who tell the world about it."

"How come they weren't at the airport when you arrived?" Whittaker asked.

Lisa laughed. "Because we leaked that I'd be on the Miami flight, which landed an hour after mine did."

"Won't they be mad about that?" Foster asked. "You need them to write nice things about your book, don't you?"

"They're not the literary critics," Lisa replied. "The critics received copies weeks ago. Their articles are already written. Most have been published before the book is even released. This crowd are the media circus who want to capture the launch hoopla and get a witty quote."

I looked at Lisa. She didn't strike me as the type who liked being in front of cameras and being put on the spot.

"No," she said, catching my eye and shaking her head, "I'm not full of fancy one-liners. Hell, it's killing me to have to wear real clothes and put on makeup. I spend most days wearing sweatpants and one of my husband's baggy T-shirts, hanging with Mr Phillip in my office. If he could use indoor plumbing, I wouldn't step outside some days."

I pictured her dog sitting awkwardly on a toilet.

A tour bus pulled up and tried to park, but the vans were all in the way. Traffic on the narrow street by the waterfront came to a stop in both directions while people poured out of the bus, led by a tall lady who looked more like she was dressed to go to a horse race than Hell. She held the large, lacy, hat-like thing on her head to stop the wind from whisking it away, and her blue and white floral dress billowed. I could tell from this far away that she was barking orders at the guests as well as the press, who tossed their cigarettes carelessly away on the dock and rushed over.

"That's your publisher, isn't it?" I groaned.

"Yes, in the dress," Lisa confirmed. "She'll soon have everyone whipped into shape."

I felt Whittaker nudge me, and I looked his way. He raised an eyebrow.

"Sir," I said quietly, acknowledging his reminder.

But he hadn't mentioned blunt-faced dogs and bossy publisher women when he'd let me volunteer for this train wreck. I wondered if I could still back out of the gig, but I knew the answer was no. Whittaker would have to ruin someone else's Christmas holiday and they'd know it was because I bailed out.

I still had no clue what I was going to buy the kid for Christmas, but if I had to deal with this mess, she'd better appreciate the heck out of it, whatever it ended up being.

5

POCKET PLASTIC AND DOGS ON DRUGS

It was decided that as I was already there and the meet-and-greet started at 5pm that Foster and I would both stay and get acquainted with the yacht and the crew for a few hours. He'd then leave at 6pm after getting an insight into the way the gatherings would go. Constable Gabriel Foster seemed like a nice guy, but it was odd working with a different partner. Jacob Tibbetts and I had each other figured out, and he'd learnt to deal with my quirks, as I had with his. Which was easy, as he was the nicest guy and generally rolled with whatever I preferred. Unless I wandered too far off the rails, and then he'd do his best to reel me back a notch. In my opinion, we made a good team.

Gabriel was mid-twenties, a little taller than me, and his suit hung from his frame in a way that suggested he was in good shape. He was Caymanian, but had grown up spending time split between the island and a town I couldn't remember the name of in Arizona. Most of his schooling had been in America, which explained his light local accent.

We made a point of meeting all eight of the crew, who were mostly American with two Brits and a French chef. Only one of them was new to the crew. The ship's handyman and mechanic,

Blake, but he'd joined before their prior charter a few weeks back. I jotted down their names and any details I felt were important and noticed Gabriel doing the same thing.

The guests were harder to vet. We were given a passenger list, but it was too late to run any meaningful background checks before the five o'clock gathering. Besides, Barbara Mitchell, the publisher's representative, had made it clear she didn't want us bothering the guests. She expected us to be invisible, not carry any weapons or police-like gear, or wear anything that made us look like police or security that might intimidate the guests. Of course, she also didn't want any harm to come to her prized novelist either, but apparently that was our problem regardless of the restrictions she placed on us.

"How do I look?" Lisa asked as we prepared to leave her cabin and head up to the salon.

"Okay," I told her. She was wearing a colourfully patterned dress which fell just below her knees and a pair of black Oxfords.

"Thanks for the glowing endorsement," she said, looking at herself in the mirror.

"I said you look okay," I pointed out. "I would tell you if I thought you looked like *dri*… if you didn't look okay."

"I believe you would, Miss Sommer," she replied, but didn't sound happy. "May I call you Nora?" she asked. "That's your first name, right? Nora?"

"Sure."

She forced a brief smile in my direction. "Calling you Sommer conjures up images of flowers in bloom and the warm sun on my face. But that's not really you, is it, Nora?"

I wasn't sure where this conversation was going, but she seemed irritated with me for some reason. If she needed gushing compliments, her security detail was probably not the people she should be asking, but I figured there was something else going on as well.

"Are you nervous?" I asked as she fussed with the buttons on her dress and mumbled things to the dog who stood on the bed, sensing something was afoot.

Lisa stopped messing with her outfit. "I am a bit, yes."

"Don't worry, Gabriel and I are both here. No one will get to you," I assured her, leaving out the part about being unable to defend her from a sniper's bullet from the shore, or even another boat. Gabriel and I had discussed line-of-sight opportunities from the salon earlier.

She laughed. "I'm not in the least bit worried about that."

"Then why are you nervous?"

Lisa looked frazzled. "Because there's a bunch of people who shelled out a good deal of money, waiting for me to be something special, and they'll probably be disappointed by the time the evening's over."

"So?" I responded. "It was their choice to pay for this trip. You can't control their expectations."

She sighed. "I know, but it still makes me uneasy." She petted the dog. "You have to stay here, Mr P." Lisa turned to me. "He's an Instagram hound, but in truth, he's not great in a group of people."

The mutt looked at me as though I had something to do with whether he got to come to the party or not. I ignored his pleading stare and moved to the door, where I paused with my hand on the knob.

"Special treat, buddy?" Lisa said to the dog, who instantly turned into a jumping bean of frenzied excitement.

She tossed him a small stuffed animal of some sort which he caught in the air. I thought it might be a hedgehog, but it was hard to tell, hanging from the side of his mouth.

A thought came to me as I opened the door. "Have any of these people come to things like this before? Have they heard you talk in interviews, or on those podcast things I've heard about?"

"Most of them, I'd say," she replied. "Perhaps all of them, I suppose. I recognise all their names, so they must have been to an event or interacted on my social media. Part of the business is being active online and all those things we have to do these days."

"So, it's no problem then," I declared brightly as I stepped outside and nodded to Gabriel, who was waiting. "They know not to expect much."

Lisa made a weird noise, somewhere between a cough and a laugh, then cleared her throat. "Thank you for that, Nora," she said, as she followed and closed the door behind her. "I see now you can be quite inspiring when you put your mind to it."

"You're welcome," I said, although her tone wasn't altogether convincing.

Regardless, I had a job to do, so I scanned the dock and the waters across the bay. Mr Phillip whined behind the cabin door while Gabriel led Lisa up the steps to the sun deck, where cheers and applause echoed off the fibreglass walls.

While I'd expected the author to be older, I was just as surprised by the age of her readers. Or at least the twelve who'd come on the cruise for the book launch. I'd thought they'd been polite letting the older folks get off the bus first when we'd seen them returning from Hell, but the average age of the group in the salon was probably sixty. It appeared Barbara Mitchell had been correct. The guests were unlikely to be a threat. Plus, why would an assailant pay all this money to be onboard when, for the price of an air ticket, they could sneak on the yacht for a fraction of the cost?

But my job was to protect her, so I stayed close and watched everyone. Which meant all the people noticed me. Most stared at me in some form of confusion. Whether it was my bruising or my mere presence, I wasn't sure. I wished I was in uniform, as at least that would explain my existence. I probably looked like a cow chewing the cud too. My tongue was incredibly sore where I'd bitten it, and I kept catching myself moving it around and puffing my cheeks. There was one man who carefully and slowly surveyed every part of my body until his lecherous gaze finally met my eyes.

He smiled at me. I did not smile back, and he shuffled off to rejoin his wife.

I was also surprised at the mixture of people. There were three couples, of which one was two ladies, a group of four women who seemed to be part of a club, and one woman and one man on their own. Lisa gave them equal time and was incredibly gracious and patient. There was a lot of laughter and just about everyone asked about her dog. Barbara flitted about in another extravagant outfit although she'd chosen a slightly less wind-sensitive hat. Between her height, authoritative voice, and colourful dress, she was easy to spot as she moved through the crowd, never too far behind Lisa.

Gabriel slipped away quietly around six. It was good we both got to see the guests interacting with the author and it gave us an opportunity to discuss areas to watch closely and anyone in the crowd we found worth paying extra attention to. It all felt like overkill, but Gabriel took it as seriously as I did, so I felt like we'd work together well. Not that we really would, as we'd only cross paths twice a day, but it was good to know I could trust any notes he passed on.

It was an easy environment to become complacent, and I kept reminding myself to stay alert. At 6:30pm the group sat at the tables for dinner, during which Lisa didn't eat much, but circulated from table to table to chat with everyone. One of the servers kept topping up my stainless-steel drinks bottle with water, although he tried to bring me something stronger. Later, he offered to fix me a plate of food, which I declined. Not only because he was trying to chat me up while I was working, but I knew I'd already have a hard time staying awake all night and the food wouldn't help. I hoped they'd keep a coffee pot going.

After dessert, everyone moved to the sun deck to watch the sunset and mingle. I noticed the solo male, a guy I'd guessed to be in his fifties – which made him younger than most – left the party for ten minutes. When he returned, he worked his way through the crowd towards Lisa, who had her back to him. I moved closer.

The man moved quickly, stepping between two women on the

far side of Lisa, and reached into his pocket. Coming from the other side, I unfortunately knocked into Lisa as I lurched past, sending her drink flying. She yelped, and another woman shrieked, but I grabbed the man's hand as it came out of his pocket. Sweeping my right leg behind his, I used my right arm across his body to take him to the ground. Pinning his wrist to the deck, whatever was in his hand clattered across the floor between the legs of the startled crowd. He wheezed when all the air was forced from his lungs, and my knee across his shoulder kept him from moving.

"What on earth is going on?!" Barbara yelled, and the crowd fell silent, standing around me and staring.

"What is that?" I asked, nodding towards where the object had flown.

A few people stepped back and one of the book club ladies reached down, picking up an object I couldn't see in the shadows. She held it up.

"This?" she said, holding up a plastic figurine of a dog. "It's a little Mr Phillip."

Fy faen. I looked at the man, whose face was a potentially problematic shade of purple.

"I was giving it to Lisa," he spluttered.

I let go of his wrist and lifted my knee, standing up.

"What the fuck were you thinking?" Barbara shouted at me.

"He came rushing through the crowd and went for something in his pocket," I replied, fighting to remain calm. "I protected my charge."

"He was bringing her a fucking toy dog!" Barbara yelled.

"Are you okay, Doug?" Lisa asked from behind me.

He didn't look particularly okay, but I reached down and helped him struggle to his feet.

"Sorry, sir," I said. "You'd better sit down for a minute."

I began helping him over to a chair, but Barbara shoved me aside.

"You've done enough. Just stay out of the way."

She and Lisa aided the guy to a chair where one of the servers brought him a glass of water. The colour in his cheeks slowly began returning to normal, and he seemed to feel as embarrassed about the incident as I did.

"I knew I'd never forget this trip," he joked.

Lisa didn't say anything to me, but she wouldn't look at me either. I figured I was probably one and done on author babysitting duty. Someone took hold of my arm and I turned to see Barbara glaring at me. She pulled me to the railing at the back of the sun deck, away from the crowd.

"I've never seen anything as unprofessional as that ridiculous display," she whisper shouted. "We'll be lucky if he doesn't sue us all."

"I've apologised, but if I'd done nothing and that had been a weapon, your author would be dead."

"But it wasn't a weapon, was it?" she snapped. "It was a plastic Boston terrier!"

I realised there was no point saying anything more. The woman was going to yell at me however much I explained myself, so it was best to keep quiet and wait to be relieved from duty.

"How long have you even been a cop?" she ranted. "I see how you got that now," she added, waving a hand at my face. "You couldn't even put a little makeup on to hide the result of your last altercation." She shifted her attention to my feet. "And what's with the tennis shoes? Don't they teach you how to dress wherever the hell you're from?"

She was a few more words away from going over the railing without a few of her teeth, but fortunately Lisa called to her.

"Be right there," she said cheerily, which I now knew was a painted on front for her cash cow.

Barbara Mitchell wasn't worth losing my job over, or being kicked out of detective training. Though I was fine with not having to come back to this gig. I'd come up with a way to get Jazzy some kind of gift.

"Nora," I heard Lisa call, and looked over. She was saying good-night to the guests.

I walked over and noticed the man was back on his feet, chattering away with a pair of ladies. I moved closer and put a hand on his arm.

"I'm very sorry, sir. My mistake, and I hope you're okay."

He smiled at me. "I'll be alright. Probably a bruise or two, so we'll look like twins."

He laughed, and the ladies laughed with him.

"Goodnight, sir."

I followed Lisa down the steps to the door to her cabin. I should have led her, and opened the door for her to check the berth, but I wasn't about to insist. She paused as she unlocked the door.

"That was a bit over the top, Nora. You know that, right?"

"I'm sorry, ma'am. I overreacted."

She nodded and thought for a few moments. When she spoke again, her voice was a whisper. "Thanks for looking out for me, though. That was kinda cool."

"That's why I'm here, ma'am."

"Goodnight, Nora."

"Goodnight, Lisa."

Maybe I wasn't getting kicked off the assignment, I thought as I watched the door close. But then Lisa screamed.

"Nora!"

I used the card they'd given me to open her door and rushed inside, looking for an intruder. But the only person I could see was Lisa, standing by the bed with her dog in her arms. Mr Phillip appeared to be out cold, his tongue hanging out more than normal and his eyes rolled back.

"Is he alive?"

"He's breathing," she gasped.

I looked around and noticed the room was a total mess, like someone had trashed the place with a strimmer. I picked up a piece of shredded… dog toy? I couldn't believe the volume of carnage the dog had made from one small soft toy. You'd think she'd left him with a life-sized teddy bear.

"He's sick from something in the toy," I suggested.

"No, no," Lisa assured me impatiently. "He does this all the time. That's why it's his special treat. I can't afford to give him hedgehogs all the time. They only last a few minutes."

Taking her word for it, I continued searching for anything else he could have consumed that had made him ill. The bathroom door was closed, and Lisa's luggage had all been put away.

"I think he's coming around," Lisa said, laying him down on the bed.

The ugly little dog groaned, and his eyes fought to focus.

"It's okay, buddy, I'm here," she assured him.

I examined the room again, checking the bathroom and the wardrobe, but nothing appeared to have been disturbed. Apart from the deceased dog toy. A picture of Lisa's husband and daughter sat on the bedside table, along with a reading tablet. I paused by the desk.

"Is there a safe in the cabin?" I asked.

"Yes, it's a small one in the bottom of the closet. Why?"

"Is that where your laptop is?" I asked, remembering I saw it on the desk where just a power cable now dangled over the edge. I'd noticed a decal on it of a smooshed-face dog like Mr Phillip.

"No, it won't fit. It's right there on the…"

"I think someone's been in here," I said, retracing my steps and everything I'd touched.

"They drugged Mr Phillip?!" Lisa realised in horror, hugging the stoned dog before looking up at me. "My new book is on that laptop. I'd just finished it on the PR stops over the last few days and the flight out here. I haven't synced it to the cloud thingy in ages, either. The last half of the book is only on that laptop."

Suddenly, I didn't feel so wrong for taking down old Doug. We had a criminal on the yacht after all.

6

PODUNK ISLAND

Rounding up a vet at 9:00pm on Grand Cayman was far more challenging than I'd imagined it to be. In the end, I called Casey, a friend with the Department of Environment, and she knew a lady who'd answer her mobile if an animal was involved. By the time she arrived, Mr Phillip appeared to be back to as normal as I'd seen him be. The vet said there wasn't much she could do and told Lisa to call her back if the dog's condition regressed.

Detective Whittaker took me ruining his evening in his stride, as usual. Our head of CSI, Rasha Howard, was less impressed. After eleven straight days working, she'd just gone to bed when I called. She was too polite in the way English people can be to say anything, but I could tell she wasn't happy about processing the cabin over what she undoubtedly considered to be a laptop we'd never see again. She'd be right if it was a random computer nicked from a house, but I sensed this was probably different.

"The door was definitely locked when you returned?" Whittaker asked me off to one side on the rear deck.

"Yes, I watched Lisa swipe her key when we returned, and I watched her close it before we left. If it's closed, it's locked. Neither of us went back to the room during the event."

"You didn't unlock the door and check the room before Lisa?"

I sighed. He'd already heard about me tackling Doug, thanks to my good friend Barbara, but letting the incident compromise my role was on me.

"I didn't, sir," I replied. "And I should have."

"Well, she had the dog in the room," he offered, which was nice of him, but still no excuse. Especially as it turned out Mr Phillip was comatose at the time. "No signs of entry through a window, which would have been difficult to do without being heard or seen, so it appears the perp had a key card," Whittaker concluded.

"Which points to crew," I added.

The detective thought for a moment. "You and Gabriel both have a key, correct?"

"Yes, sir. And I texted Gabriel to keep him up to speed. He still has his."

Whittaker nodded. "Hmmm," he murmured before looking up at me. "Have any thoughts?"

He often tested me in this way as part of his mentoring, which was annoying, but probably good for me. This time, I got the sense he was really more interested in hearing my perspective as I'd been on the yacht all evening.

"The thief is either really stupid or quite smart," I began. "A regular, devious thief would stay away from something like this. High risk, low return. If it's one of the crew, they're an idiot as they'd be the first place we'd look as they have access. I think there's more chance the thief was after what's on the laptop, not the hardware itself. Lisa told me her latest book is on it and not backed up recently."

"Some kind of publishing industry espionage?" Whittaker queried.

I shrugged. "Maybe. Or ransom."

"We need to make sure she keeps checking her email and voice-mail on her phone in that case," he replied. "The perp might contact her at some point."

"Overzealous fan," I suggested as another theory.

Whittaker looked over to where Lisa sat on a wooden folding chair outside her room with Mr Phillip on her lap. "There are much cheaper and easier ways to access Mrs Regan. Why come all the way here?"

"Maybe her house in America is guarded and super secure," I replied, but with little conviction. Lisa struck me as pretty down to earth. I'd more easily believe she'd lived in the same house for all her married life. "Brings us back to a competing publisher."

Whittaker nodded again. "Let's start with the captain and find out if anyone we're not thinking of might have access, and then we'll chat with Lisa's publishing company representative. Maybe she can shed insight into whether this sort of thing has been a problem in the past."

"Great," I mumbled, less than excited to go anywhere near Barbara.

Whittaker looked at me questioningly.

"I'll find the captain, sir."

I left while the detective checked in with Rasha, who was still dusting the cabin for prints, but I paused by Lisa.

"How is he doing?" I asked, looking at the black and white dog I now knew was a Boston terrier.

"He's conked out," she replied, looking sleepy herself.

"The captain said he'd put you in another berth," I reminded her.

She shrugged. "All our stuff is in there," she replied, throwing a thumb towards the yellow police tape across the doorway. "I'll wait it out."

Seemed better to get some sleep to me, but it was her choice. I was about to move on when I figured I'd ask another question.

"Where do you live in America?"

"Pennsylvania."

"Have you lived there a while?"

"My whole life. Why?"

"What about your current house?"

"What about it?"

"How long have you been living in it?"

"Nearly five years."

"Is it big?" I asked.

"Bigger than the little place we started with," Lisa replied. "But it's no mansion."

"Do you have staff?"

Lisa scoffed. "Sure, loads of them. I do all the laundry and make dinner every night for fun." She frowned at me. "Why is this important?"

"It's probably not. We were just wondering why someone would follow you thousands of miles to nick your laptop when they could have broken into your house in America."

Now she looked like she'd tasted something awful. Like she'd eaten a Salt Sild. As a Norwegian, I'm supposed to love the weird liquorice herring shaped sweets, but I hated them. No one outside of Scandinavia liked them either, which made me think of them when Lisa scrunched up her face. She looked like someone had tricked her into trying a Salt Sild.

"What a horrible thought. My husband and daughter are there alone."

"I'm sure they're fine as you and your computer are here," I pointed out. "Well, just you now, as the laptop is gone."

"You don't think this was neighbourhood kids?" she asked, then lowered her voice to a whisper. "Or one of the staff? They have keys to everywhere, right?"

I wanted to ask her about publishers and whether there had been incidents in the past, but Whittaker was right, Barbara the Loud was the right person to question about it. We shouldn't upset Lisa any more than she'd already been.

"You might have a good story for one of your books out of this," I joked instead.

"Not if I don't have a computer to write it on," she quickly retorted.

"*Ja*," I muttered, and scuttled away to find the captain.

To my delight, I found him next to a coffee maker in the galley and made myself a cup while I invited him to join Whittaker and me for a chat.

"I'm sure you're going to ask me about my crew," he said as we walked back through the salon towards the stern. "We do background checks before we hire anyone on the *Maureen*, I assure you, Constable."

I didn't respond. Mainly because there was no point having that conversation without Whittaker present, and also because background checks only turned up people who'd been caught. Plenty of criminals had clean records.

"Thank you for joining us," Whittaker greeted the captain, and we moved to the dock for privacy.

I was still keeping an eye out as my role of security for Lisa didn't end because of the current distraction, although someone would be foolhardy to try anything with more police present, especially as we had two constables at the top of the dock.

"I'm keen to help in any way I can, Detective," Captain Marston replied. "I was just telling your constable that I have the utmost confidence in my crew – they've been thoroughly vetted before setting foot on my yacht."

"I'm sure you've taken all the precautions available to you, Captain," Whittaker replied tactfully. "But it's not always easy to know what's happening in a person's life that could lead them off track."

The captain let out a forced laugh. "This may look like a big ship, sir, but believe me, it's a very small sphere in which eight of us live together for often months at a time. We all tend to know what's going on in each other's worlds."

"In that case, are any of the crew under financial stress?" Whittaker asked.

Marston shrugged his shoulders. "All of them. Crewing on a ship affords you travel opportunities with most of your expenses paid, and in return you're expected to work up to twelve hours a day, six days a week, for relatively low wages. For most of these young people, this is a job they'll do for two to five years before moving on to either land-based work, becoming a captain themselves, or hiring out their services to the private sector."

"What about your new hire, Blake?" I asked. "How well do you know him and his circumstances?"

The captain eyed me with an air of superiority. Perhaps he was annoyed that a female constable dared to ask him questions, or maybe he thought we should be taking his word about the crew, but it appeared I had someone else mad at me now.

"He was vetted, like the others."

"Did he come with references?" Whittaker asked, and the captain twitched.

He didn't seem to like my boss clearly supporting my line of questioning.

"He did. Spotless references and recommendation letters."

"You mentioned security cameras when we toured the yacht earlier, sir," I asked. "Where are they, exactly?"

"I mentioned we only have a few in respect for passengers' privacy, Constable."

"I know. Where are they?" I persisted.

People love to say they'll help in any way they can, but invariably they don't. Whether it is ego, defensiveness, being worried about revealing some minor mistake or infraction, or true guilt, it is often hard to tell, but anyone with a boss to worry about is usually watching their own arse.

"We have one on the bridge, a couple on the roof facing for and aft, and one in the engine room."

"Can we check the footage from the roof cameras?" I asked, and hoped the rear-facing lens covered the gangway. We would see if anyone boarded during the meet-and-greet dinner.

"I'm afraid they're not recording at the moment," the captain replied. "They automatically record when the engines are running."

"Would probably be useful to have the roof cameras recording while in dock," Whittaker said. "Don't you think?"

"Company policy, Detective. Not my call."

"How are the room keys made, sir?" I asked, holding mine in my hand.

"Standard hotel-style RFID programmed cards," Marston replied. "We have the software on our server, accessible from several enabled computers, and a card encoder. We prepare them for each guest before they arrive."

"Who knows how to run the encoder?" I asked, and he gave me the same disgruntled look again.

"We're a crew of eight, Constable; we all have to know how to do just about everything on the vessel. I believe everyone except Blake and François the chef has programmed keys at one time or another."

"What about masters?" Whittaker asked.

"The encoder can produce them, too."

"Does the software track that?" I asked.

"Of course."

Whittaker and I looked at each other.

"We'll need that record from before you left Miami please, Captain," Whittaker said, and I noticed he didn't phrase it as a question.

"Certainly," Marston replied, bristling at the continued doubts over his crew.

Once he'd realised we meant now, the captain left, and Whittaker led me to Barbara Mitchell's cabin.

"The nice Nora," he reminded me before he knocked.

I wanted to tell him no promises, but I thought it best to stay quiet and hope for the best. Maybe she'd retired to her room to get stoned and the mellow version of the publisher's representative would answer the door.

"I don't care what the idiot you spoke to in Timbuk-fucking-tu told you, I want to speak to someone at Apple in America," she was barking into the phone as she opened the door and waved at Whittaker to enter. "They track every damn thing we say in front of every damn device they make, so you can't tell me they're not picking up the location of a five-thousand-dollar laptop." There was a brief pause. "Fine. Call me back once you have a useful human being on the line."

Barbara hung up her mobile, took a swig from a wine glass, then stood with her hands on her hips. She glared at me while speaking to Whittaker. "Give me good news, Detective."

"Very early days, Mrs Mitchell. But we do have a few questions which might help us as we conduct our inquiries."

"Miss, not Mrs, Detective. I like my men to leave when I'm done with them. Make your questions quick; I have more calls to make before I'm done and I need to check on Lisa."

If her words surprised the detective, he did a superb job of hiding the fact and jumped right into the burning question.

"In the novel-publishing world, Miss Mitchell, have you ever come across any corporate espionage or theft?"

The woman laughed. "That's ridiculous! Most of us have known each other for years. Nothing like that goes on."

"Okay, that's helpful, thank you," Whittaker replied politely.

"I haven't heard about any shenanigans since that mess a few years back," the publisher added, and we both looked at her. "Some upstart new publishing house with a big backer started signing up mid-level authors and trying to buy them end of aisles in the big bookstores. It was a one-time thing."

"That doesn't sound illegal," Whittaker pointed out.

"No, no, we all do that. They got busted when they hit big with Tawny Flock. You've heard of her, right?"

We both shook our heads, although I'd half expected the detective to know the author. He did read the paper and watch the news.

"Shit. I keep forgetting I'm on a Podunk island. Tawny Flock went huge. Three books, rapid released in fantasy romance, and she's number one everywhere. New York Times bestseller list, she's on *Good Morning America*, Oprah's Book Club, the whole nine yards. Then out of the woodwork comes this nineteen-year-old kid who said she wrote all three books and someone stole her manuscripts. The publisher changed a few names and places and put them out under Tawny Flock. The kid proved she'd written them by producing her laptop with the timestamp history from the files as she'd spent the past four years writing them."

"That's significant," I said. "Could be tied to this case."

Barbara glared at me. "Why is GI Jane even here still, Detective? I thought I told you I want her gone?"

"I'm well aware you mentioned that request, Miss Mitchell, but Lisa made a point of telling me she wants Nora by her side for the rest of the trip."

"She did?" Barbara blurted, echoing my exact thought.

"Indeed, she did," Whittaker confirmed.

Barbara polished off the rest of her wine.

7

THE EVE OF CHRISTMAS EVE

Rasha was finally done, and Lisa and Mr Phillip moved back into their cabin. I thought about thanking Lisa for insisting I stay, but as I wasn't sure I wanted to be there anyway, I didn't say anything. Instead, I sat down on the wooden chair outside the cabin door. For the first hour or so I studied the printouts the captain had given us. It didn't help much. No one had created a master key recently, but records showed thirteen of them programmed in the past year by a variety of staff members. Some of whom were no longer part of the crew. Tracking down thirteen key cards would be impossible.

Unfortunately, for privacy reasons once more, the locks on the cabin doors weren't the kind which recorded or signalled a central system when a key was used. At least, the captain quoted privacy as the reason, but I figured there was just as much chance they'd bought the cheaper versions to save money. Regardless of the motivation, it meant that even if we found every master key, we still wouldn't know which one opened Lisa's door earlier in the evening.

The rest of the night dragged by painfully slowly. The Christmas lights on the yacht and on the island had long since been turned off and I sat in the dark listening to the water softly lapping against the hull. It was peaceful, tranquil, and perfect for falling asleep, which of course, I couldn't do. At least my head had stopped aching, but my tongue was driving me nuts. There's not much to be done with a wounded tongue. I tried consciously keeping it to one side of my mouth so the cut didn't touch anything, but I had to concentrate to do that, which made me more aware that it hurt.

Every twenty minutes, I took a walk around the deck, going up one level to the galley once in a while to refill my coffee. All the cabins on Lisa's deck were accessed from the exterior passageways running down both sides. The cabins below were reached via a pair of interior stairwells. By leaning over the railing, I could check the portholes of the deck below, and by midnight, all cabin lights had been extinguished.

The first mate, Helen, a quiet but confident woman in her thirties, had the night watch on the bridge. I stopped by once and saw her several more times when she made a sweep of the decks. Helen didn't seem to be the chatty type, and I'm certainly not, so the exchanges were brief but pleasant.

It was still dark when I heard footsteps along the dock. Moving quietly to the starboard side, I saw a figure approaching. He walked through a faint beam of light from one of the buildings onshore, and I recognised Constable Gabriel Foster. I checked my watch. It was 5:45am, so he was early.

"Hey," I whispered just loudly enough to be heard over the hum of bilge pumps, electronics, and the water against the yacht.

"Morning," he whispered in return as he boarded. "How did the rest of the night go?"

"Boring," I replied.

"That's good, right?" Gabriel said, setting his rucksack down by the chair.

Of course he was right. The goal was for our job to be uneventful and tedious, with no action at all, but I hated doing nothing. Although I hated it less than being yelled at by Barbara, so uneventful was fine in this case.

"*Ja*. Coffee?"

"Sure."

With more caffeine in hand, we stood on the broad swim step and I filled Gabriel in on the little we knew about key cards, Barbara's comments about intellectual property theft, and my guess that fingerprints from the cabin would yield nothing for Rasha. I'd decided whoever had let themselves in was either on the crew, in which case their fingerprints would be all over the yacht, including the cabins as most of them rotated on housekeeping duties, or smart enough to wear gloves.

"Are they proceeding as scheduled today?" Gabriel asked.

"I haven't heard differently," I replied.

Which meant the yacht would be leaving the dock for the snorkelling trip, which included lunch on the water, and then the big book release sunset dinner bash in the evening.

"Did Whittaker say anything about us both covering the event?" Gabriel asked.

I shook my head. "But it would be a good idea based on what's happened."

"Having a laptop stolen is a long way from a physical threat to our subject, but seems like we should be cautious," he agreed. "I'll mention it to him if I see him today."

"Okay, I'll see you later," I said, and headed for the gangway as the first hint of sunrise began reclaiming the sky above the island.

"Get some sleep," Gabriel offered. "And happy Christmas Eve."

I gave him a brief wave on my way to the Jeep. I hadn't given much thought to the holiday all night, but now I remembered I still didn't have a gift for the kid. Even if I couldn't get into the spirit of the festivities, I wanted her to have a chance to. I was relying on my friend AJ supplying her Christmas cheer, especially now it appeared I'd be absent for most of it.

Remarkably, my sign was still lying on the dashboard. The police presence during the evening had probably kept any opportunistic pranksters away. I was dead on my feet, but I realised I was also hungry. With skipping dinner, I hadn't eaten anything since lunch at Jazzy's athletics event. I drove north on Church Street, which soon became West Bay Road. The streets were quiet.

This early on a Sunday morning, I wondered where I could get food and then I remembered Cafe Del Sol. After passing the Marriott hotel, I turned right on Lawrence Boulevard and to my relief I saw the coffee shop in the little Marquee Plaza was open. The term Boulevard was misleading. The short street between West Bay Road and the Esterly Tibbets Bypass had a divider down the middle, so I guess the word was technically correct, but it was a long way from the broad, multi-lane thoroughfares of America. But the coffee shop was open and served the most amazing pastries and sandwiches. They made fancy coffees too, which was how I knew about the place, as AJ was addicted to the expensive drinks with Italian names and rarely passed up an opportunity to drop in.

I didn't need any more caffeine if I had any hope of sleeping, but I ordered an apple turnover for me and a cinnamon roll for the kid. Then I added a banana nut muffin as I was getting hungrier looking at all the food. The staff were still setting up, but they warmed everything for me, and I was about to leave when the door chimed as another early riser came in.

"Hello, Nora," came a thick Irish accent I recognised.

Lahana Jones worked as a reporter for the *Cayman Compass*, the islands' daily newspaper. As a rule, I despised reporters, but she was actually okay. She seemed to care about getting the facts straight, and didn't sensationalise events for no good reason. That was increasingly rarer in an industry which prioritised advertising dollars over actually delivering the news.

"Hey. You're up early," I said, pausing for a moment although I was ready to get to the Jeep.

"Heading to the office. Article due this morning and then I'm on that yacht of yours the rest of the day."

"All day?" I asked.

"They said to be there at ten," she replied. "I'm covering the snorkelling adventure, then on to the book release."

"I'll see you later then," I said and reached for the door handle.

"What was all that going on yesterday evening?" Lahana asked.

"Meet-and-greet event," I said, but her look let me know that wasn't what she meant.

"Whittaker and Rasha don't usually attend author meet-and-greets, Nora."

I sighed. My muffin and apple turnover were cooling every moment I spent there nattering. "Someone broke into one of the cabins," I admitted, although I wasn't about to give her the whole story. I liked Lahana, and we'd been diving together a few times with AJ, but I wasn't about to become her source.

"So nothing I should look into a bit more?" she asked.

I realised it was her way of giving me the opportunity of telling her something without actually telling her anything. I figured she had plenty of sources within the police department who she could push for more info. In fact, I knew she was friends with Rasha as we'd all dived together.

I shook my head. "No. Not yet, anyway."

"See you later," she said and pushed the door open for me.

Riding home, I inhaled the turnover but resisted the muffin as I figured it would crumble all over my fancy shirt I'd bought at the charity shop. Which already needed washing after twenty hours in the Cayman heat and humidity. I parked off the edge of the road by the woods and ducked through my hole in the fence. The sun was now up and the pretty chirps of warblers and vireos occasionally interrupted the harsh croaks and whistles of the grackles. In the shadows of the dense woods, several little critters scurried away from my footsteps. Either lizards or mice, but I could only hear them rather than see anything more than the movement of twigs and undergrowth.

I walked quietly up the wooden steps and slipped my key into the door. It would be almost impossible not to wake Jazzy up as we shared the only bed in the house, but I would try.

"What's in the bag?" came the kid's voice across the darkness. So much for not disturbing her.

"Something that'll wait until later."

"No way. I can smell cinnamon roll from here," she replied, and I heard the sheets fly back.

Jazzy had spent years on the streets fending for herself. When she first came to live with me, every creak or movement by me brought her instantly awake. These days, she slept more soundly, but her inner radar still wouldn't let someone enter her space without alerting her. It wasn't a trait I cared for her to lose.

The bathroom light came on and the skinny kid in a T-shirt down to her knees and with a mop of unruly hair twice the size of her head disappeared through the door. As we'd now be up for a little while longer, I turned on the kitchen light, took a small plate from the cupboard and slid her treat from the bag.

"This is good," she moaned sleepily as she chewed on the cinnamon roll.

I held a napkin under the muffin, and we both ate in silence for a few minutes.

"How was the movie?" I asked when we were both done and had washed our hands.

"Fun," she replied.

"What else did you do?"

"Nothing, really. Went back to AJ's and watched another movie on her TV."

Maybe I was supposed to feel guilty for not providing a television for the kid, but she never actually complained about it. When she hung out at a friend's or at AJ's, she seemed to view it as an occasional treat rather than something she was being deprived of. Which was good, because I didn't have plans to get one anytime soon.

"Do you have to work tonight?" she asked.

"*Ja.*"

"It's Christmas Eve," she pointed out.

"Tell that to the bad guys."

"There should be a rule about no crimes at Christmas," she announced, showing a glimpse into the small amount of innocence still hidden inside the kid.

"I agree. But they don't care about the rules. That's what makes them criminals."

She sighed and looked at me. Her expression was full of unspoken words which made me feel equal parts guilty and warm inside. I was slowly learning it was okay to be needed. Or at least wanted.

My mobile rang, and I groaned as I checked the caller ID.

"Morning, sir," I answered, seeing it was Whittaker.

"I am truly sorry to be calling you after you've just got off a long shift, Nora."

"That's okay, sir. What's up?"

"I'm even more sorry to ask you this, but Constable Foster just called me. Lisa is asking if you can come on their excursion today."

"Why? Gabriel is there, isn't he?"

"It appears she's rather nervous after the break-in and feels more comfortable with you around," Whittaker explained. "I would have said no already, but this is a big deal with the governor as you know, Nora."

"Fine," I replied, feeling too weary to figure out a good reason why I couldn't do it. Although several hovered around the edge of my mind. How useful will I be with no sleep, and spending none of Christmas with the kid were two reasons for starters.

"The yacht leaves dock…"

"At ten, sir. I know."

"I appreciate this, Nora. In a few days, it'll be over, then I promise you can have extra time off."

"Yes, sir. Thank you," I replied, and hung up.

I'd committed to the gig as I needed the extra money, but I hadn't bargained on it taking me away from Jazzy for the whole holiday. And now she was looking at me, no doubt wondering what was going on.

"I have to go back to work in a few hours."

"That sucks."

Yeah, I thought, that does suck. Except it also felt good that someone else also wanted me around. I just wished I could please them both.

"You'd better try to sleep for a bit," Jazzy suggested.

"I'm sorry," I said.

She shrugged. "That's okay. I'll get to watch another Christmas movie at AJ's."

I turned off the kitchen light, and we walked back to the bed, realising I didn't even have time to wash my charity shop outfit. Stripping down, I threw an old T-shirt on, deciding to worry about appropriate attire in two hours. I set an alarm on my mobile and slipped under the lightweight duvet.

"Hey," I said, remembering something I thought I should still be involved in with Jazzy's life. "Who was the kid you were talking to at the track meet?"

She was quiet for a few moments. "What kid?"

"The boy. Tall. Looked older than you."

"Just a guy."

"Does he go to your school?" I asked.

"No."

"What's his name?"

Jazzy let out a huff. "You should probably try to go to sleep, you know."

I'm pretty sure I realised that was an evasive answer, but I don't remember what came next, so I guess I followed her advice.

8

CAFFEINE AND DUST

I wasn't sure if my short nap had helped or hurt. I couldn't say I felt refreshed in any way. It was more like someone had shoved me in the back. I was still knackered, but stumbling down the road again. And I stood corrected. I did, in fact, need more caffeine.

Wiggling through West Bay, I directed the Jeep to the One Stop Mini Market on West Church Street, which I knew was open on Sundays. Their coffee wasn't the best, but they sold the coffee-flavoured energy drinks and I bought two, plus a pre-packaged pastry, which promised a serious sugar rush. Sitting in the Jeep, I called AJ and ripped into the wrapper while my mobile, balanced on the dashboard, rang on speakerphone.

"What are you doing up?" came my friend's voice. "Didn't you just work all night?"

I could hear wind and waves over the line.

"*Ja.* Have to go back in."

"Blimey. Aren't there rules about shift lengths and hours and all that?" AJ asked.

"Probably. But this is a weird circumstance."

I didn't feel comfortable telling her I'd been requested, as it still seemed odd to me, plus it really wasn't important. I was going back to the yacht regardless of what the policy manual said.

"Need me to check on Jazzy?" AJ asked. "I don't have a trip this afternoon."

"*Ja*. If you could. You know she can feed and look after herself, but I feel shitty leaving her alone on whatever day this is."

"It's Christmas Eve, Nora."

"*Ja*. That's it."

"Maybe we'll make some decorations," AJ suggested.

"What for?" I asked. "They'll only be good for one more day."

"Because it's fun, Miss Ebenezer Scrooge. I thought you Norwegians went all out for Christmas?"

"We do," I replied, thinking back to my childhood before my life went sideways and Christmas celebrations didn't seem very important anymore. Having a teenager in the house made me realise I should probably put more thought into special occasions.

"Well, we'll make some really cool decorations and maybe we'll force you into the holiday spirit, if they ever let you come home," AJ said. "Anyway, I'll text Jazzy and pick her up after we get back to the dock."

"*Takk*," I said, hearing voices in the background. The divers were probably coming up from their first dive about now. "I'll let you know later when I'll be home."

We said goodbye and hung up, leaving me thinking about cutting out coloured paper and glueing tinsel to cardboard silhouettes of houses. I never would have thought of doing something like that with Jazzy, but it made sense. Sure, it was more for younger kids, but she had almost certainly missed out on all those things growing up. Decorating for Christmas would have been a low priority in her life. Food and shelter were far more important.

Washing down a bite of pastry with a long swig of the coffee drink, I looked to my right where an old, beaten-up silver car pulled up and parked. The man in the passenger seat turned my way. A sudden flash of recognition seemed to hit us both at once. I managed to hit the cup holder with the can, but the pastry went flying in the general direction of the passenger seat as I leapt out of the doorless Jeep.

Shouts from the silver car told me I'd indeed been recognised, and as I rounded the front of the CJ-7, the Toyota shot backwards with tyres squealing. Backtracking as fast as I could, I fired up the inline six-cylinder engine and ground the gears as I wrenched the transmission into reverse. By the time I'd backed out of the parking spot, the Toyota was already pulling onto West Church Street and heading east. Instead of following them out the car park exit, I swung the other way and accelerated hard. The big off-road tyres left the tarmac and flew across the scrubland next door until I whipped the wheel and dodged between two fence posts, swerving onto the street.

Clifton Bush had lost the Raiders jersey, but I was sure it was him. I'd only caught a glimpse of the driver, but he'd looked familiar too. The young man from the house. The fact that they'd taken off seemed to confirm my suspicion. No reason for two men to run from a female wearing plain clothes and driving an old Jeep. I also knew why they'd chosen to bolt east. The West Bay Police Station was no more than a few hundred metres west of the mini market.

Fumbling with my mobile, I called 9-1-1 as it was easier than dialling a ten-digit number. I also had the stereo turned off, so I had to put the phone to my ear instead of using the hands free system.

"PC277, off duty," I shouted over the wind and tyre noise. I suppose I was kind of on duty, but I didn't have time to explain why I wasn't in uniform or driving a police vehicle. "In vehicle pursuit of Clifton Bush, a suspect wanted in connection with gang activity. Silver Toyota saloon car heading east on West Church… make that north on Mount Pleasant," I amended as the silver car turned left around the outside of an SUV who laid on their horn.

I overtook the SUV using the oncoming lane before steering back to the left side of the road as an oncoming car blasted their horn at me.

"Send all available backup and alert Detective Whittaker and

Sergeant Williams with the firearms unit. I'm driving a blue Jeep. Over."

The lady in despatch repeated the details back to me.

"*Ja, ja.* I have to drive now. Over."

I hung up and dropped my mobile into the storage box between the seats. I'd learnt the hard way that things placed on the passenger seat tended to fly out the side, unencumbered by a door. Pretty sure my pastry was already gone.

The Toyota was no more than a hundred metres ahead but was going as fast as the clapped-out engine would allow. Dark smoke spat from the exhaust with every gear shift, and from the engine note it was apparent the rusty silencer was either missing or full of holes. Mount Pleasant made a sharp right and the driver of the silver car used the oncoming lane to take the corner, although I doubted he could see around the fence to be sure nothing was coming. From my higher seat in the Jeep I could see it was clear, and the big tyres complained as I hurtled through the corner using all of the road.

If they stayed on this street, it would eventually tee into Conch Point by the water, which was near my shack, but I figured they'd turn before then. West Bay had a warren of small streets and lanes lined with homes, some of which dead-ended and some fed through to other roads. I guessed Clifton Bush would know every one of them intimately, and if the driver was part of the West Bay Bush Bros gang, he'd undoubtedly be just as familiar. But the little town surrounded by the Caribbean Sea was also my beat, and I felt confident I knew my way around the place as well.

The Toyota caught an old stake-bed truck overloaded with tree trimmings and swung into the other lane to pass. A blue car coming the opposite way slammed on their brakes just in time, veering to the verge as the Toyota whistled by. I timed it to pass the truck a moment after it had cleared the blue car and gained a little ground on the suspects.

From the centre console, my mobile rang, and I groaned, unsure whether to attempt to answer it. It was almost certainly Whittaker who'd tell me to call off the high-speed pursuit and wait for backup. Which was probably the right thing to do as the chase was putting members of the public at risk, but I really wanted to catch this *drittsekk*. My head still ached enough to remind me of the whack he'd given me and my face looked like the negative of a raccoon. I grabbed the mobile as I took the long left-hand curve by Meadow Avenue.

"*Ja!*" I shouted, putting the call on speaker and dropping the device into my lap.

"I was thinking," came AJ's voice, "should I plan on Jazzy staying over at my place tonight?"

"*Fy faen!*" I groaned. "I'm a little busy right now!"

"Nora? What are you doing? I thought you were driving to the harbour?"

"*Ja, ja*, and then I found the gang leader who hit me in the face!"

A sharp right turn loomed, but the Toyota didn't slow, and for a moment I was sure he was about to crash into the trees on the outside. Then I realised what he was up to. He went straight down a smaller lane, which met Parkview Crescent. His brake lights glowed red, and the Toyota lurched right, sliding with the tyres squealing.

"Are you chasing him in your Jeep?" AJ asked.

"*Ja!* Gotta go!"

The CJ-7 was no race car, and I needed both hands to downshift then persuade the beast through the tight turn. I cringed as the big knobbly tyres grated across the old worn-out asphalt. The Toyota was a rusty heap, but it still handled better on the streets than my vehicle. The road quickly swung 180 degrees with older homes on larger lots on both sides. As I exited the long corner, I just caught the boot of the silver car screeching right down another small lane.

When I reached the same turn, the Toyota was already turning left at a T-junction with Jade Drive. I was barely keeping in touch with them. In the back was my lockbox containing my radio, which would be handy about now, and my Taser, which I'd dearly love to use on Clifton Bush. There was no way I could reach back there while I was in pursuit, but it would be my priority if we ever stopped.

I slowed more than they had for the turn, not willing to risk being T-boned by another car, which lost me more ground. Jade became Bankers and would tee into Birch Tree Hill in less than a kilometre, but I guessed they wouldn't go that far. Birch Tree Hill was one of the main roads through West Bay, which wasn't saying much, but it was still likely to have more traffic and possibly a police car, so they'd try to avoid it.

Sure enough, the brake lights came on and the Toyota slid as the driver turned right with a little too much speed. Jade was narrow enough to not have a line down the centre, but the little lane they took was even tighter and a layer of dust and sand covered the asphalt. Dirt and stones flew from the left side tyres as the silver car glanced off the trunk of a tree before swerving back onto the road. I made sure to slow more, but still skated across the slippery surface, narrowly missing the same tree.

Another T-junction loomed, and I tried to recall if I'd ever been down the street before. Nothing felt familiar, so I guess they did know West Bay better than me. The Toyota turned left and disappeared from my view again. As I cleared the same corner, it looked like the asphalt ended as a cloud of dusty limestone billowed from the Toyota, leaving me blinded.

With no idea where the road went, I was forced to slow down, until two red squares faintly appeared in the haze. Hoping there were no significant obstacles between me and the brake lights, I accelerated into the cloud, knowing the Jeep now had the advantage on the rough surface. I closed quickly on the tail lights, which then suddenly went out. Steering slightly left of where I thought I'd last seen the lights, I braked hard and the Jeep's tyres locked on the gravel and ruts.

Through the cloud, I caught the rear of the Toyota just as I slid by to the left side, coming to a halt before my own dust cloud overtook me. Coughing, I jumped out and leaned over the back, fumbling with the tumbler on the lockbox with tears in my eyes from the gritty haze. Finally swinging the lid open, I snatched up the radio and swung my utility belt around my waist.

The cloud was beginning to clear. I was standing at the entrance to a construction site with trees on both sides. The doors of the Toyota were open, but no sign of Clifton Bush or the driver. I picked up my mobile from the front seat where it had ridden under my leg.

"Hello?" I said, seeing I appeared to be connected to a call.

"Nora! Are you okay?" AJ asked.

"*Ja.* Why didn't you hang up?"

"I was worried, and the line stayed open, so I kept listening in case I could do something," she explained.

"Like what? You're on a boat out at sea."

"Good point," she admitted. "But I was here for emotional support."

"I feel supported, *takk*. Now I have to go."

I hung up and switched to the radio, calling in my location. As best I could. In the distance I could hear several sirens wailing, so backup wasn't far away. Not that they could help either. The two men were gone, and I had no idea where. Their options for cover were endless, I realised, turning in a circle. I'd lost them.

9

NAKED WATERBOARDING

Captain Elliott Marston looked me over with obvious disapproval as I boarded the MV *Maureen*. Helen, the first mate, seemed slightly amused. I wasn't sure whether it was my general appearance that brought a smile to her face or the captain's reaction. His stuck-up attitude had to get under the crew's skin. He annoyed me and I'd only been around him for 24 hours.

"Are you okay?" Detective Whittaker greeted me, and I wondered why he was so concerned. Lisa was with him and seeing the look on her face told me why.

I hadn't done much to clean myself up after the car chase, so to add to the facial bruising, my hair was now a dirty tangled mess, and the clothes I'd not had time to wash were filthy from dust and dirt.

"I'm fine. Sorry they got away."

"You're a regular Sarah Conner," Lisa said with a big smile.

"Who?" I wondered aloud.

"Terminator?"

I shrugged.

"I know you're young, but everyone's heard of the Terminator,"

Lisa insisted, using an odd, deep tone and a strange accent on the last word.

"I don't own a television," I pointed out. "Or go to movies. Or read newspapers," I added, figuring I might as well give her the complete list. Well, almost complete. I left off the part about not reading fiction books seeing as she made her living writing them.

"Seriously?" she responded, looking at me like I had two heads. Or maybe just a whopping great bruise on my face.

"Seriously," I replied, still not understanding why people found it so hard to believe that I didn't own a television. Imagine all the useful things people could do if they didn't sit in front of a box of electronics for hours every day. Although, I suppose the world would be better off if the *drittsekker* stayed home and watched TV more often. Like Clifton Bush.

"The car was stolen," Whittaker said, stepping in to save me from further discussion of terminating Sarahs. "Reported a few minutes ago. Taken from outside a rental flat on Watercourse Road in West Bay."

"We need to dust the driver's side for prints, sir," I said. "I think it was the same young guy who helped Bush get away."

"Did you get a better look at him?" Whittaker asked.

I shook my head. "A brief glance. But I think it was him."

Lisa was listening carefully to our conversation.

"This is all confidential, ma'am," I reminded her.

She smiled and drew her fingers across her mouth like a zipper. "I won't say a word to anyone."

"We're giving you fodder for your next book," Whittaker said with a smirk. "Which is rather embarrassing as we pride ourselves on having a safe island."

"I'll change the names to protect the innocent," Lisa replied with a bigger smile, before her expression turned serious. "Nora, I feel bad for requesting you to be here, especially now you've had real police work to do, but thank you for coming."

I shrugged again. "Sure. But I assure you Constable Foster is perfectly capable of keeping you safe."

"I have no doubt," she replied, turning as we all looked at Gabriel, who remained at a distance, keeping a careful eye on everyone. "But Mr Phillip has taken a shine to you, and he's never wrong about someone."

I laughed, then quickly stopped when Lisa appeared to be offended.

Until her mouth curled into a grin. "He'd sell any of us out for a few treats, but seriously, I am grateful you're here."

"We'll be casting off in five minutes," Captain Marston announced, and several of the crew busied themselves preparing to release the lines.

"Call if you need anything," Whittaker said, then stepped to the dock.

I wanted to ask him what the plan was for later today and tonight as we hadn't discussed it yet. I needed to sleep more than a few hours at some point before Lisa was scheduled to leave. But now didn't appear to be the time to get my answer.

"Did you bring a swimsuit?" Lisa asked me as we walked to her cabin.

"I can watch everything more effectively from the yacht," I pointed out, although I did have dive leggings and a rash guard in my rucksack along with my radio, Taser, and truncheon.

"Well, I'm a bit nervous. Apparently, we're going out to a big shipwreck to snorkel. You'll have to give me pointers on how not to drown."

"That's easy," I said, unlocking the cabin door. "Breathe the air, not the water."

Lisa laughed and opened the door to check inside. Mr Phillip excitedly wagged his tail from the bed and made weird grunting and sniffling noises.

"See, he's more excited to see you than me," Lisa said, following me inside and making a big fuss of the dog.

Everything in the cabin appeared to be normal, so I turned towards the door. Mr Phillip met me along the way, pawing at my leg from the bed.

"*Hei, hei,*" I said, and looked down at the mutt. "What's wrong with your dog?" I asked, studying his pointed ears, bug eyes, and odd-shaped… everything.

"I'm telling you," Lisa replied, "he's usually shy or suspicious around new people, but he really likes you."

I had to agree, anyone or anything liking me was odd, but that wasn't exactly what I meant.

"No, what's wrong with him?"

"What do you mean, 'wrong with him'?"

"His face is sort of smashed and his tongue won't stay inside his mouth."

Lisa petted Mr Phillip. "That's the way they look, isn't it, my love?"

"With one tooth sticking up like that?"

"It's a Boston terrier thing."

"They're all like that?" I asked, struggling to believe that evolution had levelled off the breed in this state.

"They're a little behind in the dentistry department, I admit, but Mr Phillip is a handsome fella in the land of Boston terriers."

Lisa walked into the head, and I risked a hand scratching the dog's ears. I generally liked dogs, but bigger ones with all the parts in the right place. Maybe we'd caught this breed mid development.

"I'm sorry you're so ugly, Mr Phillip," I whispered. He wagged his tail and made more odd noises.

I smiled, and he fidgeted, wagging his tail even harder, like he wanted me to pick him up. "Not on the first date, P-Man."

"If you want to change into your swimwear, I'll ask them to wash your clothes," Lisa offered, returning with a tube of sunscreen. I was pleased to see it was the truly reef-safe kind. "They'll be clean and dry by the time we get back to dock."

I looked down at my charity shop outfit, which now looked like a challenge test for a detergent company. I really hadn't planned on going swimming with Lisa and her guests, and I was certain wearing AJ's Mermaid Divers brightly coloured leggings and top wasn't considered an appropriate police uniform. But neither was a filthy shirt and trousers.

"Okay," I said, and began stripping out of my clothes.

"Oh, right here," Lisa stuttered. "Okay. I'll, err, go change in the bathroom then."

I looked up, but she'd already disappeared. That was another thing I never understood. People get so hung up about naked bodies. Probably because in places like America you were more likely to see a bloody carcass on TV than a perfectly intact bare human. Norway didn't have that problem. You could see boobs as well as severed limbs for your evening entertainment.

It only took me a minute to trade a pile of dirty clothes for the snug-fitting gear I usually wore diving.

"I'm going to check with Gabriel before we leave dock," I called out, and Lisa slid the pocket door open. She hadn't changed yet.

"Wow," she said, looking at me.

"What's wrong?" I asked, touching my bruised face.

"Nothing," she hurriedly responded, waving her hand at me. "It's just you're so tall, and thin, and athletic and all those things."

"Is that a problem?" I asked, thoroughly confused.

She laughed. "Not for you, it's not. You look amazing."

I touched my tender nose again. I didn't feel very amazing with almost no sleep and a blue and purple face.

Lisa frowned. "I didn't mean that in a weird way, you under-stand? I'm happily married, you understand?" She blushed and fanned her cheeks.

"I'll go talk to Gabriel," I responded, as I wasn't sure what else to say.

"Good idea. I'll be in here with Mr Phillip, who doesn't mind when I say weird things."

I opened the door. "I believe men like the curvy parts more than you might think," I said, briefly pausing.

"Is that supposed to make me feel better?" Lisa asked with an eye roll.

"*Ja.*"

"Well, I suppose it did."

I nodded and started to leave.

"Because at least you're just as weird as me."

I looked back over my shoulder. "So I've been told."

We were both laughing as I stepped outside.

The big engines rumbled below decks and the crew stood by on the lines. Gabriel was blocking the gangway, which was still in place, checking the ID of someone I recognised.

"She's okay, Constable," I said, walking towards them.

Gabriel turned.

"You know Miss Jones?"

"*Ja.* Hi, Lahana," I greeted the reporter.

"Hey," she replied with a smile. "Good-looking here is being extra security conscious for some reason." She raised an eyebrow and smiled even wider. "Why is that, Nora?"

"Standard protocol we insist upon for our top authors," Barbara announced, arriving behind me. "Thank you for joining us today, Miss Jones. We do love having representation from the local press with us."

I stepped aside for Barbara to shake hands with the reporter. Today's outfit was a yellow-themed camouflage-pattern, one-piece swimsuit with a sheer cover-up. Which, needless to say, didn't cover up anything so was pointless to me. A bit like yellow camouflage, unless you planned on sneaking up on the enemy through a pile of bananas.

Blake and the guy who'd hit on me last night pulled the gangway, and with the lines released, the yacht eased away from the dock.

"Kris with a K," the young guy said, leaning in close to me. "We didn't get formally introduced last night."

He was good looking in an American fair-haired surfer kind of way, which may cause girls on holiday to fall at his feet, but I didn't have time for his arrogant flirting. His eyes did a lap of my figure while he waited for my response.

"Constable with a C," I replied flatly, "and I'm on duty."

"You look like you're ready for me to show you how to freed-ive," he beamed back, undeterred. "You won't believe the cool stuff you can see on the reef here."

I held back my instinct to laugh. While he'd been scoping out my Lycra-clad body, apparently he'd missed the Mermaid Divers logos. Or perhaps he'd mistakenly assumed I only used a scuba tank when I dived.

"Really?" I replied instead. "And you're willing to show me all that cool stuff?"

His eyes lit up. "It would be my pleasure!"

I shook my head and walked over to Gabriel, who was scanning the dock as we left.

"Heard you had some excitement this morning," he said, turning to me.

"*Drittsekker* got away," I replied. A fact that was still gnawing away at me.

"Sorry you've been called back in here," he continued. "I believe I could have handled things."

I nodded. "*Ja,*" answering both statements together. "We should speak with the guests throughout the day."

He lowered his voice. "I was thinking the same thing, although we'll have to watch out for Barbara on the prowl. She wants us to steer clear of the guests, especially after last night."

From most people, I would have taken Gabriel's reference to my tackling Doug to be a dig, but Gabriel appeared to be purely using it as a reference. And he was correct. My actions had harmed our interactions with the guests, along with straining relations with the publisher's representative. But I think they were always going to be strained.

"Maybe we need to watch her more than anyone else," I suggested, as an idea stirred in my mind.

"Barbara?" Gabriel replied in surprise. "Why would her own publisher steal a manuscript they already have?"

"They don't have the last part of the book yet," I reminded him. "And maybe she's getting ready to defect."

Gabriel chuckled. "To the Soviets?" he joked.

"She'd fit right in," I replied, picturing Barbara, hair in a tight bun and a Cold War-era Russian uniform instead of her banana camo and net curtain.

"Maybe the publishing world is a cut-throat biz," Gabriel said, clearly mulling the idea over.

"I don't know," I admitted. "But we'll waterboard her this afternoon and find out."

Gabriel laughed again and looked at me. I stared blankly back.

"You are kidding, right?" he whispered with a frown.

I kept staring.

"Nora? We can't do that," he hissed, his whole body tensing.

I finally grinned, and he groaned.

"Good one," he said, shaking his head.

We walked across the swim step to the rear deck, where Barbara was still talking to Lahana. Both women watched us approach. The reporter smiled at me. Barbara didn't.

That sealed it. I wouldn't mind waterboarding the bitch even if she didn't have anything to do with Lisa's laptop going missing.

10

——————

SHARKS AND ELF SHIRTS

The ride out to the USS *Kittiwake* took twenty minutes as the captain took his time with the big yacht. No doubt he was keeping an eye out for other boats and unskilled tourists on powerful jet skis, venturing out for a closer look at the MV *Maureen*.

Barbara buzzed around the guests who were being outfitted by the crew with masks, snorkels, and fins. Lisa appeared, wearing a lightweight cover-up over her one-piece bathing suit. I was pleased to see her cover-up actually performed the function of covering something.

"I don't know how I got talked into this little adventure," she whispered. "Are there going to be lots of fish there?"

"*Ja*. It's where they live," I replied, half listening and half focused on the guests. It was hard to imagine any of the people I was looking at breaking into the author's cabin and stealing her computer.

"I know *that*," Lisa groaned, slapping my arm. "I mean, like, fish that bite and what have you?"

I turned to her. "*Ja*. That's how they eat each other."

"Shit, Nora. You couldn't humour me and tell me I'd be perfectly safe?"

"You will be safe. But that's not what you asked."

She rolled her eyes. "You're very literal, aren't you?"

"So I'm told."

"You've been told right," she muttered. "So you're saying there's a bunch of fish all eating each other down there, but they won't eat me?"

"Not unless you give them a reason."

Lisa laughed, but she didn't seem to think what I said was that funny.

"What do they consider a reason?" she scoffed. "Looking at them in a funny way? My friend has a cat that'll take a swipe at you if you make eye contact with the damn thing. Mr Phillip learned the hard way to stay well clear."

It was my turn to laugh. "No, I mean shove your hand in a hole where an eel is hanging out or trying to feed a shark."

"Shark? There are sharks here?" Lisa said, louder than she'd intended and a notch higher pitched. Some of the guests had been edging closer to the author and now gathered around to listen in.

I shrugged. "Sometimes. But they mostly stay away from the *Kittiwake* as there are too many people splashing about."

"'Mostly' doesn't make me feel warm and fuzzy."

"The sharks aren't interested in you. People aren't their food," I reassured everyone as, much to my discomfort, we'd attracted a crowd.

"Tell that to the one-armed surfer girl in Hawaii. I watched a documentary about her," Lisa said.

"She lost an arm?" I asked.

"Bit it right off just below the shoulder," Lisa replied, using a chomping motion with her hand for emphasis.

"I saw that too," a lady from the book club group chimed in. I couldn't recall her name, but she had a shock of pink hair. "She carried on surfing once she'd healed. Went on to win competitions. Quite inspiring."

I noticed we'd come to a stop, and the crew were tying the yacht to the heavy-duty buoy on the wreck.

"Proves my point," I replied. "If the shark wanted to eat her, it would have done so."

"It took her arm!" Lisa exclaimed.

"Sure, but why didn't it eat the rest of her?"

Lisa raised both eyebrows. "I don't know! Maybe it was only in the mood for an hors d'oeuvre."

The crowd chuckled.

I smiled. "That's not how sharks work. They have sensors in their heads which gauge what they bite into. They evaluate whether it's worth the effort. Humans rarely are, unless they're quite fat."

Some of the crowd now looked more worried.

"With shark attacks near shore, they think the person splashing is a wounded fish. They take a taste bite, find out it's not any kind of fish they know, and leave. It's why people like the girl you mentioned survive. If the shark wanted to eat them, it would drag them out to sea and finish them off."

Faces winced. I wasn't sure what was going wrong, but I didn't seem to be selling the shark situation very well.

"You don't have to worry about sharks out here. I doubt we'll see one. If one wanders by, it'll stay away from you," I said, which appeared to be received a little better. "You're far more likely to be bitten by a barracuda, anyway. Don't wear any shiny jewellery in the water. They go for that."

And I lost them again.

"Constable, that's great that you have everyone together," Barbara called out as she and the captain walked up. "Why don't you give everyone a quick briefing on the shipwreck as you're a local – and a diver, I understand?"

Fy faen. I hated addressing a crowd. When I helped out on AJ's dive boat, even when I was leading the dive, she or her first mate, Thomas, always did the briefing so I didn't have to. I was about to decline when I realised everyone was looking at me and it was already too late. I tried to remember what AJ would say to the divers about the wreck.

"The USS *Kittiwake* is a former Navy submarine rescue vessel in service between 1946 and 1994. If you like small, dark spaces, the recompression chamber is still on board and you can go inside."

"Everyone will be snorkelling today, Constable," Captain Marston reminded me. "So no one will be going inside anything down there."

I wanted to point out that it was possible to freedive inside the wreck, but from the look of the gathered crowd, I decided that wasn't on the cards. Some of them weren't even in swimwear.

"The *Kittiwake* is famous for being involved in the recovery of pieces from the space shuttle *Challenger*," I pressed on. "And after being decommissioned, she was purchased in 2008 by the Caymanian government, then sunk as an artificial reef in 2011. She was originally upright, slightly closer to shore, but in 2017 Tropical Storm Nate broke her tethers and moved the ship up against the deep reef and tipped her over.

"The wreck attracts lots of fish and the visibility should be good today, so look for stingrays in the sand and eagle rays often pass by the wreck on the way to the wall."

"There's a wall?" Pink Hair's book club friend, who had blue hair, asked.

"Like an underwater cliff," I replied, wishing this was over. I'd already used more words than I'd budgeted for the day. Maybe the week.

"How deep is it?" asked the lecherous man from the party, who was now wearing shorts and an ugly Hawaiian shirt covered in pictures of Christmas elves.

"The wreck is at 60 feet," I replied.

"No," he said, waving a hand. "The cliff thing. What did you call it? A wall?"

It was going to be dark soon if they kept coming up with questions. "It goes to about 600 feet and a little farther out, it keeps dropping to 6,000."

Elf Shirt's eyes widened, and he turned to his wife, who was wearing a swimsuit covered in cupcakes. "You ain't going in there, honey. You could sink to hundreds of feet!"

"People float," I pointed out.

"Until their lungs fill with water," Lisa announced. "Then they sink until decomposition starts. That's when they fill up with gas and pop up again. A thriller writer knows these things."

"*Ja*," I agreed. "Which is why you have to pierce the stomach and lungs before dumping a body in water," I said.

"I had something about that in book ten, I think it was," Lisa enthused.

I returned my attention to the crowd. They looked even less enthusiastic about the ocean now.

"Come on everyone," Barbara said, clapping her hands. "This will be fun. Let's go play with the dolphins!"

"There aren't any dolphins in these waters," I corrected. "They're only in the *pet the jailed dolphins* bullshit onshore."

I'm pretty sure Barbara growled. She certainly rolled her eyes. "Let's get in the damned water," she hissed and marched towards the swim step.

Lahana paused by me and grinned. "Nice briefing. AJ told me your briefings are legendary."

"She said that?"

"She did. But I'm sure she meant it in the nicest way." The reporter extended a hand to Lisa. "Lahana Jones with the *Cayman Compass*. It's a pleasure to meet you."

Lisa shook her hand. "Nice to meet you, too. Thanks for taking an interest in our book launch."

"Of course. I've read several Josie Quinn books, so this is a pleasure for me as well as work," Lahana replied.

"Irish?" Lisa asked.

"I am," Lahana confirmed.

"Your name doesn't sound very Irish. I'm from Pennsylvania where we have a lot of Irish descendants. Can't say I've ever met a Lahana before."

The reporter smiled. "My dad stopped by Hawaii when he was

in the navy. Sort of fell in love with the place. Or at least the idea of it."

"Were you conceived there or something fun like that?" Lisa asked.

Lahana laughed. "No, nothing as romantic as that. My mum says he'd been drinking a wee bit over lunch before the christening and conceived the idea of giving me a name I'd have to explain for the rest of my life."

It was Lisa's turn to laugh, and I couldn't help grinning.

"And your mom went along with it?" Lisa asked.

"She told me she'd tipped back one too many as well. Otherwise, she would have stopped the nonsense."

"Are you joining us?" the coloured-haired ladies called out to Lisa.

She waved to the women, then looked at me. "You're in charge of not letting me be eaten, nibbled, or molested by anything in the water."

When I thought I'd be staying dry during this venture, I'd had a notion to let Gabriel keep an eye on the snorkellers while I took the opportunity to do something else, but that wasn't going to happen.

"Sure," I responded. "I'll meet you at the swim step."

Lisa took off her cover-up and gathered her snorkelling gear while splashes came from the guests dropping into the ocean. I hurried over to Gabriel, who was watching from the railing.

"This is our chance to check the rooms," I said, and he frowned at me.

"What do you mean? We need a warrant for that."

"Does the cleaner need a warrant?" I countered.

"Of course not, but they're not going through anyone's personal stuff."

"Neither will you," I replied impatiently. "Just help the maid tidy up."

Gabriel blew out a breath and shook his head. "I don't know. Nothing we'd find would be admissible, Nora. Besides, I can't imagine the captain would go for it. There are rules about these things, you know that."

"*Faen*," I muttered in frustration. "I see them more as guidelines than absolute rules."

"Well, they're not. They're the laws we need to abide by."

I knew all of these things, but we needed a break if we were going to make progress on the missing laptop. We'd be lucky to get anything back from the fingerprints over Christmas and Lisa, along with all the suspects, would leave the island on Boxing Day. "Call it a safety inspection. Have the captain accompany you. Come up with something, Gabriel."

He shook his head again. "I really don't think this is a good idea, Nora. Whittaker would freak if he knew."

"I wasn't planning on telling him," I replied. "Just take a look."

I left Gabriel as Lisa was looking at me from the swim step while the guests were calling to her from the water. I picked up a pair of fins and a mask on the way, wishing I'd thought to throw my own in my bag.

"No shark reports so far," Lisa informed me. "Just a big ship sitting on the sea floor."

"Good," I replied. "That's where I left it."

11

———

SHINY OBJECTS

We were lucky there were no other tour boats on the wreck, which meant our folks were the only ones in the water. Eight of the twelve guests jumped in, plus a few of the crew members who helped the snorkellers with leaking masks, ill-fitting fins, and all the other problems which crop up. Of course, Kris was one of them and he didn't seem to have taken any of the cold shoulder I'd given him seriously. He also made a big fuss about freediving down to the top of the mast on the *Kittiwake,* which was a little over 10 metres, or 33 feet down. He impressed the guests with his antics and inflated his ego even further.

In the clear water, the wreck was a 76-metre-long, haunting mass on the sea floor, tilted over at 45 degrees. The dark shadows below the superstructure added to the eerie feel, as well as the monotone hue where the water robbed the scene of its natural vibrance, leaving only shades of greens and blues. When I lifted my head to look at the big yacht, the contrast to the Christmas lights and decorations, even in daylight, was startling.

I stuck next to Lisa, who kept trying to talk to me through her snorkel.

"Ahh," she blurted, splashing about and spitting seawater.

"How are you supposed to breathe through this thing? I keep getting water down it."

"You can't swing your head around so much," I pointed out. "You're dipping the air end into the water."

She looked at me. "You don't have one."

"*Nei*. I hate them."

"How do you snorkel without a snorkel?"

"I hold my breath."

"I'm trying that, then," Lisa announced, and sucked in a lungful of air before sticking her masked face back in the ocean.

I glanced back at the yacht, but couldn't see Gabriel. I hoped he was busy going through the berths and seeing if he could dig up anything useful. In the big scheming of things, as I've heard people say, a stolen laptop wasn't the crime of the century, but it meant something to Lisa. And it surprised me to realise that it now meant something to me, too. I liked her, and she'd asked for me to be the one to watch out for her, which, while being a pain in my arse, was actually a nice feeling.

Turning my attention back to the group, I noticed they all stayed close by. Hardly surprising since they'd paid a lot of money to spend their Christmas with the author, but it made my job harder. I was looking for an anomaly. Someone who stuck out from the crowd. These people were all laughing, chatting, swimming around, and having fun. No one stood out as a thief, or as a threat to Lisa, which was key, seeing as my primary function was protecting her. Although I still didn't know from what. Everyone seemed to be here because they adored her; so as long as a strange boat didn't show up, or hitmen rained down from the skies, I figured she was safe.

"Oh, shit!" Lisa exclaimed, then dunked her face back in the water.

I dipped my mask and caught a glint from something dropping through the water column. I guessed what it was right away and tracked it to the wreck below as best I could. After 10 metres, it became almost impossible to spot except for the shiny metallic surface catching the light every once in a while. And of course it couldn't land on the deck, or drop to the sand. Instead, it fell straight down the exhaust stack midships.

"That was my watch!" Lisa exclaimed as she picked her head up.

"*Ja.* I saw it. I told you not to wear anything shiny."

"I forgot about the watch. It's waterproof down to some ridiculous depth."

"I'll get it!" Kris shouted from the other side of the group. He even gave me a wink.

I'm sure he considered this an endearing gesture as he puffed out his tanned and chiselled chest like a crowing cock. It made me want to stick my Taser down his board shorts.

"Where did it go?" he asked.

"Down the funnel," I called back, and watched the arrogance drain from his face.

"Inside the wreck?" he questioned. "What's down there?"

"It just leads to the lower decks. There's plenty of room to swim down it."

"You can't go inside there," Pink Hair gasped.

"I don't want anyone to risk themselves over my watch," Lisa said boldly, then lowered her voice as though talking to herself. "It was only a Rolex my husband bought me to celebrate my first book to reach number one in the charts."

Kris took in a few deep breaths and slowly exhaled them to oxygenate his lungs, but he didn't do it for long enough to be very effective. Ducking under, he kicked down towards the funnel, and everyone else in the water dipped their masks to watch. My guess was that ego alone would get Kris to the exhaust stack entrance, but no way would he go inside. And I was right. He grabbed the metal edge of the funnel and made a show of looking around, then bolted for the surface.

"I couldn't see it inside there," he spluttered, trying to catch his breath. "We'll need scuba gear."

"Do you have scuba gear on the yacht?" Lisa asked.

Kris nodded. "Yeah, but we don't have tanks. We rent them locally. We'll have to come back out."

"A diver will find it by then, won't they?" Blue Hair commented. "Aren't they diving the wreck every day?"

"Maybe not at Christmas," the lecherous man from the reception party said. No big surprise that he'd chosen to join the women in bathing suits for today's snorkelling session.

Since Lisa had dropped the watch, I'd been doing breath-up exercises to prepare for a freedive. Which happened to be my favourite pastime. I preferred freediving over scuba most of the time, but Kris was right, this situation would be better solved with an air tank. But we didn't have one, so I figured I'd try to find her Rolex.

"What can we do?" Lisa was asking, but I continued quietly preparing my lungs and didn't answer.

I would normally strap a couple of small weights around my waist to help me descend with my lungs full of buoyant air, but we didn't have any readily available, so I was going to burn extra energy getting below the first few metres. With a final long inhalation, I held the breath and slid under the surface.

Fat floats, so fortunately for me, my skinny arse wasn't too hard to kick deep enough for the increased water pressure to crush the air in my system until I was negatively buoyant. Being able to remain submerged in water for extended periods of time was a mental game. It feels like you're running out of air, but that's not what happens. There's plenty of oxygen in the breath hold to sustain the body for something like ten minutes, but the brain is conditioned to react to the rising carbon dioxide levels and craves a breath. Knowing this, a freediver, or apnoea diver as they're also known, must push through the urge, knowing they will be okay.

I reached the exhaust stack and entered without pausing. It was oval shaped at the beginning, and several metres across. The watch would have slid down the port side face, so my plan was to follow the obvious line of descent, which was helped initially by the curved nature of the funnel. Seams where segments were welded together during construction offered ridges to arrest a small object, but a layer of coral growth and silt had smoothed them over. Two levels down at the main deck where the funnel became rectangular, a door-sized section of sheet metal towards the bow had been removed to open up access to that level. The starboard and port-side faces continued uninterrupted down to the engine room.

Three levels down on what was known as the first platform, I approached the rectangular opening to the hold, the lowest deck containing the engines and drive systems. I was losing the ambient light and wished I had a torch. As my eyes adjusted, I could make out the housing for the propeller shaft running to the stern, but beyond was complete darkness. If the watch had fallen all the way down, I'd never find it without a light.

Below me, the murky depths of the shipwreck appeared to be moving, and it took me a moment to realise a school of glassy sweeper fish was moving through the hold. Occasional specks of light glistened off the little oval-shaped bodies as a straggler wandered into the funnel. As one passed under me, I glimpsed something metallic in the silt built up on a larger seam. Kicking a little deeper, I pulled the watch from its resting place and clutched it tightly in my hand.

Carefully turning around so as not to kick up a cloud of tiny particles and silt out the confined space, I was about to fin my way out of the funnel when I figured I might as well have a bit of fun while I was down there. By my estimation, I'd been under for less than a minute, and could comfortably remain submerged for twice that, even while swimming around. I dipped my head back down, and swam through the opening into the first platform deck, crossing over a dark hole where I knew from experience I would see the engine If I had a torch.

This section was barely lit from a single porthole on each side, but I knew my way even if it had been completely dark. The odd thing about swimming through a wreck keeled over at 45 degrees is your eyes being out of sync with gravity. Your brain sees every-thing as though it were upright, so you move along tipped over like the ship. But when floating up or descending, gravity pulls you, so you move at a strange angle compared to the interior. It is more obvious in scuba gear with the heavy tank and can make you feel slightly out of control.

I passed through a door into the next room, which was lined with tall gas cylinders from floor to ceiling. My lungs were burning, and I slowed my movements to relax my body and coax my brain into believing everything was fine. At this point in the wreck, my exit choices were back the way I came, or continue forward through two more rooms. I was at least 30 metres or nearly 100 feet of travel from reaching the surface, although I was only at half that depth.

A large dog snapper eyed me from a corner as I traversed to the other side of the next room, passing over a hatch in the floor in which I could see nothing but inky black. I recalled spearing a good-sized invasive lionfish hiding by the engine below that hatch. Finning on, more light filtered into the next room and I moved to the centre of the ship and ducked through another doorway. A shaft of light poured through an overhead hatch in the forward deck, and with a smooth spiralling motion, I ascended into surroundings which appeared tipped over until my brain adjusted.

Fifteen metres above me, a herd of masked faces peered down and hands quickly pointed in my direction. Angling back towards midships as I headed for the surface, I picked out Lisa and rose to meet her. I'd barely broken the surface when she threw her arms around me as I tried to refill my lungs with clean air.

"Oh, thank goodness!" she yelped.

I wasn't the hugging type at the best of times, but I resisted batting her away as she seemed to be worked up about something.

"Here, I have your watch," I said, after taking a few breaths.

"She's okay!" Pink Hair shouted towards the boat.

"What on earth happened?" Lisa asked, ignoring the Rolex in my hand.

"I found your watch," I answered in confusion, holding it out to her now she'd finally released me.

"But you were down there for so long," Blue Hair contributed. "We thought you'd drowned."

All the expressions looking at me appeared to be a mixture of concern and relief.

"Not really," I replied. "I stay down that long all the time."

"You must have gills or something," Kris chimed in. "You could have told me you were a freakin' pro. You let me go on about freediving like an idiot."

You are an idiot, I thought, but for once I didn't express my thought aloud. He seemed relieved I wasn't dead too.

"Thank you," Lisa said, and took the watch. "But you scared the life out of us all."

"Sorry," I said, as I hadn't intended to cause any alarm. I glanced over at the yacht where what seemed like everybody on board lined up along the stern looking at us.

"I've called off the coast guard," Captain Marston shouted.

Standing next to him, Lahana shrugged her shoulders. "I told them you were fine, but no one believed me."

"I write thrillers," Lisa said apologetically. "I tend to think the worst."

I gave her a smile. For the second day in a row, it appeared I'd caused a big fuss on what was supposed to be a relaxing Christmas event for Lisa and her guests. But this time, I didn't regret the commotion. I certainly hadn't planned it, but with a bit of luck, the hoopla had given Gabriel plenty of opportunity to snoop around the cabins. He was the one person I couldn't see on the yacht.

12

SLIM CAT SKINS

They served lunch as we motored slowly back towards Hog Sty Bay in George Town. Gabriel had finally emerged, and after making sure Lisa was settled amongst her guests for the meal, I slipped away to talk to him.

"You caused quite a scene," he said with a grin. "Was that designed to buy me time?"

"*Nei*. It just worked out that way. Did you find anything?" I asked, after making sure no one else was within earshot.

Gabriel raised his eyebrows. "I discovered people bring strange things with them on holiday. But I didn't come across Lisa's laptop."

For a brief moment I imagined what he might mean by strange, then decided I probably didn't want to know if it was unrelated to our case.

"Were you able to check every berth?"

"All the guests, yes. The book club women are sharing in pairs, so there's only seven cabins occupied."

"Plus Barbara's," I pointed out.

Gabriel frowned. "Of course, but I didn't go in hers. I barely had enough time as it was. Iris, the cute young stewardess and server, was cleaning rooms on her own as Kris was in the water with the guests. She gave me a master key and didn't seem to care where I went, but I didn't have much time, even with your distraction."

"We need to check Barbara's cabin," I said firmly. "Do you still have the master key?"

"No, I had to give it back. Nora, we need to be careful," Gabriel whispered. "Barbara would report us in a second if she found out. Whittaker would pull us both and maybe even suspend us. This isn't worth it for something that's a long shot at best. We already talked about this. She has no reason to steal the computer from her own author."

"No reason we could think of," I replied. "Would Iris give you the key again?"

Gabriel shrugged. "Maybe. I don't know. She's working the lunch now."

"Which is perfect as Barbara is there too."

"Does your regular partner go along with your schemes, or does he push back?" Gabriel asked.

"Jacob? He whines like you, then does it anyway. Usually."

His question did make me think. Jacob was a good check and balance for me, which I'd grown to realise I needed. I was finally in the detective training program and had avoided anyone's shit list for a while. I owed some of that to Jacob, reminding me when I was crossing lines. And because Detective Whittaker was determined to help me succeed as a policewoman. I hated to admit it, but I missed having Jacob with me.

But apparently Gabriel was cut from the same skin, as he was saying what I'd expect Jacob to have said in the circumstances. *'Skin' doesn't sound right.* It actually sounds rather morbid. Although the English have a phrase about skinning cats, so maybe it was right after all.

"Usually," Gabriel said, repeating my own words.

I didn't respond. We stood in silence for a few long moments.

One thing I was confident about was the fact that I could out-silence anyone, so I waited.

"Fine," Gabriel said, breaking down. "I'll see if I can get a key again, but you're going in the room and I don't know anything about it if this blows up."

"Okay," I said, and we both walked back towards the lunch with the red and green Christmas lights strung all over the ship, hopelessly fighting to be brighter than the Caribbean sunshine.

Lisa seemed to be fine, chattering away with the couple who I'd dubbed Baldy and Eyelashes as I couldn't recall their names. The woman had the most ridiculously long fake eyelashes which, if she wasn't careful, the seagulls might land on. But at least she was smiling and laughing. Baldy appeared to be a serious man, as every time I'd seen him, he was deep in thought or heavy conversation. Maybe his wife had dragged him along, as he didn't seem to be enjoying himself. My victim, Doug, and the woman who was making the trip on her own – I think her name was Margarine or something like that – took the rest of the seats at the table with Lisa and Barbara.

I kept an eye on Gabriel, who was circling the outdoor dining area, doing a good job of appearing nonchalant. Kris and Iris were topping off drinks and clearing plates so it would only be a matter of time until Gabriel would be able to casually intercept the stewardess.

My mind wandered back to the crew once more, and I wondered how far in advance this cruise had been scheduled. If taking the laptop was part of a competitor's ploy to disrupt Lisa's next book, maybe they'd approached a staff member who we knew had mostly been under the MV *Maureen*'s employ for a good while. That was a risky business. If they chose someone who didn't like the idea, the crew member could easily turn them in and the whole thing would be exposed. Getting people to turn on their employers, teams, or friends usually took time. A familiarity and trust had to be built. Which gave me another thought.

"Here," Gabriel whispered, and slid an electronic room key card into my hand.

I tucked the card into the little pocket in my leggings, which were almost dry.

"We need to get hold of Detective Whittaker," I said, leaning close to Gabriel.

He scoffed. "I think this is a great time to stay off the boss's radar, Nora."

"We need him to run checks on the crew," I persisted.

"He was already doing that, and he hasn't contacted us, so obviously nothing significant came up," Gabriel replied.

"That was criminal background checks. We're looking for something else."

"We are?"

"Anyone with a connection in any way to the book industry. Former employer. Family member. Friend from university."

Gabriel scoffed again. "Those are broad search criteria, Nora. On Christmas Eve? Two chances."

"Okay. What are they?"

"What are what?" Gabriel responded.

"The two chances?"

He laughed. "That's a phrase in English. I forget it's your second language. You've got two chances, slim and none, and Slim just left town is the whole phrase."

"There's someone named Slim? Like skinny?"

"No, well, yeah. It's a play on words as slim chance means there's not much hope of something happening, and Slim is a stereotypical name for a cowboy in the old west. It's actually an American phrase."

Faen. I didn't have time for more of this silly English language BS. Even if it was American English. I figured the gist was that Gabriel thought there was no way we'd get background info on anyone over the holiday, and he was probably right. But Whittaker was a resourceful man.

"Call him anyway," I said, and started to walk away, then stopped. "Which room is it?"

"Next level down. All the way upfront on the right," Gabriel replied.

"Next deck down, towards the bow on the starboard side," I corrected. "We're on a yacht."

"Aye, aye, Skipper," he joked.

"Call Whittaker," I repeated, and quietly eased away towards the stern, dropping down the steps to the upper cabin deck, where all the guests had their berths.

Wrapping around the swim platform, I moved swiftly down the starboard side, where fortunately the deck above overhung the passageway so no one above could see me. With a last check around me, I held the key card in front of the lock and heard the mechanism release. Opening the door, I stepped inside and closed it behind me. The room fell into darkness and I had to crack the door once more to find the light switch. At first glance, the room appeared tidy and spotless. A tablet of some sort rested on the bedside table along with a pair of reading glasses; otherwise, all surfaces were free of personal items. A towel crafted into the shape of an elephant rested on the bed.

I opened the wardrobe and was hit by a wild array of colours. Barbara had either packed for an extended trip beyond the cruise, or carried more clothes than I even owned for only a week away from home. The woman didn't appear to possess any garment that didn't scream her presence, which didn't lend itself to an undercover operative. But there again, hiding in plain sight was also a great disguise. Neatly lined up in two rows on the bottom of the wardrobe was a ludicrous number of shoes. *Who needs three options of flip-flops?* I couldn't imagine wearing three-inch spiked stilettos on a boat either. But I couldn't fathom wearing them anywhere, so I probably wasn't a good judge of appropriate ladies' footwear.

Opening the dresser drawers below, I discovered her undergarments were as garish as her outerwear. Beige or white was not in her repertoire. I laughed when I moved a stack of panties and found an adult toy hidden underneath. I considered taking the batteries out just to mess with her head, but decided against it. Gabriel was right. It would be a shitstorm if it came out that I'd been in Barbara's cabin. Plus I really didn't want to touch the vibrator. The fact that it appeared to be rechargeable was the final decider. I did wish I had itching powder on me, but it wasn't something I kept readily on hand.

Continuing, I carefully rifled through each drawer, finding nothing more than clothes. And hats. One drawer was dedicated to fancy hats like the one she'd been wearing when I'd first seen her. I checked both bedside tables, then moved to the head. It was hard to believe Barbara had brought all the garments I'd seen, plus the toiletries and hair and makeup products which filled the medicine cabinet and cupboard under the sink. But still no laptop or suspicious items that led me to believe she was anything but a bossy business woman.

Something was missing. A suitcase for one. And her own laptop. Returning to the berth, I looked around the elegant, but very small room. The queen-sized bed took up most of the space. I wondered if the crew stored the suitcases somewhere else for the guests, but that still didn't explain the lack of carry-on bag or personal laptop. I dropped to the floor and looked for drawers in the base of the bed, but didn't see any. As I lifted up, my shoulder caught the edge of the mattress in the cramped space and something moved, then banged closed. Standing, I reached under the mattress and felt a board underneath. I pulled, and the whole bed swung upwards, hinged at the head, revealing a large storage space.

I went straight for the large suitcase and unzipped every option, but it was completely empty except for a heavy coat. Presumably, Barbara had come from and would be returning to somewhere far cooler than Grand Cayman. Setting the coat aside, I picked up the case, and the weight suggested there was nothing hidden in a secret compartment. Especially a couple of kilos of laptop. I put the coat back inside and returned the case to the spot where I'd found it.

Next was a large handbag, and inside I found two laptops. Excitedly, I removed them both, but neither were the same brand as Lisa's. Checking the bottom of the bag, I found Barbara's US passport and a mobile phone. Which was weird. *Surely she'd have her phone with her?* I'd seen her constantly talking on her mobile, which I was sure was the latest television-sized smartphone. This one was a cheap off-brand. At a guess, I'd say it was a pay-as-you-go burner model.

Vibrations through the floor warned me of someone approaching a few moments before I heard their footsteps outside. Shoving the computers and mobile back into the handbag, I hurriedly placed it in the storage. In one motion, I used my body weight to close the mattress-topped boards down as I fell to the floor and lay down flat. I heard the lock mechanism release and the door open, then close. Someone walked across the cabin to the bathroom. I heard the toilet lid raise.

Closing my eyes, I tried to picture the layout of the head. *Where was the toilet itself? Could someone, who I was sure was Barbara, look into the bedroom from the loo?* If I remembered correctly, the basin was in front of the pocket door, the shower to the right, and the loo on the left. I could either wait it out and hope Barbara had only stopped by her cabin to pee and would leave immediately, or risk being seen or heard and try to sneak out. Neither option appealed, but the mental image of Barbara standing over me as I hid on the floor behind the bed sealed the choice for me. I took a peek over the bed.

From my angle, I could see the woman sitting on the loo, but only her body, not her face. As the sound of bodily fluids splashing in the bowl reached me, I knew I only had a matter of seconds. Quietly coming to my feet, I moved across the bed on my hands and knees, pausing for a moment in the middle. The towel elephant had been a victim of my bed top lift, so I stood it back up. The sound of toilet roll being dispensed sent me scurrying the rest of the way. I stepped to the door just as the loo flushed. There was no longer enough time to move carefully, so I quickly opened the door, surprised by how little noise it made.

But the bright sunlight it allowed into the room was startling, and I slid through the gap and pulled the door closed behind me.

"Kris?" I heard Barbara ask, as I swiftly moved down the passageway towards the stern.

13

NAP TIME

"You could have texted me a warning," I complained to Gabriel as I slipped him the master key card.

"I was speaking with Whittaker like you told me to do," Gabriel replied. "Did she catch you?"

"*Nei,*" I said, not bothering to describe how close it had been. "What did he say?"

"He said it's Christmas Eve, so he doubted he'd be able to find out much today, but he'd let us know. I wouldn't hold your breath. What did you find?"

I smiled inside. Knowing Detective Whittaker, he'd get back to us with something no matter what day it was, but I didn't bother saying that to Gabriel. "Barbara has two laptops and a second mobile phone. Looked like a burner."

He raised an eyebrow. "I assume neither computer was Lisa's."

"*Nei.*"

"Could be work and personal," Gabriel suggested. "And it's hardly a smoking gun to have a second phone. Could be the same thing. She has her work phone with her. You found her personal mobile."

"And I think she's screwing the American kid," I added.

"What?" Gabriel laughed. "You mean the American server guy? He's got the hots for you."

"He has the hots for anything with a skirt who he thinks might say yes."

"What makes you think Barbara is hooking up with him?"

"She thought it was him when she heard the door," I explained.

Gabriel's eyes widened. "Wait, how do you know this? Were you in the room at the same time?"

"A little bit, yeah," I admitted. "But it proves he has a master key, so they could be working together."

Gabriel thought for a moment. "It could. Or perhaps she's just having a holiday fling. Hardly the first person to throw abandon to the wind on a tropical Caribbean island."

That was true, but I wasn't about to toss out what I'd just discovered. Something about the two of them made me suspicious, plus we had literally no other leads or viable suspects, so we might as well pursue the only avenue that had opened up. It would either lead somewhere or come to nothing. We didn't have anything better to do.

"Kris cleans rooms, so he'd certainly have a master key," Gabriel added, holding up the card I'd just returned to him. "But I bet the whole crew have them."

As the adrenaline of almost being caught began wearing off, my fatigue from so little sleep fought to take its place. I felt drained, and it was still early in the afternoon. I certainly didn't have the energy to argue about the key card, especially as Gabriel was right. Somehow I had to keep going as the official book launch was still to come, and after that I'd learnt they planned a visit to the famous Christmas lights display at the Bodden House on South Church Street.

"You look beat," Gabriel said sympathetically.

I'm sure he was right about both meanings, and I touched my bruised face.

"Why don't you catch some sleep," he suggested. "I've got this covered, and I bet everyone will go back to their rooms after lunch. Should be a couple of hours to kill before the six o'clock launch."

I nodded. The thought of doubling the amount of sleep I'd had in the past 30 hours sounded appealing.

"The rest of the press are supposed to arrive at five. I'll wake you before they get here."

I looked over at the guests, who were deep in conversations. Lahana was making her way from table to table, chatting with everyone, probably getting background stories for the articles she'd be publishing in the paper. Lisa seemed to be fine, and Barbara had returned to her seat. There wasn't much we could do for a while.

"Okay," I told Gabriel and left in search of Helen, the first mate.

I found her on the bridge, working on a piece of electrical equipment with the ship's engineer, Avery. He was a quiet young American who was noticeable only by his absence most of the time. I'd noticed he'd often help clear the tables, but only after the guests had left.

"Is there somewhere I can use to sleep for a few hours?" I asked.

Helen studied my face. "You do look a bit tired, Constable."

"So I've heard."

She chuckled. Avery remained silent but had paused his work and listened to the conversation.

"I'll get you a key to one of the berths we're not using for the guests," Helen said. "It'll be on the lower cabin deck if that's okay?"

"Does it have a bed and a shower?" I asked.

"Of course."

"Then it's perfect."

Helen led me to a computer on the back wall of the bridge, where she entered a short and simple password, then opened software and programmed a key card.

She handed it to me. "Room sixteen. Go down the steps midships. It's on the port side. That's the left side."

I took the card. "Thanks. And I know which side is port."

Helen smiled. "Many of our guests don't, so it's a habit to explain it to them."

Sometimes, as a copper, it was useful to be seen as a newbie or unknowledgeable about an environment, but personally, I found it irritating. Of course, she had no way of knowing I'd sailed since I was a kid and had spent close to a year island hopping around the Caribbean. But it was unimportant, and I was exhausted, which made me more easily aggravated than usual, so I thanked her again and left. Avery watched me the whole time, so once outside the door, I paused for a moment.

"What happened to her face?" I heard Avery ask.

I walked away while Helen explained that I'd arrived that way, so she didn't know. It was easy to forget I looked like a human punching bag, which caused people to stare and probably act slightly odd around me. I gritted my teeth as I thought about Clifton Bush getting away again that morning and briefly managed to unclench my jaw enough to tell Gabriel my room number. Retrieving my rucksack from Lisa's cabin, I was pleased to also collect my charity shop clothes, which had been cleaned as promised.

The berth was a lot smaller than Lisa's, as she'd obviously been given the best room available, but the bed was comfortable and I quickly stripped and laid down. Exhausted, my brain annoyingly swirled around the missing laptop with the faces of each of the crew flashing by. I rolled to my other side as though the movement would change the view behind my closed eyes. Clifton Bush and his mysterious younger accomplice now popped into the frame, and I opened my eyes again.

How I could be so tired and not fall straight to sleep was beyond me, but I'd been afflicted with the problem ever since I'd run away from Norway. Too many bad memories lurked under the cover of my eyelids. I sat up and reached for my mobile, which I'd set on the bedside table. I dialled AJ's number.

"Hey. Are you getting to come home?" she answered.

"*Nei.* Is the kid okay, or is she being a pain in the arse?"

AJ laughed. "Not a pain in my arse," she replied. "I spoke to her, and she told me she had plans with school friends for the afternoon."

I waded through the fog in my mind, searching for the conversation where Jazzy had told me this, but I couldn't recall her saying anything about plans.

"She didn't say anything to me about that."

"Oh bugger, should I not have let her go?" AJ responded. "I figured she'd said something to you. Want me to try calling her?"

"*Nei*, it's okay. I'll try her," I replied. "I may have forgotten. We didn't cross paths for long at the house."

"Okay, well if you need me to do anything, let me know," AJ offered. "She said she'd come to my place afterwards."

"She say when?"

"She told me they might go see the Christmas lights this evening, so after that."

"Okay, *takk*," I said, and hung up.

Jazzy's mobile rang a few times, then went to voicemail.

"Hey," I started, about to leave a message asking her where she was and who she was with. But then I paused. I sounded like my mother when I wasn't where she expected me to be. It had always bothered me that she didn't trust me enough to know I wasn't doing anything crazy or stupid. Which, back then, I didn't do. Until I did. And my life would never be the same, so I guess I couldn't blame her. Still, I didn't want to come across untrusting to the kid.

"Just checking in. Text me when you have a minute."

Ending the call, I dropped the mobile back on the bedside table. I lay down once more and stared at the ceiling. I'd pulled the shade over the porthole, but light still leaked into the berth, so I could make out the darker circles where the flush-mount LED lights resided.

I lay there wondering what my mother could have done differently. Most of the time, I was either swimming or sailing, but she usually knew where and when I was doing that. The times I didn't want her to know about were because I'd been seduced by my schoolteacher and was having an affair with him. I reached for my phone, desperate to call Jazzy again and find out what she was up to, but I forced myself to stop. I could only protect her from so much. Chances were, she was with the handful of school friends she'd finally made, and they were being teenagers somewhere, having fun. I hoped so.

I guess I convinced myself enough, as the exhaustion finally took over and I fell asleep.

Waves crashed over the bow of the Hobie Cat as I fought the sails. I had to keep the little craft facing the swells, or we'd be turned over. Sitting, staring at me, doing nothing, was Jørgen Paulsrud, the schoolteacher who'd ruined my life. Blood trickled from a large gash on the side of his head. Seawater hit me in the face, and I turned to look at a door floating in the stormy sky beside us. A knocking came from the hovering door, but I couldn't reach the handle to let the person in.

"Nora!" came a voice, and I woke, blinking my eyes.

Reality quickly settled in, and I scooted out of bed, grabbed a towel, and went to the door. When I opened it, sunlight poured in and Gabriel looked at me in shock. He covered his eyes, and I realised I'd only wrapped the towel around my waist. He was far more embarrassed than I was.

"Okay," I mumbled, closing the door. "I'll be up in five minutes."

If Gabriel acknowledged me, I didn't hear him and I stumbled into the head, dropping the towel.

It took me closer to ten minutes to wake myself up under a chilly shower, dress into my freshly cleaned clothes, and find Gabriel at the swim step. He was chatting with the captain and Barbara while a few people walked along the dock, heading our way. The publisher's representative was wearing another loud sun dress, but had given up on the fancy hat program.

"We have six reporters coming aboard," Gabriel said when I joined him, and I was pleased he seemed to act normally despite me accidentally flashing him. "Check IDs against the list Barbara has, and welcome them aboard. No drama," he added, and looked me in the eye.

"Yes," Barbara chimed in. "No drama."

I didn't respond and stood to the side of the gangway awaiting the reporters. I could have done without Gabriel's comment, especially in front of Barbara, but it wasn't worth making a fuss about or I'd create exactly the scenario they were warning me about. Besides, I needed to be low key around Barbara to make sure she didn't think I suspected her of anything. If she was involved in book publishing espionage or theft, it would be my great pleasure to surprise her when I slapped her in handcuffs.

The new reporters were mainly American, having flown in at Christmastime to cover the book release. Lisa really was a big deal. All six showed us their passports and business cards, which all matched Barbara's list. She soon shepherded them away, showering them all in complements, thanks, and other bullshit.

"Sorry, I , err..." Gabriel bumbled, once we were alone.

"Yeah, that was *dritt*," I replied, glad he acknowledged his error made in front of Barbara.

"What I saw wasn't *dritt*. Is that what you said? I don't know what it means, but I can guess."

I was now confused.

"At the cabin door..." he offered. "I guess I woke you up."

"Oh, that," I responded, realising what he was talking about. Turns out he hadn't let it slide. "I'm sure you've seen a topless woman before."

"Of course," he laughed. "Just not one I work with."

"They're breasts. We all have them. Most are better than mine."

Gabriel's mouth opened, but no words came out. He may have blushed, but his skin tone made it hard to tell.

"I meant it was *dritt* what you said in front of Barbara," I pushed on. "There's a good chance she's up to more than holiday sex with Kris. We need her to forget about us, and maybe she'll screw up."

"Oh, right. I didn't mean anything by it. I was just trying to placate her. But you're probably right. It's best to stay under the radar as much as possible around her," Gabriel said. "Although I still struggle to see how she'd be behind stealing the laptop. It doesn't make much sense to me."

"It does if she's working for another publisher and wants to delay the next book." I didn't know how that business worked, but Barbara would probably know Lisa's latest progress on her manuscript, and may well know whether or not it was backed up. Not too many people would have that kind of inside knowledge.

"What?" Gabriel asked, and I furrowed my brow. "You looked like you had more to add," he prompted.

I was about to say no, but then I thought it over. This was one of Jacob's complaints, too. I didn't explain all that I was thinking about on a case. There was very little I hated more than people who blathered on about this, that, and the other, with no real point. Sharing a hundred 'what ifs' felt redundant to me and went against my nature. But it was exactly what Detective Whittaker often forced me to do. As much as I detested using more words, I was beginning to see how it might help my partner, which should help the case.

"Barbara's reason could be that..." I began, but my mobile buzzing in my pocket stopped me. It was Detective Whittaker.

"Sir?" I answered, walking across the gangway to make sure I was out of earshot of anyone on the yacht. I nodded for Gabriel to follow.

"I may have found something useful," he said, as I put the call on speaker with the volume low.

Gabriel and I huddled closely together with our backs to the MV *Maureen*.

"One of the crew members is the nephew of a book publisher in New York."

"Kris?" I blurted.

"No. The fellow's name is Blake Willshore."

14

UNDERCARRIAGE GERMS

All the guests, reporters, and most of the crew were now gathered in the salon, where Barbara addressed the crowd, introducing them to the official book launch. She stood in front of a table containing neatly arranged stacks of hardcover books, and beside her, an easel displayed a poster board picture of Lisa holding the novel. Prominent in the upper corner was Big Apple Literary Press's logo, an iconic rendition of a pen nib inside an apple.

Christmas lights twinkled above the tinted windows of the salon, and decorations adorned every table. Glittery reindeer with glowing red noses looked ridiculous during the bright, sunny daytime, but no doubt would give the room a festive cheer once it was dark outside. I thought about my little shack and the half-hearted effort I'd made to give it a Christmas feel. My little fake tree and a few strands of tinsel had been the total of my efforts, but the kid deserved better.

Captain Marston stood off to one side, looking very official in his meticulously pressed uniform. I couldn't see Helen or Avery anywhere, nor François the chef and his sous chef, but they were likely in the galley. Iris and Kris loitered in the back, waiting to serve more drinks once Barbara stopped jabbering on. More importantly, Blake was also unaccounted for.

Whittaker had told me he'd attempt to get a search warrant, but didn't think his chances were great on Christmas Eve. A judge was always on call for such things, but *on call* simply meant they were the appointed official at that time. It didn't guarantee they'd be readily available.

Barbara finally got around to introducing the person everyone was there to see and hear from, and Lisa joined her at the table of books. I could tell she was nervous. She looked my way and held my gaze for several moments. I wasn't sure whether she needed something from me, or I was simply a better place to look than her fans and the press. The room had fallen quiet and a sea of expectant faces were locked on the author, waiting for her words of wisdom.

I was the last person anyone should go to for encouragement, as my philosophy was more along the lines of *get on with it*, but I gave her a thumbs-up and a brief nod. Lisa smiled and turned to the crowd.

"I want to thank you all for being here with me today," she began, sounding far more confident and assertive than I'd expected.

Everyone applauded, and I missed whatever came next as my mobile buzzed in my pocket. Looking at the screen, I saw a text from Detective Whittaker.

I nudged Gabriel and held it so he could read the message. "I have it."

"Keep an eye out for Blake," I whispered to him. "I'll check the galley and the bridge for the others, then tell Marston we have a warrant."

"Shouldn't we wait for Detective Whittaker?" Gabriel urged.

"He sent a picture of the warrant," I replied, opening the attached photo. "We need to locate Blake and make sure he's still on the yacht."

"Okay," Gabriel reluctantly agreed. "But remember the press are here, Nora. No drama."

"So you keep saying," I muttered, and eased away, exiting the salon to the rear.

Descending the steps to the upper cabin deck, I moved forward along the exterior passageway and went back up the steps near the bow so no one in the salon would see me. As I'd hoped, Helen and Avery were on the bridge, and I passed by without stopping. Moving aft past the captain's quarters, I came to the port-side door to the galley. I glanced through the window and saw François and Jen, his young American sous chef, busy preparing the upcoming meal.

It could be as simple as Blake was in his berth, or doing service work in the engine room, but I began to worry that he'd already left the yacht. We were on an island, so his options for leaving were limited to the airport. We didn't have any international ferries as the island was too far from another destination and I couldn't imagine Blake had the means to charter a private vessel. Unless he'd slipped away earlier in the day, there would only be a few flights for the rest of Christmas Eve, so apprehending him at security should be easy. But currently, all we had was a loose connection to a publisher and a theory without a single piece of evidence.

I retraced my route down the steps, along the lower deck, ascending the aft steps to the back of the salon. Entering, I saw the crowd had left their seats and were now huddled around the table at the front, where Lisa was signing copies of her book for everyone. Several of the reporters were taking photographs of the proceedings, and Gabriel had moved to a position behind Lisa.

Captain Marston remained off to the side, keeping an eye on things. He glanced my way, and I beckoned him over. Initially, he frowned at me, but after a moment, decided to comply. No doubt he took umbrage at a young, female constable giving him instructions, but based on how defensive he'd been of his crew, he was about to be even more upset when he heard what I had to say. I opened the rear door and held it for him while he joined me on the outdoor patio area.

I opened the picture on my mobile and showed it to him. "Sir, we have reason to suspect a crew member of being involved in the theft of Lisa Regan's computer. This is a warrant authorising us to conduct a search of the crew's quarters."

He stared intently at the screen, then took the mobile from me and zoomed in to read the document.

"This is ridiculous," he finally said, handing me back my phone. "No one on my crew would be involved in such a thing."

"We can wait for Detective Whittaker to arrive with the original document," I said, ignoring his claim. "But I'd prefer to access Blake Willshore's room right away, sir. This may be time sensitive."

"Blake?" the captain echoed.

"Where is he right now?" I asked.

Marston looked stunned and perplexed. "I'm not sure. He may be in his berth."

"Let's look, sir," I responded. "Lead the way."

The captain didn't move. "This is all quite concerning, Constable Sommer. I'm not even sure your warrant is valid on a yacht under a foreign flag."

"It is while you're in Cayman Islands waters, sir. Not complying will be obstruction. Besides, would you rather help our investigation, or let Lisa Regan and her Apple Whoever Publishing Company know you're trying to protect a suspect?"

"Don't threaten me, young lady," Marston growled, his cheeks reddening. "Of course I'll comply with local laws. This is all just a bit of a shock. I should contact our corporate office and let them know. I'm sure we have lawyers for this sort of thing."

"Okay," I replied. "Meanwhile, you don't know where your crew member is, so I should put the airport on alert. He could be leaving the island with Lisa's computer."

"Damn it," Marston muttered. "We can check his berth."

The captain marched away, and I followed. Most of the crew berths were in the bow of the lower cabin deck. Marston descended the aft steps, then made his way along the exterior passageway beyond the guest rooms to a hallway running across the yacht.

Midships, he opened a door which led down more stairs to berths on either side. He rapped on the port side door and we waited.

He knocked again. "Blake? This is Captain Marston."

When there was still no reply, he took out a key card and opened the door.

"Royal Cayman Islands Police Service with a search warrant. Announce yourself if you are present," I said loudly enough for anyone inside to hear. Normally, we'd bellow the instruction, but I didn't want half the yacht to hear me. Especially as Blake could well be somewhere else on the vessel.

I switched the light on and looked around the berth. Two single beds were squeezed in either end of the oddly shaped berth with the port-side wall curving as it followed the shape of the yacht's hull. Built-in wardrobes back to back formed a half divider, but storage was minimal and there was no shower, but a shared sink and head at the bow end.

"Who else sleeps here?" I asked.

"Avery, our computer engineer and electrician," Marston replied.

I pointed to the bed with pictures of drag-racing cars and bikini models pinned to the wall beside it. "That Blake's?"

"I honestly can't say," the captain replied. "But I think that would be a safe bet."

The other bed was tidily made and a schematic of the yacht was the only wall decoration. Everything about Blake's area was slightly dishevelled and his roommate's neat and organised.

I didn't have medical gloves with me, so I looked around for something to protect myself from contaminating the scene with fingerprints. Avery had a box of tissues on his bedside table, so I pulled several out, then moved back to Blake's side, starting with his bedside table. The drawer was crammed full of charging leads and international adapters, packets of chewing gum, a couple of silver chains, and a packet of condoms. Opening the cupboard below, I pulled out mostly clothes, a technical book on diesel engines, a few stickers from places they'd visited, and another packet of condoms. As both packets felt full, his preparation appeared to outrun his success.

Moving to the bed, I checked around the edges against the wall to make sure nothing was hidden, then tugged on the foot of the bed until it rose on hinges. Underneath was a shambles. Heavier wet weather gear, a ski jacket, a laptop – which wasn't Lisa's – and six pairs of various shoes and boots.

"How would you normally locate Blake if you needed him?" I asked, glancing over at Marston, who'd remained in the doorway while I closed the bed and stepped over to the wardrobe.

"I'd text him, most likely. But that varies depending on where we are. At sea, we often don't have cell service so we use walkie-talkies."

"You're in port," I pointed out.

"Obviously," the captain groaned. "So I'd text him. Should I do that now?"

"Not yet," I replied, sliding back one mirrored door and rifling through the hanging shirts and trousers.

Finding nothing pertinent on either side, I pulled the first of two drawers open below. It was full of underwear and I really wished I had nitrile gloves. A couple of tissues might keep me from leaving fingerprints, but I wasn't confident they could protect me from Blake Willshore's undercarriage germs. Taking a deep breath, I shuffled through the garments and found nothing except clothing. Moving on to the second drawer, it yielded nothing more suspicious than his questionable taste in colourful shorts.

"Are we done here?" Marston asked impatiently. "I told you it was a waste of time and I'm offended you suspected one of my crew of foul play. We pride ourselves in honesty and customer service."

"That's nice," I muttered to myself, annoyed I hadn't found a smoking gun. Or laptop.

I looked at Avery's side of the room. The berth was so compact, it only took me two steps and I lifted his bed on its hinges.

"Hey, you said you were looking at Blake, not anyone else," the captain complained.

"Warrant covers all crew quarters," I replied, and looked up at Marston. "Which includes yours, sir."

He gritted his teeth and mumbled something under his breath, but didn't protest any further. I returned to looking through Avery's under-bed storage. Predictably, his was perfectly arranged and organised, so it was easy to spot the contents. A soft duffel bag contained his wet weather gear, and a cardboard box housed computer components and accessories. The thought occurred to me that the best way to carry Lisa's information away would be to remove the laptop's hard drive and toss the rest of it into the ocean. But I wasn't sure how to identify hers. In the top of the next box was a laptop of the wrong brand, and I lifted it to reveal another. Still the wrong brand. Underneath that was a third computer, and I began to wonder how many the guy needed. But he was their IT tech, so I suppose it was to be expected.

"Is this usual for a guy in his position to have this many laptops?" I asked, looking over at the captain.

He shrugged. "We believe in redundant systems for safety, so yes, it's normal. Each one with the *Maureen* logo on it is a backup for the ship's systems. That one in your hand is an old computer of mine. Avery rescued the data for me, and I told him he could keep it for parts."

I lifted two more out, one with the yacht's logo, and one without, until I reached the final laptop in the stack, where I paused. I couldn't believe I was staring at Lisa Regan's computer. He hadn't even bothered to peel off the Boston terrier sticker.

"Is that it?" Marston asked. "I don't believe it. Not Avery, surely?"

"Let's go to the bridge and find out," I said, taking several pictures with my phone of the location where I'd found the computer. "And now's the time to text Blake as well. Have him meet you on the bridge. Don't say why."

"Blake? Why? That's Avery's bed," Marston said, paused with his mobile in his hand.

"Just text him and let's go," I replied, carefully removing Lisa's computer with my tissue gloves.

15

SPIDER-MAN AT THE HELM

On the way to the bridge, I texted Gabriel to say we'd recovered the laptop. He'd have to wait to get the whole story as we still didn't have the thief in custody as yet.

"Blake hasn't responded," Marston said as we neared the bridge. His voice had lost all the defensive bluster he'd portrayed earlier.

It wasn't surprising Blake had gone dark, but I didn't say anything. Opening the door to the bridge, Helen looked up from a logbook she was making notes in, and Avery stared at me from behind her. I wished I had backup with me as the far door offered an escape route, but if my hunch was right, Avery wouldn't run.

"Captain," Helen and Avery both acknowledged as we entered the cramped space.

I set the laptop down on the top of the instrument panel. "Recognise this computer?"

"Is that the missing one?" Helen asked, but I ignored her and kept my eyes on Avery. The colour was draining from his face as he realised I'd aimed my question at him.

Avery shook his head. "I don't have any Macs."

"We found this one under your berth," Marston said, and I

turned and glared at him. I'd had my words carefully planned out, and he'd just jumped a few steps for me.

"You searched my room?" Avery asked nervously.

"With a warrant to do so, yes," I replied. "And found Lisa Regan's missing laptop under your bed."

"Explain yourself, Avery," Marston barked, receiving another glare from me.

"Captain, please allow me to do my job."

"It's my bloody ship," he snapped back, but took a breath and turned away to stare out the window.

Avery was as pale as a ghost. "I don't know how it could have got there," he stammered. "I didn't put it there, I swear."

"When we check for fingerprints, you're saying yours won't be on this laptop?" I asked.

Avery shook his head again. "No way. I'm telling you, I've never seen it before, let alone touched it."

"Then how did it get there?" I challenged, testing where he'd direct the blame.

His mouth opened and closed a few times like a goldfish.

"Answer her questions, Avery," Marston demanded, and the young man flinched.

"I can't, sir. How should I know who put something there that I didn't even know was there?" His eyes flicked back and forth between me and the captain.

Marston's mobile buzzed, and he looked at the screen. "It's Blake. He's asking if it's urgent as he's running checks on the engines."

I thought for a moment.

"I share a berth with Blake," Avery mumbled as though he were processing the thought. I'd wondered how long it would take him to figure things out.

"Tell him not to worry," I said to Marston, and pointed to the laptop. "Nobody touches that for any reason."

I quickly stepped outside and looked down the starboard side passageway, past the dining salon where the festivities continued.

Seeing no one, I leaned over the railing to look down the exterior passageway of the upper cabin deck. A series of supports partially blocked my view, but I noticed movement near the stern. A head poked out and looked straight at me. It was Blake. The moment he saw me, he ducked back, and I knew he was going to run.

Sprinting around the bridge on the bow deck, I headed for the starboard railing. Blake was already crossing the gangway to the pier. From the top of the gunwale railing, it was two and a half metres down to the concrete, and a good two metres across. If I missed, I'd probably smash into the side of the pier on my way into the water. But I couldn't let him get away.

"What are you doing?" came Captain Marston's voice behind me, but I didn't have time to explain.

I backed up across the deck, then took a run at the waist-high railing, leaping at it, leading with my right foot.

"You're crazy," yelled Helen, far louder than I would have liked. My plan was to grab the guy with as little fuss and *drama* as possible.

My jump was better than I thought it would be, and I got a good launch off my foot, carrying me higher than anticipated. The distance wasn't going to be a problem, but it now felt like I was dropping from the roof of a two-storey building. Out of the corner of my eye I could sense Blake running towards shore along the pier, but my focus remained on my landing. If I could stick it like a gymnast, I'd intercept him without a problem.

I attempted to absorb the hit through my legs as I dropped to a squat like Spider-Man. Unfortunately, I wasn't that graceful, and my forward momentum carried my body over my feet into a tumbling fall. Ending up on my back, I saw Blake pull up short, unsure what to do. I'd grazed skin and was pretty sure I'd ripped clothing, but I locked eyes with him and scrambled to my feet.

"There's nowhere to go," I pointed out, as he looked at water on both sides.

To his left was the space I'd just jumped between the MV *Maureen* and the concrete pier, the yacht held away by large, round inflatable fenders. On his right was a concrete sea wall up to the old tourist submarine ride building, which was now unoccupied. The steps were behind me, along with the path to the street. Blake glanced over his shoulder, where his other option would be the water, except Gabriel now crossed the gangway and began closing in.

"Seriously, Blake. It's over." If I'd had my Taser with me, it would have already been over and he'd be flopping around the pier like a fish out of water. But it was in my rucksack, so the young man had a decision to make.

And of course, he chose the dumb option. Jumping at the sea wall, he grabbed the vertical wooden balusters and hauled himself up.

"*Fy faen,*" I growled and rushed after him.

I swiped at his ankle, but he pulled it over the low fence just in time. I reached up and took hold of the wood, pulling myself up to give chase. By the time I made it over, he'd already gained ten metres on me, but I doubted he knew where he was going.

As I started after him, I called out to Gabriel. "Call it in!"

I didn't wait for a reply, but I noticed the guests had emptied out of the salon and were now watching from the railing. *So much for no drama.*

A horn honked from the road, so as I rounded the building I had a pretty good idea that Blake had crossed Seafarers Way, bringing traffic to a stop. An annoyed driver began moving again just as I ran across and he honked again as he slammed on his brakes. I reached out my right hand defensively and brushed the Christmas wreath he had tied to the front grill of his SUV.

The other lane was clear, and I looked up to see Blake disappearing down the walkway between the duty-free shops, past the fountain with the stingray sculptures. We'd relied on mobile phones between us as there were only the two of us on the yacht, but a radio would have been handy about now. I cursed Barbara for insisting we not carry any police-like stuff.

Blake had decent pace, so I was glad I had trainers on. He exited the walkway into the car park and veered left. It probably looked like there was more cover that way, but he was heading for the little downtown area where there were more likely to be police. He was sprinting at full speed, which I knew he couldn't maintain, and I fell back a little, pacing myself.

Racing by the older building at the corner, Blake found himself at the junction of Goring Avenue and Louise Llewellyn Way. These were narrow two-lane streets with early afternoon traffic beginning to build as people made their way to family Christmas gatherings. The streetlamps were wrapped in glittery tinsel and as the sun was getting lower in the sky, the festive colours and lights were beginning to shine.

Blake chose to cross Goring and head to the left side of the RBC Bank building. By luck or judgement it was the best decision as a right turn down Louise Llewellyn would have taken him to Elgin Avenue. No more than 100 metres from the central police station.

While he was running faster than me, he had to hesitate and make decisions at every new intersection, which allowed me to gain back the distance. He kept looking over his shoulder, and each time, his face looked more terrified. I knew he was already regretting his choice to run, but he was committed now and wasn't about to stop.

Dodging a passing van, he crossed Shedden Road and aimed for a narrow alleyway between the backside of a row of shops on the next street over. Cardinall Avenue. More horns blared as Blake ran into the side of a car, which was attempting to back into a parking space. The woman behind the wheel stepped out and yelled at him as I flew by. He'd turned right, which was back towards downtown, and he crossed to the far side of the street, running between the parked cars and traffic. I ran straight down the middle of the road as the cars were all moving slowly, and figured I'd make up more distance if he turned right at the next intersection.

With another glance over his shoulder, he spotted me and chose left on Albert Panton Street. I whipped across a gap in traffic to follow and picked up my pace. Blake was running out of steam and he hadn't anticipated it being a one-way street with the cars all coming towards him. Along with pedestrians on both sides, taking up the pavement. I stayed on the edge of the road and waved for the cars to move over. Being in uniform would be useful, as I probably looked like a crazy tourist chick chasing her boyfriend through town.

Seeing a square up ahead, Blake cut right across the street, causing more horn honking and shouts. He then stayed on the pavement, which was now free of pedestrians. I dodged that way and took a chance. Angling farther right, I aimed for the fountain in the middle of Heroes Square, hoping the various memorial walls and a giant inflatable reindeer would hide me from view.

Blake took the bait, cutting across the square once he'd cleared the wall, looking for me over his left shoulder. By the time he heard me to his right, it was too late. Rather than try to tackle him, I shoved his shoulder, sending him crashing into Simon Morris's lovely bronze depiction of a father and son at the helm of a schooner. Blake's outstretched left hand went through the spokes of the ship's wheel, punching the bronze leg of the younger sailor. Blake's face was the next thing to make contact with solid metal, and he fell to the ground in a groaning heap.

"Are you broken?" I asked as I caught my breath and tried to see if any internal body parts had become an external mess.

"Shit," he muttered. "I think you broke my hand."

"I didn't break anything, you *dummenikk*. It was your choice to run."

He held up his hand, and it appeared to be bleeding a bit, but all his fingers were pointing the right way.

"Get up. You're under arrest for theft and industrial espionage."

"For what?" he stammered, struggling to his feet.

"Stealing things from one company to give to another company," I said, unsure if I had my legal terminology even close to being right. Although I thought Whittaker had used that term.

I didn't have any handcuffs or zip ties with me, so I grabbed his arm.

"Try running again and I will break parts of you. Understand?"

"Jeez," he muttered, but nodded.

It took a few minutes to walk back to the pier, and on the way, I called Gabriel and told him to call off the search and ask for a car to be brought to the dock. He told me Detective Whittaker had just arrived. I wasn't excited to face the crowd back at the MV *Maureen*, but I hoped Lisa and Barbara would at least be pleased I'd recovered her laptop.

Lisa was. "You're a rock star, Nora," she enthused, jogging to the road to be the first one to greet me. "You have no idea what a relief it is to have my computer back." She stopped short of us and glared at Blake. "You drugged my dog, you little shit."

Blake stared at the ground. "It was just an over-the-counter sleeping pill," he mumbled.

"You nearly put him in a coma!" Lisa snapped. "Good job you're already beaten up, or I'd punch you on the nose myself."

I thought about offering to hold him while she did, but I knew Detective Whittaker was somewhere close by and he'd probably frown at such antics.

Blake wisely stayed quiet, and Lisa turned back to me. She frowned. "Oh Lord. Are you okay?"

"*Ja,*" I replied, then looked down at myself.

My new second-hand trousers were torn at my thigh, revealing a red-streaked graze. The upper arm and shoulder of the blouse were also shredded, and now I'd looked at the abrasion underneath, it began to sting.

"*Faen.* I just bought this shit."

"I'll buy you something new," Lisa said. "It's the least I can do."

Sirens wailed and blue and red lights flashed around the seafront as a police car pulled up close by. Whittaker and Gabriel joined us, with Barbara rushing over behind them, trying to keep the reporters at bay.

"I can take Mr Willshore from you," Whittaker said wearily. I noticed traces of coloured paint around the edges of his face.

"Sir," I acknowledged, and he caught me squinting at him.

His hand shot to the side of his hairline. "Nieces and nephews were face painting. I was at a Christmas party."

"Sir," I said again, and tried not to grin.

Detective Whittaker was the most put-together, pressed-suit, perfect-tie man I'd ever met. Not in a vain way, but purely professional. I had a hard time picturing him on the floor with a bunch of kids painting all over his face.

"Lawyer," Blake muttered as Whittaker handcuffed him.

"Certainly, young man," Whittaker replied. "And they'll have plenty of time to get here, as you'll be held until after Boxing Day when the courts open." He looked at me. "Good work, Constable."

"Can we get this shitshow moved on and have them turn the damn lights off?" Barbara huffed, throwing her hands in the air. "You've turned this book launch into a fucking circus."

"But I have my precious computer back," Lisa said in my defence as Barbara's eyes fell on me.

"Of course, of course," Barbara said, forcing a smile while looking over her shoulder at the reporters taking photos and video with their phones. "I just don't know why everything has to be Armageddon with this one." She returned to glaring at me. "She's got a screw loose or something," she added under her breath.

"You're welcome," I responded.

16

RAMBOSHIRE

I wrote up a brief report for Whittaker before he left with the other constables, Blake Willshore, and the laptop to be processed for prints. The culprit refused to say anything, but I suggested if the detective played it like the Cayman Islands had an unpredictable and corrupt legal system, then I was sure he'd start blabbing. Which of course wasn't true about our police or courts, but all he had to do was get Blake to believe it was and the little *drittsekk* would soil his shorts. Also, if we could tie him and his theft to the US publisher, then we could hand the case over to the US authorities and not have it burden our system.

Lahana grinned at me like a Hampshire cat. That might be the wrong English county, but they have too many shires to keep them straight.

"You know, I could just follow you around all the time and fill the newspaper with articles," she said, which I didn't take as a compliment despite her amusement.

"How about you tell me why a crew member on a chartered megayacht would risk everything by pinching a laptop he could have nabbed from almost any tourist in any port?"

I shrugged. "Maybe Whittaker will find out in the interview," was all I would tell her. "Check with the station in the morning."

She shook her head. "I gotta work over Christmas like you. Least you could do is throw me a bone."

I wanted to tell Lahana the truth because I liked her, and she was right. We were both stuck working instead of enjoying ourselves with family, but I couldn't. The tie to the competing publisher was nothing more than a family connection. We currently had no hard evidence, so until Blake admitted to it, or we found emails or texts to support our theory, there was no way we needed a rumour getting out in the press. Lahana soon gave up on me and moved on to chatting with the guests some more. For many of them, it would be a fun novelty to have their names in the paper. I tried to keep my name out of the headlines.

Gabriel offered to stay with me on duty for the night, or even take the shift, but I lied and told him my nap had freshened me up enough to carry on. Now all the *drama* was over, I figured I might be able to sneak another nap in the night, anyway. Helen, who was a few inches shorter than me, but otherwise about my size, kindly lent me a pair of black leggings and a lightweight sweatshirt with the *Maureen* logo across the chest. The leggings were more like capris on my long legs, and I turned down a T-shirt offer, throwing the sweatshirt on over my sports bra instead. None of it aligned with the RCIPS guidelines for dress on duty, but it was that or a nicer outfit from Lisa that definitely wouldn't fit my tall, lean frame.

Except for Barbara, who remained sour behind her plastered-on fake niceties to the press, the atmosphere on the yacht was remarkably buoyant. Lisa addressed the group and pointed out how the theft and my antics were perfect thriller fiction fodder, and she may have to include the events in a future book. It felt weird, but I seemed to have become a celebrity with the guests, who were keen to tell me how exciting it had been to witness a real-life chase and apprehension. Captain Marston was less enthu-siastic. He'd apologised profusely to Lisa and Barbara and now hung in the background, not looking as pompous as he had before.

The sunset dinner cruise was abandoned in favour of the meal served in dock, and once the sun went down, the lights on the yacht kicked off a festive feel, elevated by the decorations along the seafront. Christmas music played over the boat's speakers, and for once I didn't mind so much. I was tired and sore, but looking forward to the Christmas lights tour to the Bodden House. The main reason I'd chosen to stay was the hope I'd see Jazzy with her friends. I was feeling really guilty that I'd blown the chance to have a present waiting for her in the morning, but at least I could wish her a happy Christmas and know she'd be in good hands with AJ.

"Our ride is here," Barbara announced, and I looked to the shore, where a large shuttle-style bus had parked.

"It's a ten-minute walk," I pointed out, which Barbara ignored.

I watched the guests and visiting reporters shuffle off the yacht and make their way excitedly towards the bus. Lisa was being polite and allowing everyone to get aboard first, so I lingered with her. She had Mr Phillip on a lead, and he immediately rubbed up against my leg and looked up at me expectantly. I reached down and scratched behind his ears, but stopped when he tried to lick my hand with his funky tongue that hung out the side of his truncated snout.

"He really does like you," Lisa laughed.

"*Ja.* I'm not sure why."

"He knows you look after his mummy, don't you, Mr Phillip?" The dog wagged his stumpy tail at her. She looked up at the bus. "Although we'll be lucky if he doesn't throw up on the drive. He hates riding in vehicles he doesn't know."

"We can walk," I suggested again.

"Better not. It'll start a fuss and cause Barbara a headache."

I didn't mind Barbara having a headache.

"How are your scrapes and bruises?" Lisa asked.

I touched a finger to the bridge of my nose. It still hurt, so I presumed my face continued to sport an assortment of interesting colours. I only felt the scrapes when my borrowed clothes brushed against them. Which was anytime I moved.

"Fine," I replied.

"Well, you can relax a little now and enjoy Christmas Eve with us," she said, then checked herself. "Although I'm sure you'd rather be with family, so thank you again for looking out for me."

I nodded. "No worries."

"Do you have relatives here?" she asked as we strolled down the pier to join the others, with Mr Phillip sniffing at the abundant smells along the way.

"*Nei*," I replied. "Just a kid, an iguana, and some friends."

Lisa stopped in her tracks. "You have a kid?"

"Sort of."

"Sort of?" she echoed, looking at me strangely. "I have a daughter, and believe me, I remember all too well giving birth to her."

"We may see her at the Bodden House," I added, and continued walking.

I liked Lisa a lot; she was nothing like what I'd expected at all, but I really didn't want to get into talking about my personal life as we were about to be within earshot of a bus full of strangers. She seemed to take the hint, letting the subject go as we stepped aboard. We took seats in the front opposite Barbara and Lahana, and the dog sat at Lisa's feet.

"Hey," she whispered, and nudged me in the ribs. "Take this and keep it hidden."

I looked between us, where she was holding another condemned stuffed hedgehog in her hand. I really didn't want to have anything to do with the mutt as I had enough going on, but I didn't have much choice.

"In case he wigs out on the ride or at the place we're going," Lisa explained. "We'll win him back over with a treat. But you need to keep hold of it. If he sees me with it, he'll go nuts."

I shoved it under my leg and the stupid toy squeaked. Mr Phillip jumped up and spun around, looking for the source, growling under his breath.

"Oops," Lisa groaned. "I should have warned you."

She settled the dog back down and I looked across the aisle at Lahana, who was grinning from ear to ear. "Buckle up for a long ride," she said, and winked at me.

The journey actually took longer than if we'd walked. The Bodden House was no secret, and traffic was bumper to bumper along South Church Street until we reached the home opposite the Sunset House Dive Resort. Oohs and aahs rippled through the bus as the brightly illuminated front garden came into view. An eclectic mix of little buildings with nativity scenes, figures, and shapes were all covered in neatly arranged lights between the equally bright trees and shrubs. Despite having its own lights strung along the roofline, the sprawling single-storey residence was almost lost behind the Disneyland-style decorations. Not that I'd ever been to Disneyland, but I'd seen pictures.

The bus driver paused, blocking traffic, so we could all shuffle out, and Barbara announced that everyone should meet back at the entrance in one hour for the ride back. My guess was that everyone would want to stick close to Lisa, so rounding them up shouldn't be hard. The group was probably going to move around the garden like a swarm of six-year-olds playing football, where Lisa was the ball.

I looked around at the crowd already milling about, admiring the lights, but couldn't see Jazzy. It was a long shot we'd be here at the same time, but I'd hoped she intended to visit shortly after sunset, so she'd be back at AJ's before too long. I followed the group as they entered through the open gates in a low concrete wall protecting the garden from the road. The home belonged to the Bodden sisters, a family with a long history in the islands, and the lights had become a tradition which had grown over the years, all paid for by the family.

"I must say, I'm missing my hubby and daughter being here," Lisa whispered to me. "But the island certainly gets into the holiday season. It's very nice."

"*Ja*," I agreed, but my attention was drawn to the street.

"Is your baby here?" Lisa asked, following my gaze.

"*Ja.* That's her over there."

I tensed as I watched Jazzy walking towards the gate with a young man I recognised. It was the youth who'd been driving Clifton Bush that morning. The same guy who'd allowed him to jump me at the house during the raid. And now, I was convinced he was the kid I'd seen Jazzy talking to at the athletic field.

"I don't see a baby," Lisa said.

"She's fifteen," I replied.

"Oh. But how…?" Lisa stumbled.

"She's my foster kid."

"Really? That's amazing. Good for you."

"It's not too amazing right now," I said through gritted teeth. "I have to take care of something. I'll be right back."

"Of course," I heard Lisa reply, but I was already striding away.

As I closed on the gates, I could see that there was another couple with them, walking just behind Jazzy and the young man. A woman, who looked to be in her twenties, and beside her was none other than Clifton Bush. I moved behind a family who were making their way out and pulled my mobile from my pocket. I dialled 9-1-1.

"PC277. I have Clifton Bush and accomplice sighted."

"Again?" came the reply from the dispatcher.

"*Ja,* again!" I hissed. "Outside the Bodden sisters' place on South Church. Send backup."

I didn't wait for an answer. There wasn't time and my head was consumed with the fact that Jazzy had somehow got herself caught up with a gang. As we converged on the entrance to the garden, I again wished I had my utility belt with me. After catching Blake and recovering the laptop, I'd become complacent. I was still an on-duty constable, yet Barbara's wishes had forced me to operate without the equipment I desperately needed now. I had to choose. There was no way I could take on both suspects.

Keeping my head down, I waited for the family to pass by Jazzy and the young man, then stepped behind Clifton Bush.

"Police," I said just loud enough for him to hear, then kicked the back of his left knee. "You're under arrest."

As his leg buckled and he tried to recover, I wrapped my arm around his neck and pulled him backwards over my outstretched leg. The woman screamed and Clifton gasped as the air left his lungs. Grabbing his left wrist, I leapt over his prone body, rolling him to his stomach. Keeping a firm grip on his wrist, I dropped my knee into the middle of his back. Knowing I would have to contend with his younger accomplice, I turned to look, but it was too late.

With a fistful of sweatshirt, he dragged me off Clifton and flung me across the path. People shrieked, and in the melee, I heard Jazzy yelling something. The younger man was helping Clifton to his feet as I scrambled to mine. We faced off with the wail of sirens echoing around the town.

"Stay back," Clifton grunted, and reached for his waistband.

I was too many steps away to get to the gun before he aimed it at me, and running would put me amongst the people who had all stopped looking at the lights and were now watching us. I couldn't put them at risk. So I raised my hands.

"You're making things worse for yourself," I said, now facing the barrel of the firearm pointed at my chest.

"Maybe," he said in a thick local accent. "But it'll take more dan a skinny white bitch to take me down."

As he raised the gun to take aim at my face, movement started from behind him, and something came crashing down on Clifton's outstretched arm. The gun went off and shards of concrete leapt from the pathway as the bullet hit the ground, while pieces of shattered ceramic Father Christmas exploded everywhere. Jazzy's momentum sent her to the ground on her hands and knees as I leapt forward, punching Clifton in the throat.

A hand grabbed my shoulder, and I swung my elbow, feeling the younger man's head whip back from the impact. Tyres screeched and the flashing red and blue police lights added a weird swirling effect to the Christmas lights. Clifton was on the ground clutching his neck and wheezing, while his accomplice staggered back, holding his bloody nose. The look in his eyes told me he was done, so I reached down, picked up the gun, then helped Jazzy to her feet.

"Sommer?" one of the constables shouted as he ran up the path.

I recognised him from the George Town division.

"*Ja*. That's Clifton Bush," I said, pointing to the gang leader rolling around on the ground. "And this man has aided his escape twice," I added, indicating his accomplice.

"Are you okay?" I asked Jazzy, and she glared at me, then turned to the man she'd arrived with.

"You lied to me," she fumed in his direction.

Before I could grab her, she took a step towards him and swung a kick at his crotch. Jazzy was petite but strong for her size, and she didn't hold back. The guy dropped like a stone to the pathway, letting out a cry of pain. I took her by the shoulders in case she went for another swipe and the constable held up his hands.

"Enough, enough! Step back!"

Jazzy turned, her eyes burning spheres of rage. "He lied to me."

"*Ja*, they do that," I responded. "I'm sorry, but now you know."

I could feel her body shaking under my hands and I pulled her close, feeling her skinny arms wrap around me. All I could hope was that their relationship had been new and hadn't become physical. With everything the kid had been through, I desperately wanted her romantic experiences to be as kind and close to normal as teenage love could ever be. I wanted hers to be completely different from mine.

"You're a female fucking Rambo, for God's sake," Barbara ranted, standing with her hands on her hips.

The guests and reporters were gathered behind her, watching in shock and excitement. Plenty of mobile phones were recording the chaos as the two men were put in handcuffs. I ignored Barbara and scanned the crowd for the one person I was supposed to be protecting.

"Where's Lisa?" I asked.

Barbara turned and looked around the garden. "She was right here a moment ago. Lisa?" she called out.

"She was taking a picture with Doug in front of the gingerbread house just a moment before the chaos started," Lahana said, and we all turned to Doug.

He was standing in the middle of the crowd. "I came over when I heard the noise. I don't know where she went."

Everyone began looking around and calling her name. Then Mr Phillip pushed through their legs and trotted over to me, trailing his lead behind him. He agitatedly turned circles while staring up at me.

"*Fy faen,*" I muttered. "I need to call Whittaker."

17

POINTING A GUN AT PARENTING

The scene quickly fell into complete chaos. Other visitors to the Bodden House were freaked out by the police and the rumour which quickly spread about an abduction. People left to be replaced by new visitors who had no idea what had happened and wanted to know why they couldn't walk around and look at the pretty lights. The first constables who'd arrived on scene hauled Clifton Bush and his young friend away, and another pair eventually made it through bumper-to-bumper traffic.

"One of you take a sweep through Sunset House over the road," I ordered the first man walking in. "Check the bathrooms. Look up Lisa Regan the author on your mobile, so you have a picture."

He looked at me with an annoyed expression as his partner joined him.

"Constable Sommer," I said, and showed them my ID card. "You can do what I ask now or wait until Detective Whittaker gets here when he'll ask why you haven't done what I said already. Your choice."

The first man shrugged and walked towards the road. The other man stayed, so I continued.

"Check the house. The sisters keep it locked, but maybe Lisa wandered around the back. Before we call this a kidnapping, we need to be sure she's not having a bathroom emergency or wandered off to make a private phone call."

He nodded and headed for the house.

"I've called her 100 times, and it rang before going to voicemail at first, but now it goes straight there!" Barbara shouted at me.

I'd given her the task of calling as I figured she had the best chance of getting Lisa to answer if she was throwing up in the bushes somewhere or sitting on a loo mid stomach event. The fact that it had switched to going straight to voicemail suggested the phone had now been turned off.

"You were supposed to be watching her, damn it!" Barbara yelled at me. "Not screwing around with whatever else you decided was more important!"

"Your hysteria doesn't help anything," I responded, wishing Whittaker would hurry up and get here.

"I'm not hysterical!" Barbara bellowed at an even higher pitch. That seemed to trigger a realisation in her brain and she took a few breaths and calmed down. "You need to trace her phone."

"That takes time. There are other things we need to do first."

"How can we help?" Blue Hair asked, and I turned to see all the guests gathered, staring at me.

"Stay together, and let's get a headcount. Make sure everyone else is here."

The reporters stood close by and listened in, taking a few pictures, but from their expressions, I figured they weren't ready to take the situation too seriously yet. I didn't blame them, plus it kept them out of my hair for the time being. Half of me expected Lisa to appear and apologise any moment, explaining how the shrimp dip had hit her the wrong way, but the other half of me was far more concerned. Something about the situation felt real, and my own gut was twisted in a knot. But my lack of sleep, recent concussion, and other bangs and scrapes had me second-guessing my intuition.

Jazzy had remained off to the side since the men had been arrested. The other woman had bolted as soon as she could.

"Call Captain Marston and ask if Lisa has returned to the ship," I ordered Barbara. "Make sure he checks her berth."

Barbara didn't complain and began looking for the number, so I took the moment to walk over to Jazzy.

"You okay?"

The kid stared at the ground, and I didn't know what to do. I wasn't built for dealing with shit like this. If Lisa had been abducted, I knew I could come up with a plan and start working on it like I already had. But looking at Jazzy's little frame, clearly upset and feeling things I couldn't begin to comprehend, I was lost. I couldn't fathom if everything I could think of to say would hurt her more or help in some way. Obviously, I wanted to know what she'd been doing hanging out with gang members, but I knew how lousy people could talk good people into things. I also knew how easy it was to make mistakes and start an escalating series of events there was no going back from.

So I stood there, saying and doing nothing. Paralysed by my own fear of screwing up.

"You saved my arse," I finally said, as it felt like it wouldn't make anything worse. And the statement was true.

"Do you think he was going to shoot?" she asked, raising her eyes from the ground.

"It felt like he was going to," I replied. "I think the rule is you only aim a gun at something or someone you're intending or willing to shoot. If our firearms division were here, Clifton Bush would be dead right now instead of nursing a bruised arm."

She looked down again. "It's my fault they were here. I wanted to see the lights."

"Did you know who he was?" I asked before I could stop myself. My stupid police brain sent the words before my foster parent brain could intercept.

Jazzy shook her head. She had her mop of frizzy hair pulled back in a ponytail, which swished back and forth. She looked older with her hair like that, which I realised was most likely her intention. I'd find out how old the young man was, but my guess was eighteen or nineteen and out of line to be preying on a fifteen-year-old.

"I'd never met him before," she offered.

"But your friend knew him," I said as a statement, not a question. She nodded anyway.

I was about to explain how I'd met her friend twice before and both times he'd been complicit in helping Clifton Bush escape, but my foster parent brain managed to head that off before I could say it. Maybe it could be said later, in a less raw moment. Or not at all. It didn't matter.

"LaShaun swore he had nothing to do with the gang," Jazzy offered, which struck me as odd. Why would the question have even come up? She must have seen my expression.

"LaShaun Bush," Jazzy added. "When he told me his surname, I asked him if he was part of the West Bay gang. He lied to me."

I rested a hand on her shoulder. I could feel her pain vibrating through her little body.

"When he introduced me to Clifton tonight, I even asked if he was Clifton Bush," she continued through gritted teeth. I could tell she was determined not to cry. "I'd seen a Clifton Bush was wanted by police in the newspaper. He lied again. Told me this was a different guy."

"Constable Sommer," came Whittaker's voice from behind me.

"Sir," I acknowledged, then quickly turned back to Jazzy, wishing I could just take her home. "I'll call AJ and ask if she can pick you up."

"I can take the bus," Jazzy replied.

"No," I said firmly. "She'll pick you up."

"You don't trust me now?" Jazzy snapped back.

I sighed. This was more of the parenting crap I didn't know how to handle. One thing I liked about the police was how we had ranks. If someone above you told you to do something, that's what you did. The authority hierarchy in families seemed to work like that for a while until the kids realised they could rebel against the system and there wasn't much anyone could do about it. But I guess that was a bad analogy, as I was a perfect case of not doing what anyone told me. Family or police.

"I trust you. I'm worried about you. Wait for AJ."

She nodded and didn't talk back, so maybe I said something right.

"Fill me in," Whittaker said when I turned my full attention to him. I noticed he'd cleaned his face up properly, so I guessed the face-painting antics had been curtailed.

"I was busy with Clifton Bush. Lisa was over there by the little shack thing," I said, pointing. "One of the guests was with her. He came over to see what the fuss was about and that's the last she was seen. She hadn't said anything to anyone about an issue but I have two constables checking around the house here and Sunset House across the road in case she needed a bathroom or something like that."

"Checked with the boat?" he asked. "She could have made it back there by now."

"Barbara, the publisher lady, is calling the captain."

Whittaker nodded. "Why would anyone choose this time and location to take her?" he thought aloud. "Too many people around. Not to mention we're on an island. Where can they go?"

"She must know them," I said as the thought hit me.

"Agreed," he replied. "If she's indeed been taken. It still makes no sense to me."

"Bad people aren't always logical, sir."

"True. But it's still more likely she's somewhere close by, caught up in a conversation, or an ailment as you suggested. We're short-handed as it's Christmas Eve, but I'll see if I can get more bodies here."

While the detective called Central for backup, I took the opportunity to phone AJ.

"Happy Christmas!" AJ answered.

"Hey. Sorry to ask, but can you come and pick Jazzy up?"

"Of course," AJ responded without hesitation. "Something happen?"

"*Ja*. She's okay, but it would be good if she were with you. I'll be working all night."

"Where?" AJ asked, and I could hear the jingle of car keys.

"Bodden House."

"Urgh," AJ groaned.

"*Ja*. Sorry. Don't worry about the police lights."

"Bloody hell. Okay, on my way."

"*Takk*."

As I hung up, I decided if I ever needed to describe friendship to someone, then that phone call would be the perfect example.

Moving on, I turned to Barbara. "What did the captain say?"

"He hasn't seen her," she replied. "We should put the screws to that Blake kid. Maybe he was working with someone else."

I could believe that thirty minutes in a room with Barbara would make even the most hardened criminal confess to anything, but again, her suggestion was premature.

Whittaker must have overheard. "Mr Willshore isn't saying a word until his legal representation is present, which may not be until Boxing Day."

"Boxing Day?" Barbara queried impatiently. "That's what now? The day after Christmas Day?"

"*Ja*."

"Then why the hell don't you call it that?"

I ignored her. If she hadn't listened the first time this conversation had happened in her presence, I couldn't imagine she'd absorb the information now.

"Anything?" I asked, seeing the constable return from over the road.

He shook his head. "Nothing. No one has seen anyone fitting her description and the bathrooms are clear. I showed her picture to the bar staff and the front desk, too."

"Nothing from the house either," his partner announced, arriving at the same time. "The sisters are inside and said no one has entered or knocked on the door. I also checked the backyard."

My stomach clenched a little tighter. "Did you ask if they have cameras?"

"I did, and they don't."

"Miss Nora?" Blue Hair called to me.

"*Ja?*" I asked, having forgotten I'd asked her to get a headcount.

"We're missing one," she replied.

I walked closer. "Are you sure?" I began counting the faces I recognised.

I could see Doug, who I'd tackled. Margarine, or whatever her name was. Blue Hair, Pink Hair, and their two friends in the book club. They were easy as they went everywhere together as though they were attached by bungee cords. Letch, who still couldn't see anything but my breasts or backside, and his wife, Cupcakes. The female couple who were both librarians and the nicest people. Which left Baldy and Eyelashes... but I could only see Eyelashes, who looked mortified.

"Where's your husband?" I asked as the crowd parted, leaving her standing alone.

"He's not her husband," Barbara corrected me. "He's her brother."

"Then where's your brother?" I asked.

The woman's lips trembled. "He's not actually my brother."

"What?" Barbara snapped. "He's represented himself as your brother. What do you mean?"

"My brother got the flu before we left, so my cousin came instead. They look a lot alike, so he used Glenn's passport. That way, we didn't have to change the paperwork. You had all those checks and what have you he'd have to go through and there wasn't time."

"Damn it, Kelly, how could you lie to us?" Barbara fumed, but I stepped in front of her and held up a hand. We could handle the matter of how he came to be here later. That wasn't the pressing question.

"Where is your cousin now?"

She began to sob. "I don't know."

I turned to Whittaker, who'd stepped closer to listen. "That would be the someone Lisa knows, sir."

The detective let out a long breath before taking the radio from his belt and keying the mic. "Central, this is Sierra One at the Bodden House. I'm escalating the status of the situation here. We're officially dealing with a missing person. I need all available personnel called in and have someone set up an operations room."

The reporters took far more notice now.

18

THE IRISH ONE

It took Detective Whittaker stepping in, but Barbara finally agreed to return to the yacht with the guests. Except Eyelashes. Or Kelly Stockton, as I now knew her name was. She was staying with us and would be taken to and held at the station once we'd interviewed her. Overhead, the RCIPS Air Operations Unit's Airbus EC135 chopper loudly hovered with its powerful SX7 StarSun searchlight sweeping the area around the Bodden House. The helicopter also had thermal imaging capability, but with so many people around for the light display, it wasn't much use at the moment.

Mr Phillip also remained. He wouldn't leave my side and when Barbara tried to take him, he leaned back against his lead with all four legs dug into the ground. She was going to have to either drag him or carry him and he made a low rumble growling noise when she approached him. The last thing I needed was a dog to deal with, but I really wanted Barbara out of my hair, so I took the mutt.

I was busy and didn't have a chance to talk to AJ when she arrived, or say goodbye to Jazzy, which I felt bad about. The main thing was she was safe and in good hands, but I'd liked to have explained what happened to AJ, so she'd understand why Jazzy was upset. I also wanted to make sure the kid stayed home with our friend and didn't go out trying to do whatever I'd probably do in her place to figure stuff out or fix it.

Once a police passenger van arrived, we shepherded Kelly inside and closed the door, creating an impromptu interview room, or at least a space in which we could hear each other. A blend of police and Christmas lights poured through the windows, painting each of us in a rainbow of colours. I tossed the stupid stuffed hedgehog into the glove box and fortunately, Mr Phillip didn't notice as he lay down on the floor at my feet.

"Miss Stockton," Whittaker began once we were seated. "We need to know everything you can tell us about your cousin, starting with his real name."

The woman wiped tears from her cheeks with shaking hands. "Jeffrey."

"Last name?"

"Stockton, same as mine. I never took my husband's surname. He's my cousin on my father's side."

I made notes as Whittaker continued. "We'll come back to more details, but can you think of any reason why Jeffrey may have taken Lisa Regan?"

Kelly sobbed a couple of times, then pulled herself together. "Not really. I never believed he'd do anything like this."

Her answer struck me as an odd way of claiming her cousin wasn't capable of kidnapping. Her choice of language was hardly a solid denial of the possibility. I exchanged a glance with the detective, and he raised an eyebrow.

"Why did you bring your cousin instead of your brother..." Whittaker started, then looked at me.

"Glenn Stockton, sir," I filled in.

"Yes, your brother Glenn," Whittaker finished.

"Apparently he's sick," Kelly replied.

"Apparently?" I echoed. Her word choice was killing me. "You don't know if your brother was sick or not?"

She looked up at me. "Jeffrey told me he was."

I leaned back so my boss knew I was done interrupting his interview.

"So you can't confirm your brother was unwell?" he asked.

"I suppose not," she replied. "It was all last minute. Jeffrey said that Glenn had come down with the flu and I shouldn't go by in case he was contagious."

"Did you call him?" Whittaker asked.

She nodded. "It went straight to voicemail. I figured he was sleeping and had turned his phone off."

I was beginning to sense that our bad situation could become worse.

"So I'm clear about this," Whittaker said. "Did you have any contact with your brother before you left for the cruise?"

Kelly shook her head. "Not in the day or so before."

"And when did your cousin tell you Glenn was sick?"

"The night before we left for Miami."

"Have you spoken with or had any form of contact with your brother since then?" Whittaker asked, and my dread worsened. I knew what her answer would be.

"No. I've emailed and texted, but no reply. I'm worried he's sicker than we thought."

The detective looked over at me and I knew him well enough to see we were thinking the same thing.

"Your brother's address?" I asked.

Kelly read it off to me. A town I didn't know in Florida.

"I'll be right back," I said, sliding the side door open and telling Mr Phillip to stay.

As I stepped out, I was greeted by a sight that brought a smile to my face.

"Couple of days witout me and look what happens," Jacob said.

He was in uniform, so I guessed he'd been pulled in to help.

"Sorry to ruin your Christmas."

"Don't look like yours goin' too good either," he said, wincing at my bruised face. "What can I do?"

I handed him the page I'd torn from my notebook. "Get hold of the local police near this address and ask them to go by. They'll want to check inside."

"What dey lookin' for?" Jacob asked.

"Glenn Stockton."

"He dangerous?"

"Doubt it. Reported to be stuck at home with the flu. He's the suspect's cousin."

"I'll get right on it."

"*Takk,*" I said as I turned back to the van. Then I paused and looked over my shoulder. "I know this sucks, but it's good to have you here."

Jacob smiled. "Next you'll be sayin' you can't get by witout me."

As I climbed back into the van, I wondered if that might be true. I knew Jacob helped balance out my occasionally overenthusiastic tendencies, but I'd never considered the fact that I couldn't do the job without him with me. I guess I'd find out if I made detective.

"You three are all close?" Whittaker was asking as I closed the door behind me.

"Somewhat," Kelly replied. "Glenn and I are twins, so we've always been like two peas in a pod. Jeffrey is our age, but he's more of a loner. We don't see much of him."

"Why did he want to come along on this trip?" the detective asked.

"Well, he's a writer, too," she replied. "Not a successful one like Lisa, but he's written a couple of books."

"So he was interested in meeting her?" Whittaker asked.

Kelly shrugged. "He's read one or two of Lisa's books, but he's not a big fan like Glenn and me. My husband passed, and Glenn's been divorced for years. Books are our passion. We're both bookworms. We read everything Lisa puts out and follow her newsletters and all her posts on social media. It feels like she and Mr Phillip are almost friends, you know?" She leaned over the seat back and looked down at the dog.

"You still didn't answer why Jeffrey wanted to come," I said, tired of her wishy-washy replies.

Kelly looked up at me. Even in the odd, colourful light inside the van, I could see the fear in her eyes.

"He said maybe he'd learn something."

Whittaker gave me a subtle nod, letting me know to continue.

"Had he shown interest before?"

"That was the funny thing," Kelly replied. "He'd mocked us for paying all this money to come on Lisa's cruise. But with Glenn sick, he said there was no point letting the ticket go to waste."

"And you agreed to that?"

I could see fear escalate to terror as she faced answering that question. If I had to guess with the little we knew, I'd say she was guilty of being gullible and not much else. But her cousin wouldn't be here if it weren't for her allowing him to be, which she now realised.

"Never would I have thought he'd do anything crazy," Kelly whimpered. "I adore Lisa. I'd never want anything bad to happen to her."

"Does Jeffrey have a history of violent or unpredictable behaviour?" Whittaker asked, and I knew he was taking a different approach, hoping to unlock something that might help us understand the situation.

Kelly shook her head initially, but then her expression tightened. I pictured her brain like a mass of little gears spinning and meshing, scooping up long-discarded memories which were now being redelivered in film clips which spliced together into a different perspective. Those seemingly innocent, childish, or out-of-character actions that painted a clearer picture now they were placed end to end.

"He's always been cut from a different cloth," she offered. "Jeffrey didn't fit in much at school. He's never married, and he's very set in his ways. But I don't think he's ever been in trouble with the law, if that's what you mean?"

"Did he say anything about Lisa that, looking back, may have suggested he'd take her?" Whittaker asked.

Again, Kelly started with a head shake and then thought more about it. "He was annoying me as he was critical of Lisa's writing, but he just wasn't a fan. Glenn would have loved every moment of this trip, so when Jeffrey would say stuff like that, it just made me sad Glenn wasn't here with me."

"Critical how?" I asked, sensing there might be a thread which could help us understand the man's motivation. At the moment, it seemed like everything had been spur of the moment and unplanned. Perhaps he seized an opportunity to make a big splash on an international stage like so many crazies seemed to crave.

"He says her villains always make stupid mistakes."

"Do they?" I asked.

"Glenn and I don't think so. Lisa writes clever and complex antagonists."

"Who always get caught in the end?" I suggested, catching Whittaker's eye.

"That's sort of how a detective novel works," Kelly responded. "Josie Quinn figures it out and catches them in some dramatic way."

"He thinks he'll show Lisa how it's done," Whittaker said. More to me than Kelly, and I nodded.

"Does Jeffrey know anyone here on the island?" I asked.

"He's never been here before," Kelly replied. "I don't think he's ever been out of America before now."

"Wait here, Miss Stockton," Whittaker said, and indicated for me to open the door.

We stepped outside, where the reporters hovered nearby. So far, they'd been respectful and not pressed us too hard for information as we sized up the situation. That would undoubtedly change as time moved on.

"Is there any way there's a romantic element to this situation?" Whittaker asked me.

"No," I replied. I certainly didn't know Lisa well, but based on the time I'd spent with her, she'd mentioned missing her husband and daughter multiple times. It didn't fit at all in my mind.

"Then assuming Jeffrey Stockton has taken Lisa with him against her will, it appears he's winging it," Whittaker summarised. "What would he look for?"

"A place to hide," I suggested. "With all the police activity close by, he needs shelter, and he's moving with an uncooperative hostage."

"Which suggests they can't be far away," the detective added, taking out his mobile and opening the maps app. "Can't imagine he'd risk crossing Church Street, and there'd be fewer options to hide along the waterfront."

"*Ja*, but he might not know that, sir."

Whittaker nodded. "True, but I still think he'd stay away from the busy road. The Boddens' backyard stretches much farther back than I ever realised. Behind it is land belonging to the car dealer on Walkers Road and their repair garage. Looks like it's mainly wrecked and abandoned vehicles, then parking behind the dealership buildings." He held the screen for us both to see.

"North is woods which I bet are too dense to move through," I commented.

"Especially at night," Whittaker added. "And south is homes."

"Dealership is the obvious choice, but that's if he looked at a map, sir. If not, he could be anywhere. Can we trace either of their mobiles?"

"US accounts," he replied. "And it's Christmas Eve, so getting information and permission from the cell companies in America is going to be almost impossible, but we're trying."

The door to the van slid open, and we both turned. Kelly looked at us, and held out her mobile phone. It was ringing.

"It's him! It's Jeffrey calling!"

"Answer it!" Whittaker ordered, and we hurried back into the van and pulled the door closed behind us.

"Jeffrey?" Kelly said, hitting the speaker button.

"You alone?" came her cousin's voice. I hadn't spoken to the man, but I recognised his gruff tone from overhearing him at the tables.

Kelly looked at us, unsure of how to reply.

"This is Detective Whittaker with the Royal Cayman Islands Police Service. I'm here with your cousin, Kelly."

He didn't mention me, so I knew to stay quiet. Last thing we needed was for the man to feel instantly overwhelmed and hang up. Even so, I held my breath, thinking Jeffrey might end the call anyway.

"I have demands," he said after a few moments.

"Okay," Whittaker responded calmly. "Let's talk about what they are in a moment, but first we need to know that Lisa is okay. Can you put her on the line, please?"

"She's fine."

"Forgive me, Jeffrey, but under the circumstances, I need to hear from her to verify she is indeed okay."

"You're just stalling to keep me on the phone so you can track my location."

"That's how they play it on TV, Jeffrey, but here on our little island, we don't have those fancy capabilities. I just want to hear her voice to know she's okay."

A muffled sound came next, and I guessed he'd tried to cover the mic with his hand. He was talking in the background, but I couldn't make out what he was saying. The line cleared again.

"It's Lisa," came the author's voice. She sounded nervous but keeping it together.

"Are you okay, ma'am?" Whittaker asked.

"He hasn't hurt me," she replied. "But Mr Phillip wouldn't like it here."

The end of her sentence faded as the phone was muffled again.

"That's it, you've heard from her," Jeffrey said, coming back on the line.

"Okay, thank you," Whittaker responded. "Now what can we do for you, sir?"

"I want to talk with the reporter lady."

"And why is that, Jeffrey?"

"Because I want the truth told."

"And what truth is that, Jeffrey?"

He laughed, but I didn't hear any humour in his tone. "You'll see when she prints it. Have her ready when I call again."

"Which reporter?" Whittaker asked.

"The Irish one," Jeffrey replied, then hung up.

"Jeffrey?" Whittaker tried, but the line was dead.

Whittaker winced and looked at me. "Did you pick up on any clues to where they might be? I couldn't hear anything in the background."

"They're in a vehicle," I replied.

"How do you know? I didn't hear an engine running."

"Because Mr Phillip doesn't like riding in vehicles he doesn't know."

19

DUSTY BEANS FOR DINNER

"Miss Stockton, does Jeffrey own a gun?" Detective Whittaker asked after making a frantic series of calls and arrangements.

"Yes, but I have no idea what kinds," she replied. "He mostly builds them himself, I believe."

"Like ghost guns or 3D printed?" I asked.

"I have no idea what either of those are," Kelly replied, and I believed her.

"Ghost guns are assembled from components and pieces without serial numbers," Whittaker explained. "They're illegal in some US states. 3D printed means many of the parts are made by an additive manufacturing process rather than traditional metals."

Kelly frowned. "He has this machine in his house that he makes things with. Looks like a tall box with a glass window."

"Sounds like a 3D printer," I pointed out. "So, does he have a gun with him?" I asked the more important part of our line of questioning.

"Oh my. I don't know. I doubt it. We had to state that we didn't have any firearms or alcohol when we went through security."

"Did they scan you and your luggage at the cruise port?" Whittaker asked.

Kelly nodded. "We walked through one of those machines with everything out of our pockets, and they X-rayed our bags."

"All your bags? Or do you mean your carry-on?" I asked.

"They already had our luggage. But the paperwork said they'd go through a security check."

Detective Whittaker looked at his watch. "I'll call Captain Marston and find out. It's been nearly twenty minutes already. I'll set up the best perimeter I can with the limited personnel we have and let's see who we can send with you to start searching." He nodded towards the sliding door, which I opened.

Mr Phillip jumped up at my feet. "Stay here," I told him, but he leapt out anyway and shook. Pieces of slobber dripped from his tongue, which slapped against his little snout.

"*Faen*," I muttered. "I think he needs to pee." Grabbing his lead, I jogged to the hedge by the low wall. "Get on with it, then," I encouraged, although it came out more like an order.

"Sommer!" came Williams's voice. "Got a vest for you. Let's go."

I looked down at the dog, who stared back up at me. "What? You need privacy, or a newspaper or something. Take a piss and let's go."

Mr Phillip slowly squatted his hind quarters and performed his duty.

"Good dog," I found myself saying, to my horror. "Come on, ugly," I added, perhaps overcompensating, and led him back to the van. He let me pick him up and set him inside. I briefly petted Mr Phillip and looked at Kelly. "Neither of you leave this vehicle."

Joining Williams, I slipped on the tactical vest. My borrowed grey sweatshirt wasn't ideal for a night reconnaissance, but I wasn't spoilt for choice and the vest at least partially covered the lighter colour. Jacob came around the side of Williams's van, already wearing a vest and testing his torch.

"Where are all your guys?" I asked Williams.

"Trying to enjoy Christmas," he replied sharply. "Couldn't schedule your little disaster for a better time, could you?"

"Then arm us," I said.

As head of the firearms unit, Williams carried a sidearm and an assault rifle. He'd usually have at least three other armed officers with him.

"Not happening, Nora," Whittaker said from behind me. "By the book, and the sergeant takes lead, understand?"

"I've been to the range," I argued. "The sergeant has taught me how to use a sidearm."

Whittaker frowned at Williams.

"Thanks, Nora," the sergeant muttered, before turning to the detective. "Just a couple of times, sir. She can handle a handgun."

"Still no," Whittaker said firmly. "There's an approval and certification process for a reason, and you both know it."

"Sir," Williams and I both acknowledged.

"Remember, we don't know for sure that the suspect is armed," Whittaker continued. "Proceed with caution and if you sight them, sit tight so we can secure a perimeter. The plan is to talk our way through this."

"Sir," we all acknowledged again.

"On me," Williams ordered, and we trotted along in line as he headed around the side of the Bodden House towards the backyard.

Behind me, I heard Whittaker asking Lahana Jones to join him.

The bright lights of the front lawn soon faded behind the house as we made our way to the back of the property. Scattered trees amongst patchy grass and dirt soon shielded most of the illumination and slowly our eyes adjusted. Williams moved to his left and pointed to either side of a pair of shipping containers, which I presumed were used to store the Christmas decorations for eleven months out of the year. Jacob and I split up while Williams checked each door. He finally used a torch, shielded carefully by his body to see the locks were in place.

Moving on, we soon reached the fence at the bottom of the Boddens' lot. Two metres high, it appeared to be sturdy and well maintained, with the wooden slats varying in tone where they'd been replaced over the years. I couldn't imagine Jeffrey getting Lisa to scale the obstacle and, for the first time, I doubted our theory that he must have come this way.

Williams held up a hand for us to wait while he jogged to the north-east corner. I could follow his progress from the torch beam he kept low against the fence line, checking for possible openings. When he returned to us, we fell in line behind him as he kept moving south. Nearing the south-east corner, a large yellow mastic tree towered overhead, and the fence rose and fell unevenly where the roots had grown beneath and damaged the slats. Williams's light fell upon an opening where several of the cracked planks had been kicked in. The pale cast of the splintered edges told us it was recent damage. Williams quickly turned off his torch.

"I'll take centre. Nora left, Jacob right," Williams whispered. "Don't use your light unless absolutely necessary or to signal me in an emergency."

Jacob and I both nodded, then I squeezed through the gap in the fence.

In the distance, security lights on the back of the dealership building covered the edge of the car park, but between the fence behind me and trees and old vehicles in the scrubland, it was almost pitch black and I had to watch my footing. Moving along the fence line, I reached the corner where a less sturdy barrier of barbed wire separated the lot from the woods. I began picking my way east, stumbling on discarded junk hidden in the tufts and patches of grass and weeds.

Reaching a row of wrecked vehicles, cast aside long ago by the amount of foliage growing around them, I searched for signs of recent disturbances. By ducking down, I looked through the cars hoping to spot the silhouette of a person, but apart from the scurrying of small critters and the buzz of insects, all appeared to be quiet. In daylight, we'd have a chance of seeing tracks, but we couldn't risk the torches for fear of warning Jeffrey Stockton. If indeed we were anywhere near him, which was a pure guess and a long shot at best.

A worn path extended from the paved car park up ahead, made a U-turn around a row of abandoned vehicles, then returned on the other side. More vehicles lay dormant in the spots where they'd been dropped on the outsides of the dirt trail. I caught sight of Williams, 20 metres to my right, checking the far lane, so I pressed on, zigzagging back and forth in my lane to inspect the cars on both sides. Ahead to my left, a rusty old passenger van creaked, and I thought I noticed a glimmer of light which quickly went out. It was hard to make out details in the dim light of the stars, but I thought I could see the windscreen was missing as well as most of the side glass. The van sat low on four flat tyres and undergrowth had consumed the lower part of the vehicle.

Aiming my torch across the lot towards Williams, I cupped my hand around the side facing the van and flicked the beam on three times. Hunching down low, I waited. A few moments later and the sergeant arrived beside me.

"The van," I whispered.

"You saw him?" he asked.

I shook my head. "But someone or something is in there."

"So it could be the garage cat," Williams hissed back, and I caught the grin on his face.

"Only if he smokes," I replied, touching my nose, picking up the faint hint of burnt tobacco in the air.

He nodded. "Take position. Wait on me," he ordered, then indicated for me to move to the rear of the vehicle while he approached the front. I stayed low and eased across the dirt lane, trying to be as light on my feet as I could. Reaching the rear corner, I paused and allowed time for Williams to make his move to the front of the van. Watching over my shoulder, I waited for his cue.

"Police!" he called out as he stood and shone his torch through the front window frame.

I leapt up and switched on my light, squinting against the brightness we'd created inside the old vehicle. A figure dived for the floor inside, disappearing between the rows of seats.

"Let me see you!" Williams ordered. "Hands raised. Slowly."

On the seat behind where the figure had been, I saw several filthy duffel bags and an open can of beans whose contents now dripped to the floor.

"Not our man," I called out to Williams, then carefully moved along the side of the van until my torch fell upon the figure. I kept the beam from directly shining on him, but the old man still squinted and tried to cover his eyes.

"It's okay, sir. Sorry to disturb you."

Williams came alongside. He extinguished his torch in his left hand and lowered his weapon in his right.

"You're trespassing," he said to the homeless man.

"*Fy faen,*" I muttered. "Give the bloke a break."

Williams shrugged and walked back to the dirt lane. I fished in my pocket for my mobile and pulled out a ten Caymanian dollar note, which was the only cash I had on me. I held it through the broken side window. The old man tentatively took it from me as he hauled his bony backside up onto the shredded upholstery of the seat.

"For the meal we ruined," I said, then followed Williams.

"Sir!" Jacob called out in the dark, then flashed his torch three times in our direction.

At this point, our presence was obvious, so there was no reason not to use our lights as we jogged between the wrecked vehicles towards where Jacob stood next to a box truck which had its right front corner smashed in.

"I think they may have been here," Jacob said, shining his torch into the cab where a walk through went into the cargo section. "I heard something after we came through the fence, and the passenger side door was open when I got here."

He directed the beam at the floor. A layer of dust and dirt had been recently stirred by footprints.

"Could have been our friend over there," Williams commented.

"Look inside, sir," Jacob said.

I followed Williams into the wrecked van. Its windscreen was shattered, and the airbag laid limply from the centre of the steering wheel. We stepped between the seats into the box section, which was hotter and muggier than outside. The back roll-up door was closed and nothing appeared to have taken up residence yet, so I guessed it hadn't been here that long. We ran our lights around and I paused on the right-side box covering the wheel well.

"Sergeant," I said, circling my light on the words in the dust.

Jeff has gun.

"So much for the yacht's security checks," Williams commented, then pulled the radio from his belt and hailed Detective Whittaker. While he reported our find, Jacob stepped outside to answer his mobile, which vibrated in his pocket.

After taking a few pictures with my phone, I followed both men outside, where Jacob was finishing his call.

"Dat was da local police in Florida. Dey had to break into da brudder's place."

"Is he sick like Jeffrey claimed?" Williams asked.

Jacob shook his head. "No. He'd been tied up and left."

"He's alive?" I asked in surprise.

Jacob shook his head again. "Dey said whoever did it set up some drinking water ting, but it must've not worked. Body still warm, so not bin dead long."

"So they're treating it as a homicide?" Williams asked.

"Dey are," Jacob confirmed.

Williams unclipped his radio once more, pausing to look at me. "So, what do you think? Where's he taken her now?"

I looked around us. To the east were the dealership and service buildings, which would likely be alarmed and have security cameras. Beyond was Walkers Road, but if Whittaker had established a perimeter guard on the main streets, that wouldn't be an option. To the north, the dense woods created a barrier, and turning to the south, I saw the pale glow of lights from the houses on the backside of a quiet residential street.

"One of those homes," I replied.

20

SLOBBERY REJECTION

To reach the homes, we would have to scramble over their garden fences, so we jogged back to the front of the Bodden House to regroup with Whittaker.

"I have people placed in both directions of South Church and Walkers," the detective explained as we crammed into the police passenger van.

Mr Phillip jumped up and wagged his stumpy tail, panting excitedly at me.

"Let me get in, you silly mutt," I told him, urging him out of the way while petting him at the same time. It was a bit like having a bloke you're not interested in hitting on you in a bar. But less creepy. Although the amount of slobber seemed similar.

"What about the residential neighbourhood?" I asked Whittaker.

"Two constables in a car are about to run a patrol through all those streets," he replied.

"Call them off," I said, then remembered an important part which often slipped my mind. "Sir."

Whittaker picked up his radio and ordered the patrol to standby for now, then looked at me expectantly.

"He's in one of those homes," I said.

"You saw him?"

"*Nei*. But he doesn't have many choices."

"Makes sense to me," Williams added.

I was grateful for his support, but I now felt another knot in my stomach. This one borne out of pressure I'd just heaped on myself. It didn't slide by unnoticed that Whittaker had called off his patrol before questioning my reasoning. While his confidence in me was nice, and I'd spoken boldly, all I had was a logical hunch. And now our pursuit of the suspect was primarily focused on my suspicion. *What if I was wrong?* Lisa's life was hanging in the balance. But I was committed now.

"If you have men you could place in the repair shop's yard, tell them to have their lights on and make noise," I said.

"Where you just were?" Whittaker queried.

"Exactly. We need him worried about the backside of the house while we have time to figure out which one it is from the front," I explained.

I looked at Williams and realised I'd taken the lead when he was in charge of our makeshift unit, but he wasn't objecting or giving me the stink eye, so I pressed on. I brought up the street map on my mobile.

Jacob looked over my shoulder. "Phelan Close. An uncle of mine used to live dere. It's a cul-de-sac off South Church Street."

"Okay. Let's go," Williams announced.

As I put my hand on the door, a mobile rang. Kelly, who'd remained silent in the back, held up her phone.

"Answer on speaker," Whittaker ordered and held a finger to his lips directed at Williams, Jacob, and me.

"What do you think you're doing?" came Jeffrey Stockton's voice. He sounded agitated and out of breath.

"How do you mean, sir?" Whittaker asked.

"Don't fuck with me," the kidnapper snapped back. "You have a SWAT team roaming around looking for me."

The detective paused a moment before responding, gathering his thoughts. "What did you expect, Jeffrey?"

"I expected you to wait for my call back with demands!" he shouted.

"Please calm down, sir," Whittaker said. "I'm sure you know how this whole thing works, but I should tell you, the movies and TV shows don't depict these situations particularly accurately."

"Don't treat me like an idiot, Detective."

"I certainly didn't intend to come across that way, Jeffrey. I'm just saying, from our side we have to figure out where you are, which of course you'll have to reveal at some point if you plan on leaving the island."

My eyes met Whittaker's. It was a brave tactic, and a smart one. If we could understand his end game, we might establish a timeline we had to work with. We all waited for a response, but nothing came.

"You have Lisa, Jeffrey, so we're not about to do anything impetuous," Whittaker added. "In a situation like this, we must assume you're armed, and the last thing we want is harm to come to you or Lisa."

"I am, and don't pretend to care about me, Detective," Jeffrey retorted.

"In my home, I was raised to care about everybody, Jeffrey. Especially at Christmas."

We were surrounded by a night filled with bright holiday lights, but I'd completely forgotten it was Christmas Eve. And I still didn't have a gift for the kid. That ship had certainly sailed and would be another tick on a long list of bad parenting moments for me, but I hoped Jazzy was feeling the spirit a little now she was home with AJ.

"Can we talk about your requests, Jeffrey?" Whittaker asked. "I believe that was why you called."

"Is the reporter there?"

"She's standing by. Are you ready to speak with her?"

I'd noticed Lahana was standing by the back of the van away from the other reporters.

"You're a clever man, Detective, but I told you before I'm no fool. You don't think I'd be timing our calls? Keep your SWAT team away and wait for me to call back."

"Jeffrey, we don't have a SWAT team..." Whittaker replied, but he was talking to a dead line.

"Let's go," Williams said again.

But Whittaker halted me. "Just a moment."

"Sir?" I questioned.

"Let's take a second to think about who we're dealing with. Jacob filled me in on the report from Florida."

"He's killed already," Williams said, and Whittaker's eyes flicked to Kelly.

"Shit," Williams muttered.

"Jeffrey?" Kelly blurted. "You're saying he's killed someone?"

The woman was shaking from head to toe, and more tears came down her cheeks. For once, it wasn't me who'd put their foot in their ear.

"This must all be confirmed with official identification before we can say anything for certain, Miss Stockton," Whittaker said, trying his best to salvage the situation.

But quite honestly, we didn't have time for niceties. We couldn't help Glenn, but I sure as hell didn't want to see Lisa become his next victim and was determined to prevent it.

"It sounds like Florida was unintentional," I pointed out. "That's something we might be able to use, sir."

Whittaker scratched his chin. "Maybe. It can go both ways, though. If he thinks he's already on the hook for one, what's the downside of another?"

"Dat could be bargained down, don't you tink?" Jacob offered.

He rarely spoke up in debriefs and meetings like this, so I was both surprised and pleased. Usually he'd wait until we left, then tell me what he'd been thinking. Perhaps he was starting to realise how life would be if I did make detective and we were separated. It was weighing on my mind more and more.

Whittaker nodded. "That would certainly be the approach. I'll consider how to use the information for when he calls back."

"Jeffrey wouldn't hurt anyone," Kelly whimpered from the back. "I know this looks bad, but he's not a violent man."

"Then what does he possibly have to gain by taking Lisa?" I asked.

She shook her head, and more tears flowed. "I honestly don't know. He's frustrated by all the publishers who've turned his book down. Maybe it has something to do with that."

"Pretty sure kidnapping a famous author won't make a publisher change their mind," Williams commented.

Whittaker held up a hand, telling his firearms specialist to back off. I raised a finger and Whittaker nodded.

"Why have they rejected his books?" I asked.

Kelly wiped her face and sniffled a few times before answering. "I don't really know. If he's said, I don't remember."

"Have you read his books?" I continued.

She nodded. "Well, I read the first one, and then a little of the second."

"Why did you stop?"

Kelly wouldn't look up at me. "They're not really my taste."

I glanced at Whittaker, and he nodded for me to continue.

"Why?" I asked.

She shrugged her shoulders. "A little darker than I like."

"He writes horror?"

"No, they're not really horror, but they are graphic, and…" she trailed off and went quiet.

"And what?" I pushed.

"Disturbing," she mumbled under her breath.

I could understand why she'd tried to stop herself from saying the word, but I guess she couldn't come up with a better one.

"You love Lisa's books, and they're thrillers. They get pretty dark, don't they?"

Kelly's head bobbed as she nodded. "But they're different. Her Josie Quinn character solves the crimes. Jeffrey writes his from the killer's perspective."

I turned to the detective. "He could be building up to…" It was my turn to check myself, which for once I actually did. "Escalating his actions, sir."

"Agreed," Whittaker replied. "But keep in mind the initial evidence suggests Florida was unintentional. This could all be slipping outside of what he'd intended. We need to prevent it from getting worse."

"He's confirmed the gun, sir," Williams pointed out.

"I understand that," Whittaker responded. "But our best solution is always to talk our way out of the problem."

He looked at each one of us in turn and we all responded with a "Yes, sir".

"Alright. Now go, quickly," he ordered us. "If there's any way to locate him without being seen, it would help me out when I'm dealing with him. I'd rather he didn't feel pressured or panicked. He's unpredictable already."

I opened the van door and stepped outside. Mr Phillip followed, and I had to wait for the other two to come out before I could shovel the dog back inside. I scratched his head.

"Stay here. I'll be back. Maybe I'll have your mummy with me."

I looked up and noticed Whittaker was staring at me. With a slight grin on his face.

"On our way, sir," I muttered, embarrassed to be caught worrying about the mutt.

"Nora?" he said, stopping me.

"Yes, sir?"

"Think slowly, then act quickly."

"Sir," I said, leaving the van door open as Whittaker called to Lahana.

I jogged to catch up with the other two and thought about what the detective had said. Initially, it didn't make any sense to me. This job was no place for a slow thinker. Bad people didn't wait for you to look at situations from all perspectives. They forced issues, making you rely on your wits and think nimbly on your feet. But I realised that wasn't what he meant. Whittaker was telling me to tread carefully. We were in a time crunch, no doubt, but Jeffrey Stockton wasn't running at me, whirling an axe in the air.

We had time to pull all the pieces we knew together, which should help us make the right decisions. So what did we know? Jeffrey is a loner, almost certainly troubled and, from his reactions over the phone, angry when he feels disrespected. But disrespected for what? No one likes to think people are treating them or thinking of them as fools, but he was more specific. Jeffrey wanted Whittaker to know that he understood how police crisis situations worked.

"Do we have any background info on this bloke?" I asked as we walked briskly down South Church Street, which was finally clear of pedestrians. In the distance, in both directions, a line of cars backed up as far as I could see. We'd brought the south side of George Town to a standstill.

"Like what?" Williams asked in reply. "He had no priors in the system we have access to."

With more time, we'd dig around his social media profiles and request other records like Department of Motor Vehicles from his home state, but I guessed we were too short staffed for all of that tonight.

The situation still struck me as being unplanned. Maybe he'd decided long ago to take the brother's ticket and bluff his way here with his sister, but if that was the case, Jeffrey hadn't thought it through very far. He had no way of knowing Clifton Bush would show up and I'd create a perfect distraction for him, and he clearly hadn't planned out an escape with Lisa. No, he was winging it. Something must have tipped him over. Maybe he was at Glenn Stockton's already and whatever was said started the ball rolling, or perhaps he'd come up with the idea before visiting his cousin. But the Bodden House part had been spur of the moment, I was sure of it.

The question now was not only where he went, but what his

end game could be. He'd asked for a reporter, which meant he had a message to tell the world, and it wasn't going to be *Free Tibet*. He felt wronged in some way and wanted to set the record straight. My best guess was the backbone of the situation stemmed from his book rejection, but he should've grabbed Barbara instead of Lisa. It was the publishers he was mad at. He was simply jealous of Lisa and her success. We'd have a whole different situation if he'd taken Barbara. I doubt anyone would care what he did with her.

21

PAIN IN THE DAILY EDITION

Jogging along South Church Street we came to Phelan Close, which led inland opposite the entrance to the Jackson Point Terminal where the island's oil and petrol deliveries came ashore. It was strange to see storage tanks amongst a neighbourhood of residences and resorts, but the place wasn't very big and was well hidden behind trees. There were no streetlamps on Phelan, so the bright lights of the Bodden House and Church Street soon faded to a glow in the sky.

The narrow street turned 90 degrees left, then after 100 metres, turned hard right to continue in its original direction. The homes on our left were now the only things between us and the Boddens' backyard and then the car repair yard. Staying close to a low wall fronting the first house, I paused and looked at the map on my mobile. The screen went into nighttime mode but still felt like a beacon in my hand as we tried to remain unseen. I was assuming Jeffrey had made for the nearest sanctuary, but it was possible he'd crossed Phelan to the homes on our right. In which case he could be looking right at us as we crouched over the bright screen of my mobile. Or I could be completely wrong and he'd already made it a mile from here with Lisa.

"The fence at the bottom of the Boddens' garden is between the next two homes," I pointed out. "That leaves three more houses before the end of the cul-de-sac."

"We'll number them one through six, with one being the last home on the street, okay?" Williams said. "Means we're at home six right now."

"Den home tree is in a direct line from da van he was in," Jacob whispered. "Try dat one first?"

"Maybe," I replied as I thought it over. "But only if no one is home."

"He has a gun. Lisa told us and he's confirmed it," Williams said. "He might not be fussy."

I nodded, but my gut told me that Jeffrey Stockton was keen to avoid escalating his situation beyond where he'd found himself. Something about his voice over the phone told me he was trying to gather his thoughts and feel in control once more. Additional hostages would complicate everything, and he had to know he'd need to move again. It was only a matter of time before we'd canvass all the homes in the area. And he couldn't know we were as short staffed as we were.

"We'll knock on the door of those where people are home," Williams continued. "Then perimeter check the others looking for signs of forced entry."

He waved a hand forward, so I pocketed my mobile and fell in line behind him. Home five was easy to skip. Through the front window we could see a family playing some kind of game in their living room. I wasn't good at judging kids' ages, but they were somewhere between infants and puberty. Young enough to still want to play games at Christmas with their parents.

We moved on to home four and I pictured the map in my mind. We were now alongside the area we'd searched amongst the wrecked vehicles. These were all nice homes. Not the swanky *look at my fancy second home* you found in the newer developments on canals and the oceanfront, where rich people spent a few weeks a year, but well-built, single-storey homes with full-time families.

The curtains were drawn on home four, through which an animated glow suggested a television playing. Williams pointed at Jacob, and then at the front door. That made sense. Jacob was the only one in obvious uniform. If Williams showed up carrying his assault rifle over his shoulder, he'd scare the hell out of the residents. It was hard enough to get people to believe I was a constable when I was in uniform, and right now I looked like a civilian who'd nicked a tactical bulletproof vest.

Jacob rapped on the door, and after a few moments, a lady answered. From what I could see, she appeared to be surprised but didn't have the edge-of-panic demeanour of a citizen being held hostage and told to talk casually to a copper at the door. Jacob was keeping his voice lower than usual to minimise the chance of other homes hearing the disturbance, but by his smile and hand gestures, I could tell he was being his affable self.

Once he'd returned to the street, we quickly moved to house three. The exterior was lit by a row of Christmas lights along the roofline, but the interior appeared to be dark and void of vehicles in the driveway. I looked at the other two homes along the cul-de-sac and could make out the tops of cars in each driveway. If I was looking for a place to hide, this would be my choice.

"Nora, go left," Williams ordered, keeping to a whisper. "I'll take right and meet you around the back of the house. Jacob, stay here and cover the front."

I hopped over the low ironshore rock wall and stayed close to the hedgerow which divided the property from their neighbour. There was no way to remain completely hidden from the decorative holiday lights, so I ran to the side of the house. Vaulting a low metal and wire gate, I hoped I wasn't about to meet a snarling dog. I was banking on any animals having heard us before now and at least coming to the gate to investigate.

Along the side of the house, the building and the hedge blocked almost all the light, so I paused for my eyes to adjust. After a few moments, as the outline of objects began appearing, I moved forward, skirting around a rubbish bin and then a bicycle leaning against the house. The back garden was open, with a lawn extending beyond a concrete patio to a wooden rear fence. It was tall and from the glow of the neighbours' pool lights, I could see it was in good shape. Unless Jeffrey had found a hole or created one I'd missed, he'd have had a hard time penetrating the barrier. Especially with an unwilling hostage in tow.

Easing along the patio, I watched Williams approaching from the other side and we met by the back door. We both shook our heads, acknowledging we'd seen no evidence of a break-in. I softly tried the door handle, but it was locked. Looking at Williams, I wondered what we could do now. Without clear evidence that someone was inside, we couldn't break in ourselves, but if we didn't get to check every room, we couldn't know for sure. The back door could have been unlocked when Stockton arrived, then he locked it himself after entering.

We both looked around. The faint sound of voices reached us from the neighbours in house four, and in the other direction I was sure I could hear more annoying Christmas music. Muted rustles came from all around us as birds, lizards, and other small critters moved about in the night. An underlying buzz of insects and the hum of cars in the distance completed the low-volume backdrop over which I could hear us both breathing. Laughter erupted from the game players, accompanied by the muffled sound of a door sliding closed.

"Let's check the other two houses," Williams whispered, and I had no reason to disagree. And yet my feet were reluctant to move.

Forcing myself to follow, we made our way around the side of the house to the street where Jacob waited, but I could almost sense Lisa close by. The feeling was strong, albeit completely illogical. As we moved to house two and Jacob once more rapped on the front door, I'd convinced myself that my imagination and desire to find her were playing tricks on my mind. The lack of sleep was also undoubtedly contributing, and as the adrenaline ebbed, the soreness from the bruises and grazes made me walk stiffly.

Jacob soon returned after speaking with a bewildered older man who hadn't seen or heard anything unusual, and we briskly moved to the last house on the street. Thicker shrubs and small trees hid the building, and while the one car I'd seen was parked in the driveway, it was set to one side as though making room for another. Solitary decorative fake candles burned in each window; otherwise the house appeared to be vacant.

"Same drill," Williams said, and we split up, moving either side of the home.

I'm not sure which of us triggered it, but we'd only made a few steps towards the front when floodlights came on, bathing the area in bright white light. I jogged ahead, finding the shadows alongside the place, where I halted. Once again I needed my eyes to adjust and they took longer this time having been momentarily blinded. I also wondered what other security measures the homeowner had in place. If similar motion sensor lights were set up in the rear, it would almost guarantee Jeffrey would have run a mile from this place.

Carefully making my way forward, I listened for sounds inside the house as I neared the rear corner. My heart skipped when the air conditioning compressor spun up next to me in a sudden whirring and creaking of pipes. Around the back I peered into a window, cupping my hands on either side of my face to shut out the faint ambient light and stars. Something moved inside, but all I could see were vague outlines of furniture. From the silvery glint, it appeared I was looking through the kitchen window over the sink.

A face suddenly shot towards the glass and I stepped back. The cat's mouth opened and closed, but I couldn't hear its meow through the double panes. I wondered how Mr Phillip felt about cats and the idea of bringing him back to chase the feline around the house seemed appealing.

"Anything?" Williams whispered, arriving by the back door.

"*Nei.*"

"Okay," he said a little louder. "The theory was good. We should knock on doors across the street on the way back."

I nodded, but stayed put and looked around me as Williams walked away.

"Hey," I hissed, and he turned.

"What?"

"You and Jacob knock on doors. I'll hop the fence and walk the backside of the car repair shop lot. Maybe I can see where he might have found a way through."

Williams groaned. "We should stick together, Nora. If we had a fourth, we could pair up, but I don't want anyone on their own with an armed fugitive on the loose."

"We just checked every house. He's not here," I pointed out. "I'll meet you on the road by house six. If I find a way through the fence, it might give us a clue where he went."

"Maybe there isn't a hole in the fence," Williams countered.

"Then we'll know he couldn't have come this way at all."

In the dim light I could still tell Williams was shaking his head. "You're a pain in the ass, Sommer."

"Thank you, sir," I said, and moved towards the rear of the property.

"I wasn't agreeing, Nora," Williams grunted.

"Close enough, sir," I replied and kept going.

Maybe my sleep-deprived gut wasn't working properly, but I'd been sure Stockton had headed this way. It wasn't just his best choice; it was just about his only one.

Houses one and two backed up to the paved car park of the car lot and a two-metre stone wall divided them. The homeowner had planted shrubs to hide the ugly wall, but they probably preferred the wall to a view of vehicles and the accompanying noise of the dealership and repair shop. I shoved branches aside and jumped to grab the top of the stone, then pulled myself up using my feet on the face of the wall to help. Fortunately, there were no glass shards or barbed wire along the top, and I lowered myself down the other side, landing in long grass.

As I stood, a beam of light whipped along the wall, pausing on me.

"Stop dere! Police!" came an accented voice.

"Shhh!" I hissed back. "Constable Sommer. Stop yelling and turn the light away from me."

"ID," the constable responded in a quieter voice, and he dipped the torch, but didn't turn it off.

I took out my badge and held it up. "Light?"

He finally swung it away. "What are you doin'? Where's Sergeant Williams?"

"Williams and Tibbetts are checking across the street. I'm seeing where the perp may have cut through."

"No one come dis way," he said indignantly, as though I was accusing him of not being vigilant.

"No, he left this way," I explained, and began moving down the wall to look for access points.

The constable followed. "Need the torch?"

"*Nei.*"

"You'll be able to see better," he insisted.

"*Nei,*" I said again. "The suspect wouldn't have had a torch, so I'm seeing what he could see."

"Oh," he mumbled, but kept following.

The wall ended but a wooden fence continued behind house three. To my right, the paved lot turned to an open grass pasture with a few trees. On the far side of the property was the wrecked car dirt lot we'd searched. Everything pointed to Jeffrey leading Lisa across the pasture to the fence. At that point, he should have been looking for the empty house, which was number three. But as I walked along the property line, I couldn't see any access point other than going over the top. Which, like the wall, seemed unlikely.

Reaching house four, their pool lights made everything more visible. The tall wooden fence turned towards the street, running between the two homes. A lower white picket fence lined the back garden of home four. But lights were clearly on in the house and we'd spoken to the lady. I kept walking, treading carefully on the uneven ground with overgrown grass and weeds up to my knees.

At the far side of the back garden was a small pool house, big enough for a lounge area and probably a bathroom. It had large sliding glass doors across the front facing the pool.

"Stay over here," I ordered the constable, who seemed determined to follow me everywhere.

"Where you goin'?" he asked redundantly as I hopped the picket fence.

As I crossed the deck surrounding the pool, I could see one side of the sliders was slightly open, and I stopped. If Jeffrey was in there, he had to have seen me approaching, so there was no hiding my presence. The pool lights were reflecting off the tinted glass, preventing me from seeing inside, but anyone in the little building would certainly be able to see out. There didn't seem much point in playing games.

Taking my torch from my belt, I walked up to the slider, pushed it open, and switched on my light. To my left was a bar with bottles lined up on shelves behind. On the right, a door, which would surely be a bathroom. Between, a plush sofa and two recliners looked out over the pool, with a coffee table in the middle of the room. On the coffee table sat a newspaper, a pen, and two empty glasses.

I turned to the constable by the fence. "Use your radio. Call Williams and tell him Stockton was here."

22

UNDERLINED AND SO CLOSE

A few minutes later, Williams arrived by the pool, leaving Jacob to interview the residents in the main house. Through Detective Whittaker, I'd sent the constable who'd followed me and his partner to finish canvassing Phelan Close because I'd pulled Williams and Jacob away before they'd finished. I sat staring at the items on the coffee table.

"What do we have?" Williams asked, stepping inside.

"Lisa sent another message," I replied without looking up.

"What does it say?"

"I don't know yet."

I could tell he wanted to ask more, but to his credit he stayed quiet and poked around the little pool house, careful not to disturb anything or leave prints.

It felt good to have correctly guessed the general direction and purpose Stockton had taken, and it was nice to know my gut instincts were functioning despite my fatigue, but now I needed to do it again. Lisa must have only had a few moments to use the pen on the newspaper, as she'd underlined a handful of words. I assumed she hadn't just written her thoughts somewhere obvious on the page, as she didn't want Jeffrey to see what she'd done, and couldn't rely on us figuring out to check all the pages if she wrote it on the inside. Which was disappointing, as the first thing I did was check every page.

"There's a drawer open in the bar," Williams said. "Looks like a kitchen junk drawer. You know, pens, Sellotape, batteries."

"Maybe the pen came from there," I thought aloud, but didn't know why Jeffrey would have let Lisa get a pen. Unless he left her alone for a moment to use the bathroom or something and didn't notice.

Williams's mobile buzzed, and he answered the call. "Sir?"

He listened for a moment, then put the call on speaker. "We're both listening, sir," he said.

"Stockton called and spoke with Lahana," came Whittaker's voice. "He does indeed appear to be disgruntled about being turned down by the publishers. He wants her to write an article about the lack of respect given to many of the brilliant minds who have chosen to exercise their intelligence in what we deem illegal."

"Which he considers himself?" I asked.

"It seems that way," Whittaker agreed. "Anyway, naturally we agreed to get to work on the article, which buys us some time."

"That was his only demand?" Williams asked.

"No. He wants a plane off the island by midnight."

I looked at my watch. It was 9:38pm.

"To where?" I asked.

"Wouldn't say. Capable of 1,000 miles with one pilot and no one else aboard," Whittaker replied. "I don't imagine we could pull that off by midnight even if we chose to. Digging up a pilot who hasn't had a drop to drink and a plane we could use will take far longer than that. I've also reached out to the US authorities, as both Stockton and Lisa are US citizens. But they won't be able to assist us before midnight either. So, it's on us to find him. What do we have there?"

Williams looked at me.

"Four words underlined in a newspaper, sir," I replied.

"Which say?"

"Don't. Trust. Ride. False."

"Don't trust ride false?" the detective echoed. "What could that mean?"

"There are two empty glasses here, sir," Williams said. "Perhaps he's drugged her. That could be the don't trust part."

"He would have needed to bring something like that with him," I pointed out. "Unlikely if this was an opportunistic move."

We all fell silent in thought for a few moments.

"Is there any chance those markings were already in the newspaper?" Williams suggested. "Maybe they're not from Lisa at all."

"They are," I said firmly, but realised I had nothing to support that theory. "But we should ask the family," I added.

Williams moved to the sliding door, leaving his mobile on the coffee table. "I'll find out."

"I think he was there when you checked the house," Whittaker said, letting out a deep breath. "He was talking to us when he became agitated and went quiet. Then he said he'd call again and hung up."

"He's also been timing the calls," I thought aloud. "Could be he just ran to the end of his self-allotted time that he thinks we need to trace him."

"Perhaps. But something in the way he reacted made me think he'd been disturbed."

"*Fy faen*," I groaned. "I heard him. We were in the neighbour's back garden and I heard a door sliding. It was him leaving the pool house. We were right here."

"Means we're getting closer, Nora," Whittaker said. "Now we need to interpret what Lisa is trying to tell us."

I pushed aside my anger at having walked right by their location and looked again at the words underlined on the front page of the newspaper.

"She wouldn't have had a perfect choice of words," I said as I thought through what it would have taken Lisa to mark the paper while Jeffrey was close by. "We don't know how she intended this to be broken up."

"You mean she could have intended 'don't trust' to be one part and 'ride false' another?" Whittaker asked.

"*Ja*. But ride false doesn't make any sense. Does it?" I added, wondering if I was missing a weird saying or phrase. The English language has lots of them.

"He has to get to the airport somehow," Whittaker offered. "Maybe that's the ride part and false is separate again."

"That would mean going to a more major road and waiting for a vehicle," I replied. "Or a bus."

The idea that Stockton would risk exposing himself on a public street didn't feel right. Besides, he had to believe we had the streets either cordoned off or at least patrolled.

"He could be stealing a car from one of the homes," Whittaker suggested. "Although the bus idea is a possibility, they run all over the island along the main roads, but their schedule is loose at best. I'm not even sure how many are operating on Christmas Eve."

"He's never been to the island before and he wouldn't have used the public transport in the few days he's been here on the cruise," I mentioned. "Seems risky to rely on something he could have only researched online."

"These four words could mean a thousand different things," Whittaker said with a sigh.

"And we can't be sure of the order of the words," I replied, scanning the front page.

"Right. Her intention could be the words in a completely different order. Like don't ride, false trust. Except that makes even less sense."

"But ride has to be a vehicle," I muttered.

"Could refer to the plane he's demanded," Whittaker responded. "We also don't know whether Lisa made these markings before or after Stockton called me. She may have heard him demanding the plane."

"What if 'ride' is the bus that dropped us all off at the Bodden House?" I said, as the idea hit me. "Where did he park?"

"Hmmm, I'm not sure, but I'll find out," Whittaker replied. "But wait, the bus left to take the group back. It's gone."

"*Dritt.* That's right. I wonder if there are any other groups who were shuttled to the Bodden House?"

"We've sent everyone home and closed off the grounds," Whittaker responded. "But I suppose there could be a group waiting around or that went to My Bar at Sunset House instead. Hold on."

The line went silent as Whittaker muted his mic, so I returned my attention to the newspaper. There was a derelict school bus in the wrecked vehicle lot, but the constables we'd placed there had been obvious, so I doubted Jeffrey would have risked going back there. And I couldn't attach ride too closely to bus. Whittaker was right. It could be the plane or any other form of transport.

I shifted my thinking. *Where would he have gone when he left the pool house?* If he avoided the pasture and the car lot, and moved away from the direction we were heading, he had to either hop back garden fences or cross the street behind us. I was pretty sure some of the dividing fences were too high to drag Lisa over, which left the road.

The thought that the two of them had slipped by us in the night made my jaw clench. I was usually aware of my surroundings enough to catch something like that. Opening the map app on my mobile, I studied the options. Crossing the street directly in front of house four meant navigating through back-to-back homes, then another small street before more homes. It looked complicated and too many opportunities to be seen creeping through people's property. Moving west and following the dogleg turns of Phelan Close made more sense. Empty tree-covered lots provided cover to reach several neighbourhood streets over.

"Nora?" came Whittaker's voice as he unmuted.

"*Ja.*"

"The driver for Lisa's group parked at the entrance to the Sol Petroleum building. But like I said, he's gone. I have a constable running over to Sunset House to see if there are any groups still there who might have chartered transport."

I looked at my map. A second set of storage tanks belonging to a different company were one lot south of those we'd turned by. I'd always thought they were all part of the same complex. Now I could see they belonged to a different petroleum company.

"Let me know," I said. "I'm going to follow the path I think he must have taken from the pool house."

"10-4, and we'll keep thinking about her message. Maybe something will come to us," Whittaker replied, and hung up.

I took Williams's mobile with me and walked around to the front door of the house, which was open.

"The residents didn't mark the newspaper," the sergeant said, coming out when he saw me.

I handed him back his mobile. "I'm going to follow the path I think he took next."

"I told you, we need to stick together, Nora," he replied. "Wait until we have someone here to secure the evidence and we'll all go."

"We need to get a step ahead instead of running around after him," I retorted. "Besides, I'll just be ruling out a theory. He won't be there."

"Tibbitts!" Williams called into the house, and Jacob appeared from the kitchen. "Go with Nora and don't let her do anything crazy."

"I'll do my best, sergeant," Jacob grinned and joined me outside.

"I'll call with what we find," I reassured Williams, who didn't look convinced.

"Where are we heading?" Jacob asked as we jogged away.

"Best escape route I could see from the map," I replied.

We followed Phelan around the first bend and hugged the trees on the empty lots to our left. When the narrow street turned again towards South Church, I kept going straight through another empty lot. It was dark, but an obvious walking trail led us to the end of Pebble Lane, where it crossed Glen Eden Road. Here we had a choice of turning either way, or continuing straight across on Pebble Lane until it dead ended.

If I was in Stockton's shoes, I'd want to avoid South Church for as long as possible, so I continued straight. We passed a small apartment complex on the right corner which bled colourful Christmas lights across the intersection, then a few more homes on each side before we came to the end. An extended garden from a sprawling bungalow on the corner seemed like an obvious route until it met a tall hedgerow at the back. Without the map on my mobile I couldn't have known Clayton Drive lay beyond, but armed with a little blue dot marking my location, I watched it cross the lawn as we ran that way.

It wasn't hard to find a gap in the hedge, then I turned right on Clayton, finally heading towards South Church. Across the wider road I could see the entrance to the Sol Petroleum Plant, where tucked back from the road was a large, green passenger van. I held up a hand, and we both slowed to a walk, staying close to the hedgerow, remaining in the shadows. South Church was lit by occasional streetlamps, so we'd be easily spotted crossing the road. My mobile buzzed in my hand and I turned around so my screen wouldn't be seen as I answered.

"*Ja?*"

"We found a group at Sunset House who say they had a minibus drop them, but they have no idea where he's waiting. They're supposed to call when they want to leave," Whittaker explained.

"I'm looking at him," I replied. "Parked at Sol like you thought."

"Any sign of Jeffrey or Lisa?"

"*Nei.* But it's hard to see much. We need to get closer."

"Should I send more people?"

"*Nei.* We'll risk spooking him if he is here. I'll let you know."

"Okay. Is Williams with you?" Whittaker asked.

"Jacob is, sir. Williams is following," I said, stretching the truth. "Has Stockton called back yet, sir?" I asked, hoping to change the subject so he didn't order me to wait for Williams.

"Not yet. Be careful and keep me posted."

"Sir," I acknowledged and hung up.

We'd been too rushed to get radios and earpieces organised, which was making things trickier, but also a blessing. There was nothing worse than voices blathering in your ear when you were trying to concentrate.

"We'll cut through the front of the house on the corner so we can cross South Church out of view," I whispered to Jacob.

"Okay," he agreed, then grabbed my arm. "Wait."

I looked over at the van, partially hidden by the shadow of the Sol Petroleum administration building. It was now running and its headlights came on.

"Maybe he got da call to pick up da people at Sunset House," Jacob suggested.

The van pulled forward to the road, now backlit by a motion sensor light which flicked on and silhouetted three figures inside.

"Call Whittaker!" I shouted, before sprinting for the road.

23

GOT AN APP FOR THAT?

I looked straight into the eyes of the driver as he turned right onto South Church Street and motored away faster than I could run after him. Momentarily lit under the streetlamp, I could see the man was terrified. All I could make out in the darkened rear was the outline of two figures, who both animatedly moved in their seats, appearing to swing around as they watched me.

Coming to a stop, I looked around for any form of transport I could commandeer. The backed-up traffic had finally cleared and apparently word was out to avoid South Church Street, as there wasn't a car in sight. Leaning against the front of the Sol building was one of the green and white electric rental scooters which seemed to be lying around all over the island lately. They'd become a pain in the arse. Not only were people flying around like lunatics on them, mostly drunk and almost all incapable of controlling them properly, they abandoned them wherever their batteries died or their rental time ran out.

"Jacob!" I shouted across the road. "Do you have the app for this piece of shit?"

He jogged across South Church, hanging up the call to Whittaker as he did so. "Somewhere I do," he said, fumbling through his apps to find it.

"Come on," I urged, watching the passenger van disappear around the curve heading south. It struck me as strange that the driver wasn't speeding away, but he was probably trying to blend in by keeping under the speed limit. Regardless, it gave me hope I could still catch them.

"Here it is!" Jacob announced and began typing something on his mobile. He held the phone up to a QR code on the scooter. "Okay, how long you need?"

"How would I know?!" I replied.

"I put in one hour," he announced, and finding the thumb control for the throttle, I squeezed hard.

The thing took off far faster than I'd expected, and I barely hung on to the handlebars with one foot on the deck and the other swinging wildly in the air to maintain my balance.

I'd never ridden one before, but it seemed like it would be something akin to a skateboard. Except with handlebars, completely different wheels, and a motor. So, not much like a skateboard, but at least I'd had one of those as a kid, so maybe some of the dynamics translated.

An LED screen lit up and a somewhat useless headlight came on. As I shot down the road with the thumb throttle pegged, I found a button to turn the headlight off. The battery level showed one quarter, so I couldn't afford to waste the energy on seeing where I was going. I needed speed. The van was out of sight, so my next problem was guessing where they were heading. I passed several small neighbourhood streets on the left, but up ahead was Denham Thompson Way. My beat was West Bay, so I wasn't nearly as familiar with this area towards South Sound, but I had a feeling Denham Thompson cut over to Walkers, which led back into town.

Reaching for the lever with my left hand, I wondered what brakes the scooter had. If I grabbed only the front brake I'd likely be picking my teeth out of the pavement, so I squeezed gently and was relieved to feel the scooter slowing quite effectively with both wheels. I shuffled my feet to move my weight rearwards on the deck, making sure the back tyre didn't get light and lock, then leaned the scooter into the turn. Up ahead, I caught tail lights glowing red as the van braked for an intersection half a kilometre away. The driver indicated, then turned right without stopping, heading away from town.

Now I really wished I had a radio. I could hear police sirens wailing in the distance, so Whittaker had sent whatever cars were available, but there was no way to cover the warren of streets in this part of the island. The van could be heading towards the east end of the island, or wriggling through the neighbourhoods and still looping back towards the airport. Stockton wanted off the island on a plane, so he had to get to Owen Roberts International at some point, which was north-east of where we were now.

I was glad of the Christmas lights throwing enough illumination across the street for me to see. A decent-sized rock or a fizzy drink can would trip the little wheels up on the scooter, and without any protective gear, I'd be accumulating more grazes and bruises, or worse. The little machine was hurtling along at what felt faster than the 38 mph it claimed on the LED speedometer.

At the junction I slowed but was able to see nothing was too close to stop me from rolling through the intersection and accelerating again. Walkers ran straight for as far as I could see, and in the distance was a set of tail lights. But I was sure they didn't belong to the van. These lights were smaller and lower, like a car. Another vehicle coming towards me honked their horn in protest at my lack of lights while theirs partially blinded me. The air rushing over my face was making my eyes water, and I'd already swallowed a bug or two.

Frantically, I tried to recall where the roads to my left went. We were just beyond Jazzy's school so I'd driven around here before, sometimes having to get creative in rush hour traffic as I always seemed to be late for whatever event she had. But that was typically in daylight. At night, with watery eyes on the scooter, I was struggling to recognise landmarks.

Taking a guess, I turned on Academy Way. The road led to the backside of the school, then turned hard right and met Aspiration Drive. The van was either too far ahead or had gone a different way, but I was committed now. I turned left on Aspiration and breathed again when I caught sight of tail lights in the distance. It looked like the van, and seeing a second pair of lights, it appeared they'd caught a car.

Aspiration met Fairbanks at a three-way stop sign, and the van suddenly veered around the car, turning right on the wrong side of the road. I had no clue if the driver had spotted me in pursuit, but the move seemed overly dramatic and risky after how steady he'd been driving. The car sat stunned at the stop sign for a few moments, then moved forward just as I arrived. The driver slammed on his brakes and blasted his horn at me as I surged by without pausing at the junction. I waved a hand in the air, displaying my apology, then refocused on the road ahead.

The van was back to driving at a sedate speed. I was easily gaining on them, so he couldn't be going more than 25 mph. If Stockton was worried about me, he certainly had a strange way of showing it, although I wasn't sure how I could stop even a slow-moving van with an electric scooter. His plan could be to shoot me as soon as I pulled up close, but I had to take that risk.

I glanced down at the LED screen as Fairfield gently curved through a residential neighbourhood. The battery was now in the orange part of the gauge. The electric motor was sucking down juice when running at full speed. My top speed wide open was down to 34 mph, but I was still reeling in the passenger van.

We curved left around a tighter corner, and I was pretty sure up ahead the road led into a newer roundabout south of the airport. He was aiming there after all and had cleverly avoided Walkers near the Bodden House, where undoubtedly we had road blocks or patrols. I recognised a round-shaped church on our left and was now sure of where we were. Not far now and we'd meet the round-about, but I'd catch them before then at this rate.

The battery gauge was dropping closer to the red, but I was

almost to the bumper of the van when a female face appeared in the tinted rear window. She looked desperate, full of fear, and mouthed the word *help*. But she wasn't Lisa Regan. *Fy faen! Who the hell was this lady? Maybe a bystander caught up in Jeffrey's getaway?* I was sure I'd only seen three figures inside the van, but I supposed she could have been hidden on the floor.

Flirting with the edge of the red on the gauge, I pulled alongside the van, squeezing tightly to the side as a car passed going the other way. The handlebars bumped the metal side of the van and the scooter went into a speed wobble, veering into the oncoming lane where another car just saw me in time and swerved. Regaining control, I eased closer once more and looked in through the side window. Somebody flicked on an interior light and now I could clearly see the woman, plus a man I didn't know, and the driver.

The woman slid the side window open. "You have to help us!"

"Stop the van then," I yelled back and moved closer again as another car approached.

"We can't!" she screamed and pointed to the floor. "It'll blow up if we stop!"

The car flew by with a rush of wind and I saw we were nearing the roundabout. There was no way we'd negotiate the curves like this. I'd end up underneath the van or in a ditch. But it didn't matter. The scooter beeped three times, then died. On pure reflex, I leapt from the deck and grabbed inside the open window. The woman screamed, but the man immediately took hold of my arms, which saved me from slipping out. My feet dragged on the tarmac, saying goodbye to my running shoes as the thin material ripped and wore away.

The man pulled, and I clawed with my feet at the side of the van until between us and from the force of the van turning left into the roundabout I was heaved half inside. I thought I was safe until the driver had to turn right around the middle of the roundabout, which tried to launch me back out the window. The woman finally got the idea to help and with them both clutching my arms and the van turning back to the left, I rolled inside, landing in a heap on the seat.

"Why can't you stop?" I asked as I pushed myself upright.

The man pointed to a small canvas bag zip tied to the driver's seat. "There's a device in there that'll explode if we stop. It'll disarm only once the GPS senses we've reached the airport car park."

"Where did it come from?" I asked, knowing what the answer would be.

"Some bloke with a gun held us up as we were walking home and forced us into the van."

"He had a poor woman with him," his companion added.

I wanted to ask where they went, but I figured I should deal with one thing at a time. Looking up, I saw we were closing in on the traffic lights where we'd turn right to go to the airport. The runway would shortly be in view. So was a lot more traffic.

"Did you open the bag?" I asked.

"He said the zipper was rigged," the man said.

I stared at the bag. It was dark blue with the Big Apple Literary Press's logo on the side. Every guest had been given one stuffed with swag like T-shirts, pens, and bookmarks. I reached down and unzipped the top. The woman screamed again and the man dived over the back seat. Nothing happened. Inside was a small clock taped to some batteries and what looked like part of a blender.

"You can stop the van before you crash," I told the driver.

"What about the bomb?" he replied, still cowering over the steering wheel.

"It's a hoax," I said, pulling the bundle from the bag.

The woman screamed once more.

I threw the device out the window, and the driver finally braked to a stop.

"It wasn't real?" the man in the back said. "I don't believe it. I thought we were all going to die. The bloke was so convincing."

"Who are you?" Screaming Woman asked.

"Constable Sommer," I replied, as I fished my mobile from my pocket and dialled Whittaker.

"Where did the man go?" I asked, while I waited for him to answer.

"He told us to drive, then we never saw him again," the driver replied.

"Nora?" Whittaker answered.

"*Ja*. He sold us a decoy. He was still at the Sol building, sir."

"Really? We just diverted what few resources we have to chasing the van."

"*Ja*. Sorry, sir. He set us up. Sent these people down the road with a fake bomb."

"Good gracious," Whittaker mumbled. "Is everyone okay?"

"I think we owe the rental company a scooter. Otherwise all good, sir. But we're back to square one on Stockton."

I heard the line cut out for a moment.

"Nora, I'll call you back," Whittaker said. "That's him calling me now."

24

REASONABLE DEMANDS

After retrieving the bag I'd tossed out the window, I placed it on the pavement, away from the van. All three occupants were still nervous that the blender and batteries without any form of explosive could go boom. The words of a young, skinny blonde out of uniform didn't appear to convince them otherwise.

"You must be who she meant," Screamer said while we waited for a patrol car to show up.

I looked at her quizzically.

"The woman he had with him," she clarified.

"She spoke to you? Why didn't you tell me?"

Screamer quivered and looked like she was going to fall apart again.

"It's okay," I lied, annoyed but trying to hide it as best I could. Which I doubt was very well at all. "What did she say?"

"Tell her not to trust him," she replied.

"Lisa said that to you?"

"If the woman he had hostage is Lisa, then yes. She whispered it to me when the man was tying the device to the seat. She must have known you'd be coming."

I had another of those nervous good feelings. Lisa had more confidence in me than I currently shared. That was nice, but from my perspective, I was floundering around one step behind Stockton, whose location I now had no clue about. He certainly wouldn't have stayed at the Sol building while he had us charging around town.

There had to be more to her clues than we'd figured out. She'd repeated the 'don't trust' part and now referenced Stockton himself, but was that old news? I'd believed he and Lisa were in the van. He'd already tricked me.

"Thank you, by the way," the husband said from the back seat. "I guess we were never in actual danger of being blown up, but I might have had a heart attack before we'd reached the airport."

"*Ja*," I said, trying to shut out the distractions around me. I didn't want to appear rude, but Lisa was relying on me, and unless I could figure out Stockton's play, I was about to let her down.

I thought about the four underlined words once more. Don't, trust, ride, false. Lisa had been limited to the words available in the front-page articles, and I doubt she had time to hunt through every line. Added to that, she would have had barely any light to see. The words could be synonyms or approximations of what she'd really intended. They may also have applied to what just happened, with no bearing on his upcoming actions.

Stockton had already tricked me, so there was the 'don't trust' part. 'Ride' turned out to be the passenger van. Jeffrey couldn't have known the minibus had been waiting by the Sol Petroleum building, but his intention must have been to secure transport of some sort. Lisa didn't know what kind because, at that time, he didn't either. 'False' could be the only word she'd found instead of hoax or fake, referencing the device. He'd thrown it together using tape and batteries from the drawer in the bar, and a clock and a little blender which he could well have found in the pool house. She realised his plan was to find a vehicle to put the device in as a decoy.

Which relied upon the police knowing about it. Stockton

couldn't know I'd show up just as the van was leaving, but he'd probably figured we'd have more people patrolling the area and would try to stop whatever vehicle he'd sent. Especially when the driver couldn't bring the vehicle to an actual stop. It was a safe bet that at some point, the van would create a diversion.

So, the actions of her four words had already happened. Then why repeat 'don't trust him' to Screamer? By the nature of the situation, we were unlikely to trust the words of a murdering kidnapper, yet Lisa reiterated the phrase. I tucked that thought aside and returned to what could be next. Stockton had created a diversion to what end? It bought him time and space to move about. He was certainly trapped in the area around the Bodden House, so this may have given him the freedom to move farther away.

I'd become oblivious to distant sirens as it seemed like they'd been going all night, but the sound grew much louder and the van was soon bathed in red and blue flashing lights. I exited the van as Jacob got out of the passenger side of the patrol car and rushed over.

"You okay?"

"*Ja.* We need to get back to Whittaker. He's talking to Stockton now."

Jacob nodded. "Where da scooter?"

"It sacrificed itself," I replied, as a second patrol car arrived.

It only took a few minutes for the constable to drop Jacob and me at Central Station, where Detective Whittaker had relocated to take advantage of the incident room. Such as it was. The main advantage was access to coffee. Otherwise, the station was relatively empty of personnel and unburdened by too much high-tech equipment. Being able to easily search using our computers instead of the limited access by mobile phone also helped.

"What did he say?" I asked Whittaker when we entered the room.

The detective held up a hand for me to wait a moment while he finished typing on his keyboard. Mr Phillip heard my voice and appeared in a flurry of nails scratching on the concrete floor.

"Hey mutt," I greeted him and knelt down.

His tongue bathed any piece of exposed skin as he made what I assumed to be happy grunting noises.

"Sorry, working with the US authorities to get cell tracking permission," Whittaker said when he was done.

I stood. "Any luck?"

He shook his head. "No, and I doubt we will get much joy until this is all over, but I have to try."

Privacy was great, right up until it helped the bad guys more than the good ones. I understood rules had to be in place to safeguard against abuse, but with Lisa's life on the line, the red tape seemed ridiculous.

"He wanted to hear Lahana's article," Whittaker continued. "So I had her read what she'd put together so far."

"Did he approve?" I asked.

"Somewhat. He asked for changes skewing more sympathy in his favour."

"Will dis article ever run, sir?" Jacob asked.

"We've promised it will in the morning," Whittaker replied. "Gone are the days of telling him we've missed the paper's printing deadline for tomorrow, as of course, it can be released on their website and social media at any time."

"Did he mention the minibus or the fake bomb?" I asked.

"He did not, and neither did I," the detective replied. "I decided it best to not give him any more information than I had to."

"Any clues to his whereabouts?" I asked, with Mr Phillip shoving his stocky body against my leg for more attention.

"Outside was all I could determine by the distant sound of cars and perhaps the ocean," Whittaker explained. "He's demanded to be picked up and taken to the airport by car."

"Picked up where?" I asked, thinking it to be a strange demand. Putting himself in our hands seemed risky on his part. Various methods of incapacitating him raced to mind, even if it meant knocking Lisa out as well.

"He'll let us know, and we'll have five minutes to deploy three taxis to three different locations simultaneously."

"Clever," I thought aloud. "Stretches us thin."

Whittaker nodded. "Precisely. And with time pressing on, it gives us very limited abilities to prepare the vehicles. Being this late on Christmas Eve, we're working on it, but I'm not even sure we can round up three taxis in time."

"He knows all these things are tying us up," I commented. "He hasn't asked for anything completely outlandish or impossible. If this is all on the fly like we think, he's playing it well."

Whittaker frowned. "That may be, but he's not leaving the island tonight if I can help it. We have a plane and a pilot organised, which we'll drag our feet on to buy time. Let's figure out where he could have gone after the Sol building." He brought up a map on his computer screen. "We know where he was around 30 minutes ago. If he's still on foot, with Lisa, meaning he has to stay somewhat hidden, how far could he have gone?"

"Two, maybe three kilometres at most," I suggested. "And that would be distance travelled, not a radius from Sol."

"I think that's probably on the tall side, too," Whittaker commented. "Remember, he doesn't know where we have people or patrols."

"Where would be da most likely direction he'd want to go?" Jacob asked. "His goal is da airport, right? I'm sure he'd prefer da shortest ride in da taxi possible. Give us da minimum time to do anyting."

"Agreed," Whittaker nodded. "And I feel it's unlikely he'd head back towards the Bodden House, as that's most likely where we'd have people."

"The water?" I questioned. "If he could get access to a boat, he could cover far more ground."

"We have the Joint Marine Unit patrolling between the harbour and South Sound. Casey from the DOE is with them too. She's been flying their new drone over the shoreline. They haven't seen any strange activity or noticed boats missing. The only real options are Sunset House's dive boats along that stretch."

"And they're moored on buoys 100 metres out," I noted. "I don't see him swimming out with Lisa in tow, even if he did know how to hotwire and drive the boat."

"Dat leaves da south and da east," Jacob said as we stared at the screen.

"Which is where I just ran around chasing his decoy."

Jacob sighed. "Dat ain't dat big of an area and it's still a needle in a haystack."

"Maybe we start at the Sol building and see if we can find any traces there," I suggested.

"Agreed," Whittaker responded. "I'll see how well I can tighten our patrols and guards on the roads around there, but honestly, I'm too short staffed to create a true perimeter. Even with the extra bodies we've called in."

It still felt like we were splashing around in Stockton's wake, reacting instead of predicting or getting ahead. But there wasn't much else we could do at this point.

"Get us radios, Jacob, and I'll find us a vehicle."

"Sure," he said, and left the room.

"Take the van we had," Whittaker offered, holding up the keys. "It's out front." He looked down at the dog still leaning against my leg. "Feel free to take him with you, too. I haven't had time to figure out what to do with him."

As soon as Mr Phillip caught me looking at him, his stubby tail wagged, making his body shake. "Fine," I conceded, feeling bad for the mutt.

"What about Williams, sir?" I asked, picking up the dog's lead.

"He's helping patrol," Whittaker replied. "I'm not sure which area. Sergeant Hadley has been coordinating the little manpower we have."

"I meant, can we use Williams and any of his firearms division, sir?"

"As snipers?" the detective questioned.

"*Ja.*"

Whittaker rubbed his forehead. "That's a last-resort approach in my view, Nora, but it's on my mind. He's managed to bring one of his group in, but the others are either off the island or unfit to join us until the morning."

"We need three to cover all the taxis."

"Exactly, which means we either gamble on the two we think are most likely, or wait until Stockton reaches the airport."

"Where the gunmen could take two advantageous positions," I suggested.

"We don't usually refer to the good guys as gunmen, Nora, but yes, that's my thought." He sighed. "But I hope it doesn't come to that. The risks are high."

"If Stockton is smart, he'll make the taxi meet the plane on the runway, nowhere near buildings or elevated places for a sniper to hide," I said as I thought it through.

"I think the man has proven he's sharp enough to think of most details, even if he is making it up as he goes along."

I was about to leave but paused, and Mr Phillip tugged on his lead before turning back to see what the hold-up was.

"You think about new and different ways to investigate cases, don't you sir?" I said. "Even when you're not working a case that might involve the things you're thinking about."

"We all try to improve ourselves and the system," Whittaker responded, looking at me quizzically.

"Jeffrey Stockton has been writing about crimes from the criminal's point of view, sir. It appears to be his passion. Which means he's planned, worked out, and thought through who knows how many scenarios and situations in his mind. He may well have committed multiple crimes before now which he's never been a suspect for."

"Good points," Whittaker agreed. "So, even if grabbing Lisa, and potentially the opportunity of coming on the cruise in the first place, wasn't planned, he's still pulling from a playbook of ideas he may have perfected in theory."

"*Ja*. And Lisa keeps reminding us not to trust him, sir."

We stared at each other for a moment in silence.

"When you have little to go on, Nora, all you can do is work with the little you have," he finally said.

25

SQUAT FOR CHRISTMAS

Jacob drove us from Central Station through George Town waterfront. The MV *Maureen* looked resplendent with her Christmas lights glowing on the still, dark waters of the bay.

"Sorry you're not spending Christmas Eve with your family, Jacob," I said as he continued on South Church Street. It was typical of Jacob to have both arranged to be with his wife and kids for the holidays and then sacrificed that time when he was needed.

A year ago, I probably wouldn't have given his circumstances a second thought, as we were all doing what needed to be done. But I'd learnt to appreciate how our actions often caused a ripple effect, reaching farther out than I'd ever considered.

"I'm sure you'd prefer to be wit Jazzy," he replied. "Sooner we get dis guy, den sooner we can all go home, right?"

I nodded and opened the glove box. Taking out the toy, I turned in my seat and looked at Mr P. He stared up at me with his bug eyes and tongue poking out one side, which still didn't look right to me. I handed him the ill-fated stuffed hedgehog and braced for mayhem. Instead, he gently took it from me and dropped it between his paws, resting his chin atop the stuffed toy.

"Yeah. I'm bummed too," I told him.

Facing front, I grabbed my mobile and spun it in circles in my hand. It was late. I hadn't heard from Jazzy or AJ, but that usually meant good news. They knew I was working and didn't have time for personal calls and texts. Uncharacteristically, I called AJ.

"Hey," she answered, and I realised I'd probably woken her up.

"Sorry. It's late. Just wanted to check on the kid."

"No worries," she replied softly. "We just crashed out."

"At your place?" I asked.

"Yeah."

"She okay?"

There was a brief pause, and I kicked myself for not thinking this through. If they were at AJ's little cottage, Jazzy was either sharing AJ's bed or sleeping on the sofa, which was only three metres away. Either way, the kid could hear at least AJ's side of our conversation.

"She will be," came AJ's measured reply. "Did you get the guy yet?"

"*Nei*," it pained me to admit, and brought my head back to the case as we passed the Bodden House. "Thanks. I'll see you both tomorrow."

"Be safe," she replied, and we hung up.

One way or another, I would see them tomorrow as there was a limit to how long I could function on only a few hours' sleep. And then it would be Christmas Day, and I'd be empty handed.

Jacob slowed the van and pulled over outside the Sol Petroleum building. We got out and walked around the side to the entrance gate, which was set back twenty metres, giving room for a vehicle or two to park there. The motion sensor security light tripped on and I squinted through the sudden brightness.

"I don't see how dey left here by any way except da road," Jacob said, examining the tall wire fence with his torch. "Dis place is secure." He looked at me and shook his head. "Which means dey were right here when da van left and you went after dem. I shoulda seen dem."

"They waited until you turned away or left," I replied, double-checking there were no holes or gaps in the fence.

My torch beam stopped on a small piece of material tied to the wire. It was cream coloured.

"Lisa wearing dat colour blouse, right?" Jacob said, seeing me examine the strip of polyester.

"*Ja*. He doesn't have her restrained," I noted.

"Don't suppose she could tie dat if she was," he agreed.

"Or tear it from her blouse."

"Okay, but we already knew dey here," Jacob mused. "Question is, where dey go next?"

"Where did you go?" I asked, and swung my torch around to look at South Church and then Clayton Drive, the street we'd run down earlier which was slightly north of us.

"I backtracked to find Williams," Jacob replied.

We stood by the road and looked both ways, then I opened the map app on my mobile. I'd looked at it enough by now to know where most of the buildings and streets were, but I didn't want to overlook anything.

"Assuming he didn't risk following you, he had to move north or south on the main road," I voiced.

"South is da park by da water," Jacob noted. "Easy to hide in dere."

That was true. He could easily remain hidden and wait until he was ready to go to the airport and use the park as one of the three locations at which he'd demand a taxi. I looked directly across the road. Another tall wire fence surrounded a small self-storage complex. They mostly appeared to be garage-sized units with roll-up doors. Dim security lights made everything visible, but weren't so bright as to disturb the surrounding homes. Beneath one roll-up, I could see a sliver of yellow light.

"Someone leave a light on in dere," Jacob commented.

"Or someone is in there," I countered, and walked across the road.

Jacob followed, and we began examining the fence for places to enter. It didn't take long. The main gate was loose enough on its hinges to tilt both sides in opposite directions and slip through a gap formed between them. Jacob held the gates while I entered, then I returned the favour.

Quietly, we moved to the unit with the light showing, and listened carefully. I couldn't hear anything from inside. I rapped on the door, which rattled loudly in the still night. And then I heard movement inside.

"Police. Open the door slowly," I ordered, and both Jacob and I took a step to the side, clear of the door.

A lock slid, and the door began rising. I crouched to see how many people were inside, and could only see one pair of feet. In flip-flops with bare legs, so I hoped I was about to see some clothes. I stood and grabbed the base of the door and pulled hard, sending it flying up. Inside, a young local man stepped back in surprise. I turned to leave, already moving on, as we hadn't found Stockton.

"Is dis your storage unit?" Jacob asked.

"Yes, sir," the man replied.

I stopped to tell Jacob we needed to go, but noticed what was inside the little garage. Boxes and furniture filled half of the space, but in the front was a single mattress set on a modified shipping pallet. Next to it, a box served as a table with a paperback book and fast food drinks cup sitting atop. A power cord, rigged from the light fixture, hung down and connected to a single electric burner.

"Pretty sure you're not allowed to squat in dese storage units," Jacob said.

"Dat's true, sir," the young man replied. "But dis is all I got right now."

"What's your name?" Jacob asked.

"Devlin, sir. Devlin Oldham."

Jacob turned and looked at me. My first thought had been that a guy sleeping in a storage unit was nothing we needed to mess with at the moment, and I still felt that way. But now I took a moment to absorb his circumstances.

"How old are you?" I asked.

"Eighteen, ma'am."

"You have family here?"

"On Da Brac, ma'am. But I couldn't find work dere. Got me a job here, but I can't afford da rent."

"Why did you bring all this stuff with you if you couldn't afford a place to live?" I asked.

"Not my stuff, ma'am. 'cept da mattress and a few tings."

"You said it was your storage unit," Jacob pointed out.

"Tis, sir. I helped dis lady clear out her attic, and she need a place to put stuff, so I rented it for her. Took my last money for da deposit. She going to pay me da fee each month. I gotta stay here till I find a cheap room to rent."

Rent prices on the island had gone crazy over the past few years, so his story was believable. Housing for locals on minimum wage had become a huge problem. I looked at the boxes. Each one was carefully labelled with its contents in poor, but legible handwriting. Two strings of silver and red tinsel draped across the pile of boxes. Devlin's attempt at seasonal decorations.

"Hear anything strange across the road earlier this evening?" I asked.

"Bin sirens and what have you all night, ma'am. Figured someting big goin' on. I mostly kept my head down. Only turned da light on a bit ago. Wanted to read my book for a spell."

"Didn't see anyting at all?" Jacob pressed.

"Not much, sir."

"Not much?" I echoed. "Which means you saw something," I pointed out.

The youth shrugged his shoulders. "Just some people on bicycles. Only noticed 'cos dey didn't look too steady on dem."

"A man and a woman?" I asked.

He nodded.

"Describe them."

"Like I say, I didn't pay much attention, ma'am. Best I keep myself to myself, you know?"

"They have three eyes and bright orange hair?" I asked.

Jacob looked at me strangely.

"No, ma'am," Devlin laughed. "Dey regular white folks, best I could tell."

"Was the woman wearing a green shirt?"

Devlin thought for a moment. "I don't tink so, ma'am. More pale coloured, I reckon."

"Where were they going?" I continued.

"Town," Devlin replied, nodding north.

"You sure?" Jacob asked.

"Yes, sir. I know dat 'cos I watched da man wobblin' on da bike. Looked like it much too small for him."

"Thanks," I said, now glad Jacob had kept us there talking to Devlin.

"You bustin' me, ma'am?" the young man asked.

"*Nei*. But someone will at some point. Be careful with the light."

"Yes, ma'am," he replied, relief written all over his face. "Happy Christmas," he added, glancing at his cheap wristwatch.

I looked at mine. It was gone midnight.

"Happy Christmas," I wished him in return.

Jacob slipped the young man some cash from his wallet. "Take care, Devlin."

"You both most kind, tank you."

He pulled the door down as we walked away, and for a moment I let my mind drift to Jazzy and how she had lived like that, or worse, for several years. It made me feel even more lousy for not organising a Christmas present, although she probably wouldn't care if she too thought about where she'd been in the past.

"Call it in?" Jacob asked.

"*Nei*," I replied, taking my mobile from my pocket. "I'll phone Whittaker and tell him. We don't want half the police on duty converging on South Church Street all at once."

"Think they stole the bicycles?" Jacob asked as we walked to the van.

"*Ja*."

"Pretty bold to ride down da main road."

"*Ja*. Pretty smart, too. Hiding in plain sight."

We hopped in the van and Jacob turned around in the street while I called the detective.

"Constable Sommer," he answered.

"We believe they left Sol on bicycles, sir. Heading north."

"Towards town?"

"*Ja*."

"That's bold," Whittaker commented. "I can redirect resources there, if you're sure."

"I'd prefer he not know we're on to him, sir."

"Fair enough. But his radius just widened if we know he has transport. Even if it's only a bike."

"Sure, but he still needs to end up at the airport, sir. No reason for him to move farther away."

"True." The line went quiet for a moment before he continued. "That's still a lot of territory to cover and he's had over an hour's head start, Nora."

The detective was right, but for some reason in my mind, I couldn't see Stockton going farther than the waterfront.

"Have you spoken to anyone on the yacht, sir?" I asked.

"Not since I asked the captain about their security procedures and bag scans."

"Which were shit," I said, expressing my assumption.

"Below ideal standards would be how I'd phrase it, Constable," he said, correcting my language. "Can you think of any reason Stockton would return to the yacht?"

"*Nei*," I responded, but a couple of ideas did spring to mind. "Did you find three taxis, sir?"

"Yes, they're standing by, and each has a vehicle tracker. We also have a plane courtesy of a wealthy resident who's kindly made it available. His pilot is on his way to the airport now."

The line cut out for a moment again.

"That's him," Whittaker said. "I think this will be his three locations."

"I'll take anything he gives you on South Church area, sir," I blurted before the detective hung up.

"Where to?" Jacob asked.

"Slowly towards town," I replied. "And look for abandoned bicycles."

26

THE DEAFENING CRIES OF SILENCE

Jacob drove slowly as directed along South Church Street, and we scanned for signs of Stockton, Lisa, or discarded bicycles. We both knew our chances were almost zero, but it gave us a purpose while we waited to hear about the phone call.

"Watch for anything odd," I said absentmindedly.

"Odd like what?" Jacob asked.

"Odd like not normal."

"Dere ain't been much normal about dis evenin'."

I groaned to myself as I couldn't explain odd beyond things that weren't as they usually should be, but Jacob was right. The fact that we were driving the streets of the island in the first hour of Christmas Day looking for a kidnapped author ruled out normal.

"Stockton is on the phone with Whittaker, which might be an opportunity for Lisa to try signalling or escaping," I said, explaining the thought which had prompted my comment. "Like a flashing light."

We continued in silence, occasionally interrupted by a squeak from Mr P's toy.

"What do you tink he plans on doin' wit her?" Jacob asked.

It was a question I'd been replaying in my head all evening. He wasn't asking for anything more than an article in the paper. Sure, he was demanding an aeroplane on which to escape, but he wouldn't need it if he hadn't taken her. He hadn't demanded money, or someone released from prison, or the other things most kidnappers bartered a person's life for.

"No idea," I replied, as the only answer which seemed to make sense was unthinkable.

Jacob jumped when the radio came to life, and he pulled to the side of the road.

"Sierra 1 to all units. Taxis are being deployed. Observe, follow, but do not engage suspect. I repeat, do not engage suspect. Over."

"No way Whittaker gonna let did guy leave da island, surely?" Jacob queried.

"*Nei,*" I muttered, hoping he had Williams and his firearms unit partner in a good location at the airport.

It would be a bold play to shoot Stockton, but I had no sympathy for the man. It was Whittaker and Lisa I was worried about. Too many things could go wrong when relying on a last-ditch effort in such a dynamic environment. If the sniper missed, how would Stockton react? What if they accidentally hit Lisa? It would certainly be a long-range shot across the airfield which had a constant strong breeze.

My mobile rang, so I turned down my radio and quickly answered. "Sir?"

"Location Two is closest to you. Front entrance to the hospital," Whittaker rattled off quickly. "I have a car heading there, but you can join them."

"The hospital?" I questioned. "Where are the other locations, sir?"

"The Lobster Pot restaurant, and the High School. I have to go. Report anything you see and don't engage, Nora."

The line went dead.

"Da hospital?" Jacob asked.

"*Ja,*" I confirmed, but something didn't feel right.

Jacob accelerated, then indicated to turn on Memorial Way.

"Go to Boilers," I ordered.

"Dis is faster, Nora," he complained.

Jacob knew the island as well as anyone, so I had no doubt he was right. We had to cut over to Walkers Road, then follow it as the road curved east and led to the hospital. Boilers Road was beyond that curve but angled back to it.

"Take Boilers," I reiterated, and texted Whittaker.

"Did you speak to the captain?"

Jacob caved and accelerated down South Church while I waited for a response. I knew I was asking a lot as the detective had his hands full, but the three locations didn't add up. We reached Boilers Road and Jacob indicated again.

"Stop at the corner," I ordered.

"What we doin', Nora? You know we don't have time for dis."

"We'll just be another vehicle following along," I replied. "That's if he's actually at the hospital."

Jacob braked to a stop at the turn. "On a bicycle, he coulda reached any one of dem places. He gotta be at one of dem."

I opened the passenger door. "Maybe. Go to the hospital. I have my mobile and radio."

"What are you doin'? We should stick together, Nora. We don't, and Whittaker gonna be mad when dis all over."

Hopping out, I turned to my partner. "It's okay. Whittaker has a plan for the airport. We won't be able to help. I'm just covering one other angle."

Mr Phillip squeezed between the front seats and around the bulge over the engine. He came to the open door, but I held out my hand and stopped him.

"Den I come wit you," Jacob announced. "Where to?"

"Don't get yourself in trouble, Jacob. Go to the hospital."

He shook his head. "We stick together. If you won't go wit me, den I'm coming wit you."

His resistance and willingness to risk getting in trouble for me made me second guess my idea. I could handle whatever shit came my way, but I couldn't deal with it landing on Jacob. Problem was, I couldn't shake the feeling that something else was going on. From where we sat, I could see across the waterfront to the bay, although the buildings mostly obscured any boats.

"You're an idiot for following me," I told him as I pushed the dog back and climbed into the van. "Keep going on South Church, but stop the van in front of Off The Wall Divers' building."

Jacob drove the few hundred metres to the white, yellow, and blue dive shop, parking on the pavement. We both got out.

"Stay there, mutt," I told Mr Phillip, who keenly tried to follow me again, the hedgehog hanging from one side of his mouth. Well, he at least made an effort, although I don't think he was about to make the leap to the pavement. His short legs didn't look like they'd make good springs for landing.

Jacob came along as I jogged toward the dock where the MV *Maureen* was right where we'd last seen her. Except now, the Christmas lights had been turned off for the night. I wondered what the other guests were doing without the famous author amongst them who they'd come all this way to see. A dim light glowed from the bridge, where I knew someone would be on overnight watch, but most of the cabin windows and portholes were dark. *Maybe they'd all simply gone to bed?* Seemed strange with Lisa still missing.

My mobile buzzed and I read the text reply from Whittaker. "No."

No, he hadn't been able to reach the captain, or no, he hadn't got around to trying?

"What are we doin' here, Nora?" Jacob asked, keeping his voice low.

Fair question. *What were we doing there?* All seemed calm and normal on the yacht. Which in itself was odd to me. Lisa was being held at gunpoint by a man who was someone they'd spent the past days with. *Despite their shock and concern, they'd all turned in for the night?*

"Something isn't right," I replied.

"Don't see anyting going on," Jacob replied, studying the yacht from where we stood in the shadows of the building.

"Exactly."

"Yeah. Too quiet," he acknowledged. "How 'bout you stay outta sight, and I'll go aboard. Take a look."

I hadn't considered that option. Someone had to go aboard, but I had planned on it being me. Or us. "What happened to not splitting up?"

Jacob laughed. "You're teachin' me to embrace bad ideas."

It didn't feel right, standing back and watching while Jacob took point. But my problem was that I wanted to be the person going in and I also wanted to be the person ready to react to whatever situation arose. I think that I would be considered a Type A personality. Maybe A stood for arsehole, I wasn't sure. While I wrangled with the idea, Jacob walked away and was soon striding down the concrete dock towards the stern of the MV *Maureen*.

Staying on the street side, I moved past a wooden souvenir building to a small terminal servicing the dock. From there I could hide in the shadows cast from the streetlamps and watch the yacht. Jacob had reached the gangway leading to the swim step. He momentarily paused before continuing aboard. I caught movement on the bridge, where a silhouette crossed behind a window. Whoever was on watch may have noticed Jacob approaching.

All remained still, and I impatiently scanned the decks for signs of activity. I realised Jacob hadn't been on the MV *Maureen* before, so wouldn't know the layout or where to find the crew. Another reason I should have gone instead of him. Or at least briefed him.

I couldn't believe how quiet it was, then realised I still had my radio turned down. Gently twisting the volume knob, I held the radio to my ear and listened to the various units all reporting from the three locations Stockton had provided.

"Zulu Three in position at Lobster Pot. No activity. Over."

"Zulu Six at hospital. Have taxi in sight. Over."

If I was Stockton, having chosen one of the three locations to get in the taxi, I certainly wouldn't run right out into the open. I'd wait and watch for a while. See what trap was being set for me.

"Dis is Zulu Four at da school. Taxi in place. No movement. Over."

"Sierra One," came Whittaker's voice. "All units continue standing by. Report suspect sighting. Over."

The radio fell quiet once more. Jacob had been aboard for several minutes now. Plenty of time to have made contact with a crew member, yet I couldn't see any activity. I checked my mobile, but I hadn't missed any texts or calls. Even with the volume up on the radio, everything had returned to an eerie silence. For a short time.

"This is Zulu Six. Man approaching taxi. Over."

I listened intensely. Zulu simply meant the car was George Town based, and Six was the vehicle designation. Zulu Six was at the hospital, if I remembered correctly. Stockton could easily have cycled there in the time he'd had. There were also plenty of places to hide out around the hospital buildings and car parks, even in the middle of the night. But the call had been about a man. No mention of Lisa. Without a hostage, Stockton had to know he'd be instantly arrested.

"Zulu Six. False alarm. Some guy tried to take the taxi. Driver sent him away. Over."

A low rumble emanated from the bay, and for a moment I was confused about where it was coming from. Until I realised the MV *Maureen*'s big diesel engines had started. The crew member who'd been trying to chat me up, Kris, appeared at the swim step, followed by the chef, François, and his sous chef, Jen. I looked for Jacob but couldn't see him. The three crew members stepped across the gangway, then dragged it to the dock and left it before hurrying to the large mooring bollards. Jen freed the slack bow line, then François the mid line.

"Sierra One, this is PC277. Were you expecting the *Maureen* to be leaving the dock, sir? Over."

I was already on my way to the yacht when the reply came.

"PC277, this is Sierra One. Negative. You're sure it's leaving? Over."

"Throwing off lines now, sir. Over," I responded, breaking into a run.

"Hey!" I shouted at Jen, who hadn't returned to the stern to re-board.

She turned and looked at me, her face a mixture of fear and confusion. Without saying anything, she glanced up at the bridge. Following her gaze, I could see several figures, but it was impossible to identify them.

"PC168, this is PC277. Come in. Over," I called for Jacob over the radio.

I reached Jen and grabbed her by the shirt. "What's going on?"

"I don't know," she replied. "Captain told us to cast off and stay on the dock."

"Why?"

"I've no idea! He told us to just do it."

"PC277, this is Sierra One. Is the target there?"

"I don't know, sir. Trying to board now. Over."

I ran past François, who looked just as confused as his assistant. Before I reached Kris, he'd thrown the stern line to the swim step and now stood staring up at the yacht. His mouth opened in surprise. Swinging around, I looked up towards the bridge once more, where I saw a figure standing outside by the rail. They were silhouetted by the glow from the side window of the bridge, but I could make out the outline of a cap. It was either the captain or Jacob. Another figure stood behind them, and I watched that person raise a hand.

For a moment, the world around me seemed to evaporate as I fixated on what I couldn't believe was happening. A glint of light reflected off the face of the man at the rail, and by his dark skin tone, I knew it was my partner. My radio squawked, and I'm pretty sure Kris shouted something, but all I could see and comprehend was the raised hand. Which held a gun. In what felt like slow motion, the butt swung violently against Jacob's head, and my partner crumpled over the rail. The attacker, who I could only presume was Stockton, reached down and picked up Jacob's limp legs, tipping his body over the side.

Jacob's unconscious form plummeted the three metres into the dark water of the bay, crashing through the surface with a violent splash.

27

SOGGY SOCKS AND BIRDS IN DOG SEATS

Jen looked over the side of the dock where Jacob had gone in. I sprinted that way, peeling off the borrowed sweatshirt as I ran. Without slowing, I dropped the radio and my mobile to the ground, sending them skittering across the concrete before diving into the bay.

Immediately enveloped in darkness, I forced myself to calm down and began sweeping my arms around, searching by feel for Jacob. Providing the impact hadn't crushed the air from his lungs, he should float back to the surface even if he remained unconscious. But I couldn't guarantee that would happen before he swallowed water and drowned without ever wakening. I tried opening my eyes and keeping them closed, but neither mattered. Blurry and dark were the same as plain dark.

The sound of the diesel engines droned on all around me as my brain couldn't decipher the direction through water. I needed to be aboard the MV *Maureen*, but not before I found my partner. I should never have let him be the one to go first. Jacob, the family man, who lived for his kids and his wife. A woman whom he adored and I'd only briefly met as I felt uncomfortable invading his personal time and space, no matter how often he invited me to cookouts and gatherings. A woman who looked at me with suspicion and unease. For this very reason, I was sure. I brought an added level of risk and danger into their lives.

Images of Jacob waving goodbye to his family as I picked him up outside his house flashed through my mind, quickly followed by his body falling from the MV *Maureen*. I had to find him.

With lungs burning, I opened my eyes, and after a few moments of adjusting, I detected a faint light to my right. I'd become disorientated in the dark and from suspension in water, and now had to force myself to believe the light was coming from the surface. *Where else could it be coming from?* Turning, I kicked in the direction my senses told me was sideways, and soon broke through the surface.

The three crew members had gathered together on the dock and were yelling all at once.

"Has he come up?" I asked, trying to clear my lungs with long steady breaths before I dived again.

"No!" Kris shouted.

"He went in farther over there," Jen screamed, pointing.

François was on my mobile, hopefully calling 9-1-1 which would eventually filter the message to Whittaker. We needed the marine unit to give chase as soon as possible. I pulled my shredded trainers off and threw them on the dock. They were doing nothing except weighing my feet down.

Following Jen's directions, I dived under once more and the voices instantly disappeared, replaced by the drone of the yacht and the inky blackness of the bay at night. Keeping my eyes open with the faint glow above, I swam in what I hoped to be a large circle. The fall couldn't have taken him more than a couple of metres down, so by windmilling my arms, I prayed I'd hit a body part at some point. Just as I was about to go up for another breath, my fingers brushed something soft.

Willing my lungs to wait a little longer for fresh air, I kicked to my right and reached in the same direction again. My hand struck the same soft material and then something firmer. I grabbed hold of what felt like an ankle or a wrist. I didn't care which; we were both going to the surface.

Bursting above the water, gasping and sucking in air, I pulled on the limb, using my other hand to take hold of anything more I could reach. The effort of dragging Jacob's limp form up drove me back under, and for a moment I had to let go and again claw my way above the surface.

We were several metres from the dock, where outstretched arms waited, but my partner was face down, bleeding from his scalp, and still out cold. At least I hoped he was only unconscious. Roughly shoving his forehead, I lifted his mouth from the water and pushed his body towards the dock. The three crew members soon had hold of Jacob, hauling him to the dock where they manhandled him out of the water onto the concrete.

Swimming over, I pulled myself up and looked over my right shoulder. The yacht had moved away from the dock and was in the process of rotating to face the open water. Water frothed from the starboard bow as the thrusters swung the heavy yacht around within its own length. The swim step was passing by within ten metres of the dock. It was my only chance.

Looking up, I couldn't see anyone standing outside the bridge, which was now facing directly away from me. If I could get aboard without being seen, maybe I could disable the yacht and stop Stockton from making international waters. I turned back to Jacob, who the crew had laid out on the dock with Jen listening closely to see if he was breathing.

"Is he dead?" I asked, and all three looked up at me.

I couldn't tell if they were shocked by the question or scared to give me the bad news.

"Is he?" I snapped.

Jen shook her head. "It's shallow, but he's breathing."

"Then stop the bleeding," I said, pointing to the gash.

"Where are you going?" Kris asked as I stood up.

I ignored the question. "Use that radio. Ask for Detective Whittaker. Tell him what's going on."

"What is going on?" Kris asked. "I have no clue what's happening right now."

"Your yacht's being stolen," I replied and began jogging down the dock.

The MV *Maureen* was now at 45 degrees to me and the stern was more than 20 metres away. It was about to stop spinning on thrusters and switch to the main propellers. I'd never be able to fight against the water thrown back from the screws.

I leapt once more into the black water, using a proper dive this time for distance. With my hands outstretched and overlapped, I dolphin-kicked for all I was worth. Surfacing, I'd cut the distance to 15 metres. There was no time to waste and if I didn't reach the stern before the yacht made forward motion, I had no chance of catching her. Holding my breath and keeping my head down and streamlined for five strokes at a time, I sprinted freestyle, knowing I needed pure speed.

I was anaerobic, meaning I was using more oxygen than my lungs were taking in, which meant I'd become exhausted in short order. But it didn't matter. If I didn't reach the swim step, then I'd have all night to recover while Stockton, Lisa, and his yacht full of hostages motored off into the distance. Forcefully stopping a megayacht or any large boat was no simple task. All the marine unit could do was fire intimidating warning shots or try to board the vessel in motion. A very dangerous venture with little chance of success. All the pilot of the yacht had to do was keep manoeuvring unpredictably so the police couldn't transfer a team aboard.

Through the water, I heard the drone of the engines change, and ahead, the water stirred. I was still four metres away and the main props had been engaged. I'd been aiming for the centre of the swim step and now altered my course, moving outside the direct line of thrust from the screws. Now breathing every three strokes, I was sucking in as much air as I could, but still losing the battle with the amount of energy I was expending. Maybe in my swim team youth I could have held on longer, but these days I freedived, a completely different discipline of breathing.

I felt my pace slowing, both from the rush of water off the propellers and from being unable to maintain the effort. Grabbing another breath, I peeked forward and saw I was no more than two metres from the fibreglass swim step. Dipping my head, I swore I wouldn't lift it again until I either touched the yacht or completely ran out of air. Four more strokes and I was sure I'd reach the stern, but my thrashing hands grabbed nothing but more seawater. My eyes stung and my lungs were about to burst when my right-hand fingers finally grazed the swim step.

Reaching it was one thing, but getting hold enough to pull myself up was another. My left-hand fingers hit it next, but it did nothing more than throw off my stroke. Forced to take a breath, my next stroke swept through water once again. I'd lost ground, and the yacht was picking up speed. I risked two more deep breaths between steady strokes in the hope of pulling the last ounces of energy from my body, then powered ahead at full effort once more.

My left hand hit, and I clutched at the textured curvature of the swim step. As my right hand arched over, I stretched for all I was worth and landed a firmer grip on the top surface of the step, where little indented channels helped drain water away. Like a rock climber hanging to the wall by the barest friction of their fingertips, I carefully pulled myself forward while still frantically kicking with my legs. My tired arms screamed in pain, but I refused to let go. Lunging with my left hand, I found a better purchase and my chest was now against the step. Using my forearms on the textured face, I crawled from the ocean and lay in a wheezing heap on the stern of the MV *Maureen*.

After probably a minute of watching George Town fall away into the distance while my aching chest recovered, I wiped the spit and bile from my face and sat up. The thought of the bloody gash on Jacob's scalp took my breath away once more, and I gritted my teeth to shove my fear aside. There was nothing more I could do for my partner right now, but I'd made it aboard the fleeing yacht and needed a plan for how to stop Stockton from making it to international waters.

I reminded myself that none of this would be happening if I hadn't taken my eyes off Lisa at the Bodden House. Anger had a way of pulling me into sharper focus, and right now, I had an abundance of rage. Half directed at myself, and the rest at Jeffrey Stockton, who'd turned Lisa's celebration of her latest book into a deadly disaster.

Staying low, I scurried up the steps to the rear of the cabins where Lisa's berth was located. For the first time, I was glad the yacht didn't have decent security cameras and couldn't see me. Wiping my dripping wet hair back, I reset the simple black scrunchie holding my ponytail in place and looked down at my attire. Borrowed leggings, a sports bra as I'd discarded the sweatshirt, and one sodden sock as the other had come off at some point. I tossed the second one aside.

Mentally, I ran back through who I could expect to be aboard. From the crew, Captain Marston, First Mate Helen, Avery the engineer, and Iris the stewardess. Stockton had been smart in ditching the other three at the dock. Fewer people to keep up with but enough to run the yacht. And the eighth crew member, Blake, had already removed himself from the picture, as he was sitting in our jail cell.

I had to assume all twelve guests were aboard, two of them being Jeffrey and his cousin, Kelly. Plus Barbara. Unless Stockton had already thrown her overboard, for which I couldn't blame him. The bridge wasn't a large space, but maybe he could cram all four crew in there in order to watch them, but what about the guests? Somehow, he had to contain them, watch them, and make sure they weren't sabotaging his efforts. Where could he put them? I thought about the layout of the yacht and quickly realised how I would control the crowd once the yacht was underway. If I was right, I'd have a large amount of freedom to move about the vessel without running into anyone.

The question now was whether to disable the yacht, or to disable the gunman. Stopping the yacht could keep us in Cayman waters, but I'd still have to tackle Stockton at some point. Pushed, who knew what he was capable of, and he had plenty of sacrificial bodies if he chose to start shooting. He still sat in the dog-bird seat with the upper hand, and the only thing I had in my favour was surprise.

Assuming that he didn't know I'd made it aboard. And there was only one way to find out. Gingerly scaling the steps to the salon and bridge deck, I paused to peek over the top. Only a handful of dim accent lights were on inside the salon, but enough to see that the room was empty. I couldn't think of another enclosed space on the yacht large enough to fit all the guests. Unless they were crammed shoulder to shoulder into a larger berth. But I chose to believe my theory was correct, and I knew where they'd be.

At this point, I had no choice but to move forward using my best guesses at the circumstances, or the lack of information and answers would leave me paralysed and unable to do anything. It was bad enough that I didn't know what the hell a dog-bird was.

28

______

DASHING IN LEGGINGS AND A SPORTS BRA

Quietly opening the sliding door, I stepped inside the salon and grabbed a large cushion from one of the sofas. On the wall behind the bar were vertical mirrored strips, and holding the cushion to the end one, I punched it as hard as I could. It hurt my knuckles like crazy but didn't break the glass. Picking up a rum bottle, I repeated the process using the full bottle instead of my fist and I heard a cracking sound. Slowly pulling the cushion away, I could make out a series of lines criss-crossing the mirror, but no pieces fell down. The panels were glued to the wall. Finding a knife in a drawer, I pried and wiggled until a small section of the glass popped off and promptly shattered on the counter.

"*Fy faen,*" I grumbled and tried prying another piece, this time holding a bar towel below.

A small, jagged section of mirror fell into my hand and I returned to the drawers, which were frustratingly neat and not full of clutter. I needed tape of some kind and could only find a variety of special silverware and tools for making drinks. I'd have to make do with what I had, but I kept the knife, wrapping it in the bar towel and tucking in the waistband of my leggings.

Stepping out of the sliding door at the rear, I trotted up the stairs to the sun deck. Moving forward, I passed under the hard canopy covering the middle section to the forward area with a Jacuzzi tub and lounge chairs. Nearing the curved front rail, I slowed and lightened my steps, hoping anyone below wouldn't hear me. The wind whistled over my damp hair as the MV *Maureen* headed east at what I guessed was its top speed.

Crouching down, I stayed low as I approached the waist-high railing overlooking the bow section of the main deck. Peering over, I saw the guests herded together as I thought they'd be at the bow. He may have kept them in the salon while at dock, but moved them upfront once the yacht was in motion.

Directly below me was the bridge from where Stockton could watch his hostages. I noticed Helen, Iris, and Avery were amongst the crowd, leaving the captain as the only person on the bridge with the kidnapper. And Lisa, of course. At least I hoped she was still aboard somewhere, as I knew he wouldn't have released her. Anyway, I now knew who he had close by, as they would be most at risk if the gunman decided to start shooting.

Leaning over the railing, I stretched my arm down the sloped facia which created a weather overhang above the bridge windows. Angling the little piece of mirror, I could see the helm where Captain Marston stood. His hands weren't on the wheel, so he must have set the course and speed into the ship's computer. Rotating the mirror, I scanned the rest of the bridge, spotting Stockton against the back wall. Perfect positioning to keep everyone in view. I rotated the mirror again, feeling the sharp edge of the shard digging into my finger. I almost jumped when I found Lisa. She was standing directly behind the console and while her head was facing forward, her eyes looked straight into mine.

"Up there!" came a woman's voice.

I flinched and felt the broken glass cut my finger as I quickly withdrew my arm, dropping the mirror in the process. The sound of it smashing on the deck seemed to echo in the night, somehow louder than the wind, diesel engines, and the idiotic woman combined. I looked at the crowd to see who had been stupid enough to call out the only person trying to save their sorry arses, and spotted Kelly. Jeffrey's cousin. She pushed by the others and kept pointing in my direction. The first mate Helen, and Doug, the guy I'd tackled, both grabbed her by the arm and tried pulling her away as others crowded around.

There was no point sticking around to see if Jeffrey had seen the commotion. He'd have to be blind to miss it, but as I eased back-wards, I heard a door below me open.

"I'm tired of your BS!" Lisa shouted. "Go ahead, shoot me, you chicken shit."

I moved to the port side and looked over the edge. Lisa was outside the door to the bridge and she briefly glanced up and frowned at me, subtly nodding for me to get away.

"Come back inside," Jeffrey ordered. "Or I'll shoot the captain, not you."

Lisa threw up her hands. "Okay, okay! I'm coming back in. I'm sorry."

I stood and stole a look towards the bow. The group had somehow silenced and subdued Kelly, who was hidden from view. Maybe they'd thrown her over the side. I couldn't tell, but I'm sure she would have screamed. Helen caught my eye and with both hands on her head as though in shock, she flicked a thumb up.

If I was reading the signal correctly, between them they'd distracted Stockton and shut his cousin up before he'd noticed what was happening. I now knew where everybody was, and he still didn't know I was aboard. But there was no way they'd keep Kelly both quiet and out of sight for long, so I needed to regroup with a plan. I returned a thumbs-up to Helen, and as I backed away, I noticed Barbara was sitting on the cover for the anchor winch with what looked like Kelly's dress at her feet. Maybe the big woman with the shitty demeanour was coming in useful after all. It was good Jeffrey hadn't tossed her in the drink.

Moving back along the deck, I saw bright lights in the distance directly behind the MV *Maureen*. The boat was gaining on us and I knew it had to be the marine unit. Several of their guys were firearms trained, but I couldn't see how they'd get anyone aboard without Jeffrey knowing and reacting accordingly. Meaning, if he was willing to shoot people, that would be the time to start. Surprise was key, otherwise he'd have time to make it known he'd start killing someone every time the police boat came close. I was still Lisa and everyone else's best bet.

But I needed a weapon of my own. The knife was a good way of taking a bullet before I could even get close enough to use it. The ship would have flare guns, but they were most likely kept on the bridge. Recalling they had dive gear aboard, I wondered if they had spearguns. I ran down the steps to the salon deck, quickly checking there was no one around, then continued down the next flight to the upper cabin deck, where I could access a storage area from which I'd seen Kris retrieve the snorkelling gear.

The door was locked. When I was on duty, I carried around a lockpick set, but that was currently at home in my shack.

"*Dritt*," I groaned and looked at the police boat's lights drawing closer. They would be within 100 metres in a minute or two and I wondered if they could see me yet. Which gave me an idea.

Rechargeable torches sat in holders on the wall at the entrance to most of the yacht's passageways in case of a loss of power. I jogged along the starboard side outer passageway to the hallway across the ship, which led to the stairs to the lowest deck. Snatching the torch from its holder, I ran back to the stern and sat on the steps to the swim platform.

"*Faen*," I swore again, trying to recall my Morse code. I could cause a mass of confusion and delays if I screwed the message up.

Wishing I had a paper and pen to write this out instead of winging it, I began flicking the switch on and off in short and longer periods for dots and dashes.

Dash, dot, dot. Dot, dot, dash…

"*Faen!*" I growled once more, having messed up already. I flashed the torch back and forth, hopefully conveying that I was starting over.

Dash, dot, dot. Dot, dash, dot. Dash, dash, dash. Dash, dot. Dot.

After a few moments, a light flashed back. Dot, dash, dot. That was the letter R, so I waited for what would come next. Nothing did. R? Then it hit me. A plain R was a shorthand prosign for *Roger*, meaning the message had been received.

I held up the torch and concentrated on what to send next. Dot, dot, dot. Dot. Dash, dot. Dash, dot, dot. I couldn't recall how many beats the space between words was supposed to be, so I counted to six and started the next word. Dash, dash, dot. Dot, dot, dash. Dash, dot.

Letting out a long breath, I waited. And I waited. No doubt Ben, who was head of the Joint Marine Unit, was calling Whittaker and perhaps even Williams before answering. Just as I was sure I must have screwed up, or they were hatching a different plan, as they were taking too long, a light flashed dot, dash, dot.

Strictly speaking, *Roger* didn't mean the message had been understood or agreed to. Only that it had been received, but the boat had noticeably slowed to maintain its distance, so they were preparing for something. Sitting on the stern doing nothing, while Lisa and the others were expecting me to do something at any moment was agonising. I had no idea if Kelly had pointed me out as a dumb reaction, or if she was now helping her cousin. It was odd she'd be amongst the other hostages if she was aiding Jeffrey, or perhaps she was trying to win favour. Either way, she was off my Christmas list and I doubted Lisa would let her attend any events in the future. If there were any. First, Lisa had to survive this mess, and after that I was pretty sure Barbara wouldn't be able to talk her into dropping by a bookstore, let alone a cruise with a bunch of strangers. She and Mr Phillip might never leave the house again. He was in for one unique new potty training.

My mind whirred on exactly what I could do if the powers that be agreed to my plan. Because it was hardly a plan. More like a means to execute a plan, thoroughly devoid of plan-like substance. The light from the marine unit flashed again, and I scrambled to keep up with the message. Dash, dot, dash, dot, dash.

That wasn't a letter that I could remember. Was it a number? I didn't think it was a number either, but I knew it from somewhere. I watched for the next set of signals, but nothing came.

Attention! That's what it meant. It was a general procedure prosign often used at the beginning of a transmission to literally get the receiver's attention before the main body of the message. Still nothing came, until I heard a hum, barely audible above the diesel engines. I looked up and could see nothing except the night sky peppered with stars.

And then I noticed it. Slightly off the stern and above, a small group of the stars went dark. Then a few others and the buzz grew louder. I took the torch and pointed the beam down at the broad swim step. My heart began beating faster, and I silently cheered Casey on as she guided the drone from a boat 100 metres astern, onto a target no more than two metres wide at the back of the yacht.

When the military grade drone settled, I jumped down and carefully held it so it couldn't slide off the back. The rotors spun down and stopped, allowing me to untape the package on the underside. Taking the wrapped knife from my waistband, I tossed it towards the cabins and replaced it with the gun.

Standing clear, I swirled the torch beam on the swim step and the rotors soon spun up. A moment later, the drone was airborne and as quickly and silently as it had arrived, it was lost once more to the darkness.

29

BEST-LAID PLANS

The Glock 17 felt weighty in my hand. I was relieved to see it was the same brand and model of service piece I'd fired at the range with Williams. Trotting back up the steps to the salon deck, I mentally re-ran through the information and instruction he'd given me. Running my finger down the right-hand side of the slide, I felt for the loaded chamber indicator. I was hardly an expert after a couple of half-hour sessions, but it felt to me like the extractor was flush with the slide. It would be slightly proud with a round loaded. It made sense that they'd send it without one for safety, but it left me a round short. Still, seventeen in the magazine ought to be enough. I was hoping the threat of one would be plenty.

I pulled the slide back and chambered a round. No safety, I reminded myself. The Glock had a two-stage safety trigger instead, which had seemed like a half measure to me, but I was now glad I couldn't screw up and leave a switch in the wrong position. That was it. All I had to do now was not miss if it came to it.

The firearm had a strangely intoxicating power and feeling of infallibility, yet I was still nervous and unsure. I would likely have one attempt at subduing Stockton before other people would become victims, so quite how to go about storming the bridge was tricky. In theory, I opened the door and aimed at the suspect, but as I walked through the salon, getting closer, the move-by-move logistics were making me pause. What if he wasn't standing where I'd last seen him? If there were still three people in the somewhat narrow space, picking him out from the other two would be essential and not so easy. And of course, bad guys didn't tend to stay still and play nice when facing arrest. Stockton's reaction would be unpredictable.

By the time I stopped by the door to the outdoor passageway on the port side, I had a knot in my stomach and my hands were shaking. I'd been bugging and joking with Whittaker since I'd become a constable about getting firearms trained, and now I had what I'd asked for. Both over time and in the past ten minutes. I still couldn't quite believe they'd agreed. Drone and gun had been the two words I'd sent in Morse code.

Taking in a deep breath, I pictured Jacob plummeting over the railing, and the sight of him unconscious, bleeding on the dock. With my mind furious, crisp, and refocused, I eased out of the door and started along the passageway, with only six paces to reach the bridge. Suddenly, the bridge door swung open, and Kelly appeared outside. She screamed and froze in place, staring at me. And just like that, my whole plan went to *dritt* in a heartbeat.

How she'd escaped Barbara, I had no idea, but I was now convinced she was helping her cousin. Coming up with the only thing I could think to do, I raised the gun and aimed at the terrified woman.

"Move to the bow," I ordered in a low voice.

She turned her head to look back inside the bridge. "Jeffrey?" she squealed.

For a split second, I thought I'd accidentally fired as Kelly lurched back against the railing. But as she slid to the floor, clutching her chest, I realised her own cousin had shot her from inside the bridge.

Shouts, screams, and cries came from the group at the bow, and Kelly gasped and wheezed, slumped on the deck with her legs propping the door open. I was a sitting duck. All Jeffrey had to do was hang his gun around the door and fire. Chances were he'd hit me. Running away down the passageway gave him the same target until I reached the salon. Leaping onto the railing, I grabbed the overhanging roof, pushed off with my legs, and hauled myself up. Several more gunshots echoed loudly in the night, and from the sounds of hits below me, he'd tried doing exactly what I'd guessed.

It wasn't pretty, but I clambered over the sun deck rail and tiptoed across to the starboard side. With the overhang, I couldn't look down and see the full width of the exterior passageway below, so I had no way of knowing if he'd heard or predicted my movement. I looked towards the bow. Barbara pointed to the port side, and I hoped she was telling me where Stockton was inside the bridge. Trusting her, I lowered myself over the side until my feet found the salon deck railing. If the gunman checked the starboard side now, I was dead.

As quietly as I could manage, I dropped to the deck. I glanced forward at Barbara again, and she frantically pointed to my side of the bridge. The bridge doors hinged from the bow end, so if Stockton pushed it open, he'd immediately see me. For a moment I contemplated waiting to see if he'd do just that and shoot before he had a chance to react, but what if he made Lisa or the captain open the door? Dropping low, I scurried forward past the door and crouched around the corner below the bridge windows.

I heard the door creak open and looked at Barbara again. She held up a hand for me to stay where I was. I then noticed that everyone else in the crowd was staring right at me, no doubt wondering what I was about to do. I was also wondering what I was about to do, but I really wished they'd quit staring at me and giving my location away. Barbara must have thought the same thing as she growled something, and the group all looked away. The woman was proving to be invaluable after all.

"Show yourself!" Jeffrey shouted. "Give yourself up and no one else need be hurt. If you don't, I'm going to shoot one of them every minute until you do."

Fy faen. This was exactly the situation I'd dreaded and tried to avoid with my surprise plan. Such as it was. He'd just shot his own cousin, so I had no doubt he'd begin slaughtering these strangers if I didn't stop him.

"Let me help Kelly," Helen shouted.

The door creaked again. "Stay up there where I can see you," he yelled back, much to my relief.

I appreciated what Helen was trying to do, but coming to the bridge meant she'd be his first victim. Lisa was his star hostage, and he needed the captain to pilot the yacht. I shook my head at Helen, but it was too late.

"Okay, you," Stockton shouted. "Only you. Come here and see if you can help Kelly. The rest of you stay there."

Helen held her hands up and began walking across the deck. I wondered how accurately I could shoot through the glass of the bridge window. Surely it would be some stupidly strong laminated glass to withstand a storm and flying debris? Helen had almost reached the bridge on the port side. She was carefully avoiding looking my way, which I now wished she'd do. I could hear Kelly groaning, but Helen wasn't going to be able to help her, despite her good intentions.

The door creaked again, and I looked at Barbara. She nodded to the port side. Stockton had gone back inside the bridge. I was certain he'd walk over and shoot Helen before she even had a chance to check on Kelly.

I scurried back around the corner and reached up for the door handle. Taking a deep breath to settle myself, I counted down from three for no good reason except I needed something to shove all my doubts aside and get me to move. Carefully turning the handle, I started to slowly and stealthily open the door, but the damn thing creaked, so I yanked it the rest of the way. Staying low in a crouch, I brought the Glock up and aimed at the captain, who was now perfectly blocking my view.

As I rose up to stand, Marston suddenly went sprawling across the console, bowled out of the way by Lisa, who grunted as she too hit the control panel. With the obstruction gone, I could now see Stockton on the far side of the bridge. His gun was aimed at Helen, but he quickly swung around, hearing the commotion behind him. Any fear of hitting the bystanders evaporated as my mind laser focused on Jeffrey Stockton, who was bringing his gun to bear on me. I fired twice, as Williams had instructed me.

His head jerked backwards and blood splattered across the inside of the windows as his body slammed against the port-side door jamb. I rushed across the bridge with the Glock still aimed at Stockton as he crumpled, his firearm clattering across the floor. Lifeless eyes stared up at me from his bloody face, his nose disfigured from where one of the bullets had hit. The man was stone dead, but with the image of Jacob on my mind, I desperately wanted to pull the trigger over and over again.

"Good God," Marston muttered, and I was finally aware of the others around me.

Helen had tears running down her face, kneeling by Kelly, who was still wheezing, so I guessed she wasn't dead yet. I dropped the gun to my side and turned.

"What have you done?" Marston said. He looked white as a ghost.

Lisa shoved the man again, impressively hard, considering her diminutive size. "She just saved your ass, you idiot."

She took two steps over to me and threw her arms around me. I didn't know what to do. Every nerve in my body was tingling and adrenaline still pumped like a fire hose.

"It's okay, Nora," Lisa said softly, and my muscles slowly began to relax.

It had been years since I'd completely submitted to an embrace from another human. Since my love Ridley had been torn from me by the kind of violence I'd just brought to the bridge of the MV *Maureen*. Lisa's firm yet tender hug felt like my mother's when I was so young that I barely remembered. I melted into her arms.

"He was going to shoot me," I heard Helen say in a shaky voice, and I pulled away from Lisa.

"*Ja,*" I mumbled.

"Don't just stand there," Lisa barked at Marston. "Slow the boat and radio the police."

The man came out of his stupor and began working the controls.

"Is everyone okay?" Barbara asked, and I noticed all the guests and crew had gathered around the front of the bridge.

"Ewww. That's a mess," Barbara added, looking at Stockton's body on the floor. "Where's the medical kit?"

"You can't help him," I said.

"No, but we need to help her," Barbara replied, pointing at Kelly.

Maybe I should have felt bad for Kelly, but I didn't. For whatever reason, she'd chosen to help her cousin and had almost cost me my life as well as the others.

Helen pulled herself together and stepped over Stockton, opening a cabinet in the back of the bridge to retrieve a large medical box. In the background, I heard Marston's voice calling over the radio and Ben on the Joint Marine Unit boat answering. Like a curtain falling on a stage play, I took a deep breath and felt my wits return as the tension drained away.

I looked at Barbara. "*Takk.*"

She shook her head. "Shit, kid. I hope I never have to go through anything like this ever again, but if I do, I hope your crazy ass is with me."

Reaching over, I took the radio mic from the captain. "Ben, it's Nora. One dead, one critical. Gunshot wound to the chest. Get the helo coming if they're available. The yacht is secure. We can run hard for port in case the helo can't make it. Over."

I forgot most of the protocols, but it felt good to have my feet back under me.

"PC277, this is Joint Marine Unit one. Copy. Calling for helo. We'll follow. Over."

"Joint Marine Unit one, this is PC277," I said, keying the mic again and remembering the lingo this time. "Update on PC168 please. Over."

"PC277, this is Sierra One," came Whittaker's voice. "Transported to hospital. He's conscious, Nora. He'll be okay. Over."

I couldn't remember ever feeling so relieved in all my life. I handed the mic back. "You heard," I said to Marston. "Turn for port and run hard."

I turned back to Lisa and forced myself into a smile. "Mr Phillip is wondering where you got to."

30

—————

NON-FANCY BREAKFAST

It was a little after 6:00am by the time I left Central Station and walked to the Jeep in the car park. I'd parked there after the car chase several days ago, which now felt more like several weeks ago. I was dead tired and glad to be leaving. Turns out there's a lot of paperwork and procedural BS that has to be addressed right away when a police officer is involved in a shooting. Especially a fatal one. Even more when the constable in question is not officially certified to carry a firearm. Whittaker assured me I wouldn't be in any trouble as a senior officer had made the call to arm me. That officer being him, when Ben had called him from the water.

Letting the old CJ-7 warm up for a few minutes, I contemplated where to go. My whole body ached and felt like it had been used as a punching bag. I needed to sleep for a week, but the sun was now rising on Christmas Day. The decision really wasn't hard. I hadn't had a chance to see Jacob yet, so I drove the short distance to the hospital where he'd been kept overnight. The place was surprisingly busy and I think I'd arrived around shift change.

A man dropped a bundled stack of newspapers on the front counter and I noticed the front-page headline 'KIDNAPPER THWARTED. RCIPS recover famed author Lisa Regan and others in daring overnight operation.' I didn't know if Stockton had his article posted online at some point, but I was glad to see Lahana got to tell the real story in the printed edition. I guess she'd lied about the deadline after all.

Word overnight had been that Kelly Stockton was expected to live, although she was still in the intensive care unit. Her cousin's bullet had narrowly missed her heart, but she'd lost a lot of blood. If Helen hadn't stemmed the flow when she did, Kelly wouldn't have made it. On the ride back to the dock, Lisa had told me that Jeffrey had demanded Kelly join him on the bridge, forcing Barbara to release the woman, but apparently she'd not said a word to him about being restrained. In both moments, it appeared she'd simply reacted without thinking when she'd spotted me on the sun deck and in the passageway near the bridge. On hearing that, I was less indifferent about her pulling through.

The police sweatshirt Whittaker had found for me so I didn't have to sit around the station in a damp sports bra, along with my badge, helped the front desk agree to let me visit Jacob's room despite not being family. And the early hour.

The door was open, but I hesitated, out of sight in the hallway. I didn't know what I'd say or how to handle any aspect of seeing my partner in a hospital bed. I felt guilty, relieved, and frustrated all in one, until my stomach clenched and my feet didn't want to take the final few steps. His twelve-year-old daughter appeared from the room and looked at me.

"You're Nora," she informed me.

"*Ja.*"

"Are you here to see daddy?"

"*Ja.*"

"He's asleep," she said.

"I'll come back," I replied, discovering my feet were far keener to leave than stay.

"You can wait with me," the young girl said, extending a hand.

I had little choice but to accept her invitation and let her lead me into the room. Her younger brother was curled up asleep on a blanket on the floor. I envied some kid's ability to crash out at anytime, anywhere.

"I'm Nyah," the girl told me.

"I remember."

Which was sort of true. I recalled her name once she said it. How it wasn't ingrained in my head from all the time Jacob talked about his kids was a sad reflection on me.

"What happened to your face?" Nyah asked, and I touched a hand to the bridge of my nose. It was less sore than yesterday, but apparently I was still bruised. I hadn't looked in a mirror lately.

"I ran into a bad guy at work," I said, which was pretty much the truth.

Jacob had a bandage around his head, otherwise he appeared fine. No tubes down his throat or anything scary, just a few wires from a heart rate monitor. It was still unnerving to see him lying there, made more so by the obvious fact that his family had spent the night in his room. Just as I wondered where his wife was, she entered the room, stopping short when she saw me.

"Hello, Nadine," I said, fortunately recalling her name. I readied myself for an icy greeting, or worse. I wouldn't blame the woman for throwing me out. It was my fault her husband was lying there with his head bashed in.

But she didn't say a word. Instead, she walked over and hugged me. I needed to work on my frosty don't-hug-me look, as it seemed everyone wanted an embrace from the one person who was thoroughly uncomfortable with open signs of affection. I patted her back to offset my rigid muscles, hoping she wouldn't think I was shunning her gesture.

"Thank you for saving Jacob," she said softly as she let me go.

I wanted to explain how he wouldn't have been in the water if I hadn't let him go aboard instead of me, but I stayed quiet. Beneath my feelings of guilt was the knowledge that we had no idea what could have happened if I'd gone first. It didn't matter. Jacob did his job and Stockton chose to assault him as a show of strength. Jacob would go home with family later today and Jeffrey Stockton would be burnt into dust and be lucky to have anyone show up for his funeral.

"He would have done the same for me," I said.

Nadine grinned. "He would have tried. But he's not a fish in the water like you are. He's lucky you were there."

I nodded, feeling more uncomfortable with the compliments than if she'd thrown my arse out.

"Tell Jacob I came by," I said. "I'll check on him later."

"You can wait with us," Nyah offered.

"You'd be welcome to," Nadine reiterated.

"That's okay. I need to get home."

Nadine smiled and nodded. "You have a daughter too, don't you?"

"A kid I foster," I replied, startled by the term daughter.

"Very brave of you," Nadine responded. "We wish you both a merry Christmas."

"Happy Christmas," Nyah echoed.

"You too," I said, and slipped out of the room.

I wished I could have spoken to Jacob just to hear his voice and see him conscious. I was told he'd be fine, but I was yet to see him open his eyes since he had been bludgeoned and thrown from the yacht.

Reaching the automatic doors at the front of the hospital, I was surprised to see Lisa, Barbara, and Constable Gabriel Foster walking in.

"Are you okay?" I asked Lisa, looking her over.

"I'm fine. I just wanted to thank the poor fellow who got smacked on the head."

"Jacob. He's my regular partner," I said, nodding to Gabriel.

Apparently, my temporary partner had been charged with keeping an eye on Lisa today.

"I think they gave him the good stuff," I added. "He's fast asleep."

"Oh, of course, my sense of time is a little thrown off at the moment," Lisa said. "I can come back later." She smiled at me. "Can I buy you breakfast?"

"Have you slept?" I asked. She didn't look like she'd slept.

Lisa brushed her blouse self-consciously. "A little, but I couldn't wait to get off the yacht. Can't say I can relax there anymore. Where are you heading?"

I wasn't sure she'd ever had a chance to relax with everything that had taken place. "Home."

"Then let me buy you breakfast on the way."

I thought for a moment. "It's Christmas Day. Everything is closed."

"Of course. Merry Christmas," she replied. "Everything's closed?"

"Except for some restaurants in the hotels, but they won't be open yet," I explained. "Caymanians take their holidays very seriously. Almost all the shops still close on Sundays."

"Is it Sunday?" she asked.

"I've no idea," I realised. I'd only remembered it was Christmas Day as people had wished me such.

"It's Monday," Barbara offered.

"Well, good for them for closing on Sundays and holidays," Lisa said, although she seemed disappointed about the breakfast thing. I think she was looking for a distraction more than anything else.

"Do you drink coffee?" I asked.

She laughed. "Duh? I'm a writer. We live on coffee."

I looked at Barbara, and she must have read my expression.

"I think we can rely on Lisa being in safe hands with you. Gabriel and I will head back to the yacht for our breakfast." She turned to Lisa. "Call us when you need picking up."

"You don't mind?" Lisa asked.

"I'm not supposed to leave you alone at any time," Gabriel pointed out.

I raised an eyebrow at Barbara, and she winked in return.

"Come along, Gabriel, Lisa will be fine. Why don't we see if we can keep ourselves amused for a while?"

Gabriel looked lost for words, but he turned and followed Barbara out the doors. He might be getting more for breakfast than he knew.

"Where are we going?" Lisa asked.

"Home," I replied as we walked outside.

"Oh, just a minute. I left something in Barbara's car."

I kept walking to my Jeep and a minute later Lisa met me there with Mr Phillip trotting along on a lead. Crouching down, he sped up to me and did his grunting, slurping, greeting thing. I lifted his tubby butt into the back.

"This is yours?" Lisa asked, looking over the faded blue paint and big off-road tyres.

"*Ja*," I replied, climbing in.

"Someone stole a bunch of parts off your car," Lisa joked as she hauled herself up into the passenger seat. "Like the roof and doors. It's very *you*."

I wasn't altogether sure what that meant, but I laughed. Which in my exhausted condition came out more like a gurgle than anything associated with humour, but Lisa didn't appear to notice. She dropped a tote bag she'd brought with her on the floor in the back and made sure Mr P was ready to roll.

"Do I get to meet your daughter?" she asked as I took Hospital Road to Elgin.

"Foster kid," I corrected, and realised Jazzy was actually at AJ's place. Which gave me an idea.

I dialled AJ and waited a while for her to answer.

"Hey," finally came her sleepy voice through the Jeep's speakers.

I slowed a little so I could hear her over the wind and tyre noise. "What are you doing?" I asked mindlessly.

"Sleeping until you woke me," she mumbled, then seemed to remember everything that had been going on. "Hey, so did you get him? What happened? Everything okay?"

"Do you have coffee?" I asked.

"Do you even know me?" she replied with a laugh. AJ loved

coffee.

"Got something for breakfast?"

"Nothing fancy."

I looked over at Lisa.

"Do I look like a fancy girl to you?"

"Who's with you?" AJ asked.

"We'll be there in ten minutes," I said. "Put the coffee on and be ready to make non-fancy breakfast."

I hung up before AJ could quiz me any further.

"You have a roommate?" Lisa asked.

"*Nei.* Well, the kid. That was my friend. Jazzy stayed with her last night."

I picked up the speed on West Bay Road, causing Lisa's hair to swirl out of control in the wind. With that plus the tyre noise, she had to shout for me to hear her.

"I'm incredibly thankful, but I still can't believe you figured out he was taking the yacht."

"I wouldn't have without your notes and messages," I replied.

"The first one was the best," Lisa said with a broad grin. "I knew you'd get it."

I looked over the back, and Mr Phillip stared at me from the rear seat. He appeared to be fine and I was glad he wasn't puking everywhere.

"They were all clever," I said, turning to face the road.

"Well, I have to admit I cheated," Lisa announced, still grinning.

I looked at her quizzically.

"You'd know if you'd read my novels, Nora."

I laughed. I'd talked to Whittaker about Stockton having thought through various scenarios and situations, but I hadn't considered the same being true for Lisa. She spent her life writing about devious crimes, and how to catch the perpetrators.

The streets were mostly empty, so it didn't take long to arrive outside AJ's place on Boggy Sands Road. We got out and I lifted the mutt from the back.

"Boy. That's a fancy house for a non-fancy-breakfast type of girl," Lisa commented, looking up at the sprawling main house as Mr Phillip cocked his leg on the tall wooden fence.

"That's not hers," I said, opening the gate.

We walked across the garden with the morning sun glistening off the ocean beyond Seven Mile Beach.

"Wow," Lisa commented, taking in the view.

AJ's place was a studio-style guest cottage in the grounds of the multi-million-dollar oceanfront home. By default, she shared the same amazing location.

"AJ keeps an eye on the place for the owners in America, and gives them free diving when they're here," I explained, opening the sliding glass door, which was also the only entrance.

"Happy Christmas!" AJ greeted us, and her gaze shot to Lisa.

"Bloody hell! You're Lisa Regan!"

Lisa laughed. "Yes, and thanks to Nora, I'm still around to be her. I like your shirt. Is that a dive mask?"

AJ beamed. "Yes! Isn't it fun? I had them made for my customers."

The shirt was typically AJ. One of those round yellow smiley faces from the 70s with a dive mask over its eyes.

A pile of covers on the bed moved and Jazzy's mop of curly hair appeared, flipping back to reveal her startled face.

"Lisa Regan?" she blurted with her jaw hung open. "And Mr Phillip!"

AJ fussed and began picking up stuff around her little home. "I'm so sorry the place is a mess. Please, sit down, sit down," she said, directing Lisa to one of the two chairs at her minuscule dining table.

"Coffee?" I urged.

"Yes, yes, it's brewed. Let me find enough clean cups."

Jazzy plodded over and stared at our guest while dropping to the floor and petting the dog.

"You must be Jazzy," Lisa greeted her. "I've been dying to meet you."

"Nuh-uh…" Jazzy mumbled in disbelief. "I've read three of your books and I'm waiting for the library to get the next one."

"That's so kind of you, thank you," Lisa responded. "Your…" she turned to me, unsure. "Nora, is kinda like Josie Quinn, huh?"

"Yeah, except Nora has a super-cool chick living with her who keeps her in line," Jazzy said and beamed from ear to ear.

I rolled my eyes. AJ and Jazzy continued to pester and bother Lisa with a million questions, all of which she answered with a smile. Mr Phillip revelled in the pets and attention, and I couldn't believe both Jazzy and AJ knew about the dog.

"He gets more fan mail than I do," Lisa joked.

The coffee tasted good after police station tar all night, and we feasted on a mixture of slightly stale cereal and bagels. AJ loved bagels almost as much as she loved coffee.

After, while AJ brewed another pot of coffee and Jazzy took Mr P for a walk around the garden, Lisa and I stepped outside and sat in the chairs on the little patio. The sound of the ocean tickling up the beach just 20 metres away could have easily put me to sleep.

"That was truly something special you did last night, Nora," Lisa said in a soft tone. "I'm forever in your debt."

"You don't owe me anything," I replied. "None of that *dritt* would have happened if I'd done my job properly at the Bodden House."

She reached over and put a hand on my arm. "You were doing your job. You were arresting a gang leader as I understand it. Stockton would have found another moment to make his move if it hadn't have been there."

That was probably true, but it didn't make me feel much better. My primary task had been guarding Lisa.

"You know," she continued, "I've written about cruelty, crime, and violence in all my books, and I try to relay the visceral feeling of being a victim, or someone close to the dramatic events. But I've never experienced anything like last night before. I hope I never do again." She looked over at me. "I can't believe how decisively you handled the situation. You never flinched."

I wondered if it truly looked that way from her perspective. It hadn't felt that way from my side of things.

"If you hadn't shoved Marston out of the way, it wouldn't have worked out the way it did," I said, making sure she gave herself credit for saving Helen's life.

I had no regrets about killing Jeffrey Stockton. He forced the situation on himself, but I wasn't sure how the jarring violence of the moment would affect me. I didn't think it would keep me awake at night, the way the memory of seeing my boyfriend Ridley gunned down before me does, but only time would tell. It wasn't the first time I'd taken a life, and I was sure the events would live inside the dark recesses of my mind forever. The others did.

"I have no doubt it'll change the way I write, Nora," Lisa said. "I don't think I'll ever be the same after last night."

"I think that's okay," I responded softly. "We shouldn't be the same after such things."

Lisa nodded, squeezed my arm again, then reached into the tote bag she'd brought and lowered her voice again.

"I feel terrible, Nora. I brought special books for you and your partner at the hospital, but I didn't think to bring extras."

She pulled a hardbound copy of the new release book, but I could see it wasn't the same as the copies which all the guests had received. The end of the pages had been sprayed with an amazing design as though the cover continued around them like the spine. The dust jacket design also sported raised features, giving it a three-dimensional effect.

"Give it to Jazzy," I gushed. "With everything going on, I screwed up and didn't get the kid anything to open this morning. Would it be okay if you gave her the book?"

Lisa smiled. "I tell you what. How about I sign it to Jazzy and give it to you? Then you can give Jazzy a Christmas present."

My first reaction was that it felt like cheating. I'd failed to get the kid anything, which was on me.

"That's very kind of you, Lisa, but that's an amazing present which I had nothing to do with. It should come from you."

Lisa looked at me sternly. "Nora, I wouldn't be here to give anyone anything if it weren't for you. Please allow me to do this."

She was writing in the book before my tired brain could say anything more, and handed it to me as Jazzy returned with Mr Phillip, who was panting furiously in the morning island heat.

"Happy Christmas Jazzy," I said, passing the book on to the kid who clutched it as though she'd been given the Holy Grail itself.

Her face lit up with pure joy, and in that moment, I realised how the act of giving could be the most rewarding act for everyone involved. It was probably the exhaustion playing a part, but I don't think I'd ever felt as happy as I did seeing Jazzy's unadulterated delight.

Not even AJ turning on the annoying Christmas music in the kitchen could ruin the moment.

Thank you for reading *Festive Sommer*!

Not ready to be done with Nora?
In return for joining my newsletter list, I've written a fun bonus scene you'll find by using this QR code…

Grab the next book in the series, *Missing Sommer*

ACKNOWLEDGMENTS

My sincere thanks to:

My incredible wife Cheryl, for her unwavering support, love, and encouragement.

My family and friends for always being there.

Lisa Regan for allowing me to fictionalise her and Mr Phillip in this story. She's a brave lady! Lisa is one of those amazing storytellers I will always strive to emulate, as well as being a lovely lady. Click on this link to discover her wonderful books.

My reporter friend in Grand Cayman who allowed me to use her alter ego character name!

My marvellous editor Andrew Chapman at Prepare to Publish for his diligent work and wise suggestions.

Lily at Orkidedatter for her Norwegian advice.

Casey Keller, Craig Robinson, and Alain Belanger for their help with all things Cayman Islands related.

Special thanks to Richard Morcombe for showing me around the RCIPS Air Operations Unit Airbus helicopter and advising on its capabilities.

Shearwater Research, Dive Rite, Reef Smart, and Cayman Spirits for their friendship and support.

The Tropical Authors group for their advice, support, and humour. Visit and subscribe at www.TropicalAuthors.com for deals and info on a plethora of books by talented authors in the Sea Adventure genre.

My beta reader group has grown to include an amazing cross section of folks from different walks of life. Their suggestions, feedback and keen eyes are invaluable, for which I am eternally grateful.

Above all, I thank you, the readers: none of this happens without the choice you make to spend your precious time with my stories. I am truly in your debt.

LET'S STAY IN TOUCH!

To buy merchandise, find more info or join my newsletter, visit my
website at
www.HarveyBooks.com

If you enjoyed this novel I'd be incredibly grateful if you'd consider
leaving a review on Amazon.com
Find eBook deals and follow me on BookBub.com

Catch my podcast, The Two Authors' Podcast with co-host Douglas
Pratt

Find more great authors in the genre at TropicalAuthors.com

Visit Amazon.com for more books in the
Nora Sommer Caribbean Suspense Series,
AJ Bailey Adventure Series,
and collaborative works;
The Greene Wolfe Thriller Series
Tropical Authors Adventure Series

ABOUT THE AUTHOR

A *USA Today* Bestselling author, Nicholas Harvey's life has been anything but ordinary. Race car driver, adventurer, divemaster, and since 2020, a full-time novelist. Raised in England, Nick has dual US and British citizenship and now lives wherever he and his amazing wife, Cheryl, park their motorhome, or an aeroplane takes them. Warm oceans and tall mountains are their favourite places.

For more information, visit his website at HarveyBooks.com.